**Silver Mo**

HAVE
OF 78 GREAT NOVELS
OF
EROTIC DOMINATION

**If you like one you will probably like the rest**

A NEW TITLE EVERY MONTH

**Silver Moon Readers Service**
109 A Roundhay Road
Leeds
LS8 5AJ
United Kingdom

http://www.electronicbookshops.com

## If you like one of our books you will probably like them all!

Write for our free 20 page booklet of extracts from early books
- surely the most erotic feebie yet - and, if you wish to be on
our confidential mailing list, from forthcoming monthly titles
as they are published:-

### Silver Moon Reader Services

109A Roundhay Road

Leeds

LS8 5AJ

United Kingdom

http://www.electronicbookshops.com

or leave details on our 24hr UK answerphone

**08700 10 90 60**

**International acces code then +44 08700 10 90 60**

### New authors welcome

**Please send submissions to**

**Silver Moon Books Ltd.**

**PO Box 5663**

**Nottingham**

**NG3 6PJ**

**or**

**editor@electronicbookshops.com**

# INSIDE THE FORTRESS
## by
## John Strenes

# CHAPTER ONE

## The Lady on the Train

The young officer strode briskly along one of the platforms of the St.Petersburg Station in Moscow. He was an impressive sight in the uniform of the Tsar's Lifeguard, and drew admiring glances. The white tunic and close-fitting breeches were topped by a lancer's cap, whose black shine was matched by his riding boots. His luggage had been loaded into the rear van, and he was looking for a first-class carriage. There was a hiss of steam from the great locomotive and the railway guard raised a whistle to his lips.

The officer gestured him to wait, and the man obediently dropped his arm. Without hurrying, the lieutenant walked along the train, tapping his stick in his hand and idly scanning the first-class compartments. If he could find an empty one, he would be spared the tedious duty of having to make conversation with his fellow travellers. Suddenly his eyes met those of a woman, gazing back at him. That gaze seemed to have possibilities, he thought, and without a flicker of hesitation he opened the carriage door and entered. Before shutting it behind him, he gave a curt nod to the guard, who blew on his whistle.

As the train began to move, he turned to his travelling companion. She was a good-looking woman, perhaps in her late twenties - some years older than himself, anyway. She was smartly dressed in the height of fashion: a greyish beige skirt and jacket, unbuttoned to show a lace-trimmed blouse. From the hem of her skirt peeped delicate, well-made boots and she had laid her hat on the seat beside her. The delicate smell of her scent filled the compartment.

Her hair was brown, drawn back into a small bun with a few curls on either side of her face, which was attractive rather than beautiful. She was regarding him with an amused twinkle in her eye.

'Isn't it considered impolite to enter a lady's compartment without asking her leave?' She addressed him in French, as any Russian aristocrat would.

'I have to admit it is, dear lady,' he drawled 'but the train was about to leave and I thought it worse manners to keep you waiting.' He placed his shiny cap and stick on the opposite seat and sat down.

She smiled at this obvious lie, holding her head to one side, coquettishly. 'Well, lieutenant, this is the express to St.Petersburg. The only stop is for lunch at Bologoye, so we have each other's company for at least four hours.'

'Indeed, madam, and perhaps for the rest of the journey also. I am glad to have such a charming companion on what might otherwise have been a dull journey.' This was untrue, as he had tucked a slim volume of French pornography into his tunic with which he had hoped to while away the time. He stood up. 'Perhaps I should introduce myself?'

'Really, lieutenant, that is not correct etiquette. You must know that a gentleman can only be introduced to a lady by a mutual friend.' Her eyes had a sparkle of amusement.

He gave a slight bow. 'Well, shall I just say I am an officer of the Tsar's Lifeguard?'

'So I see'. Her eyes ran down his uniform. The officers of the regiment prided themselves on the tightness of their breeches. The lieutenant had made his tailor use a slightly stretchable material - a cad's trick, the other officers thought, but now his breeches fitted as tight as a skin, without a crease or wrinkle. Of course, he could wear nothing beneath them, and the bulge of his genitals was prominent beneath the snow-white material.

She stared fixedly for a moment, then swallowed hard. As he sat down on the seat opposite her, her gaze did not

6

leave the front of his breeches. He sat with his legs slightly apart to give her a better view.

'Lieutenant, a lady alone in a railway carriage with a strange man may think herself in danger.'

'Danger? What danger can you fear, madam?'

'Why, violation.'

'Do you think violation is likely?'

A curious eagerness came into her voice. "Oh yes, indeed. I heard that on this very line, not a month ago, that a young working girl got into a third-class compartment with five soldiers, and by the end of the journey they had all raped her several times.'

'Several times?'

'Yes, and in different ways. I believe, for instance, that one man was using her mouth while another entered her from behind.'

'How remarkable!' To hear tales of sex from the lips of an attractive woman was far more entertaining than any pornographic book. Already his penis was beginning to swell and straighten in his breeches, and he knew she could not help but notice it. 'Do you know any other details?'

'Yes. Apparently she struggled at first, but they were too many and too strong. Two held her back against the seat while two others pulled her legs apart. The fifth man penetrated her, and when he had finished, one of the others took his place.'

His penis slowly uncoiled and hardened beneath his breeches. 'How do you know of this? I don't remember seeing any such thing in the newspapers.'

'Oh no, the girl wouldn't dream of reporting the rape. The shame of other people knowing would be worse than the ordeal.'

'Then how do you know about it?'

'Ladies talk of these things, naturally. Gossip is sure to

get round.'

'Well, madam, nothing you would not wish can happen to you. You have the protection of an officer of the Tsar's Lifeguard.'

For a full minute she stared at the long, hard outline pushing out the material of his breeches. She ran her tongue quickly round her lips.

'The Tsar's Lifeguard is always smart, but I think such tight uniforms must surely be uncomfortable.'

'Not always, my dear madam. But when an officer meets an attractive lady, sometimes it happens that he finds his breeches growing too tight. It is the way of the world, as I'm sure you understand.'

She nodded.

'Yes, that must be inconvenient' she murmured, her gaze never leaving the massive bulge. There was silence in the carriage, the rumble and clatter of the train partly muffled by the expensive velvet upholstery.

She spoke again. 'Lieutenant, it is very rude of me to see you so uncomfortable while doing nothing to assist you. If you should wish to rearrange your clothing, I would raise no objection'.

'Madam, you are very kind. I was hoping you would be so gracious.'

Slowly he undid his breeches. The flies were fastened with small, flat buttons which were carefully concealed to avoid spoiling the smooth outline. He reached inside, and drew out his erection. It was very long and thick, and stood stiffly upright from his body, a drop of clear fluid gleaming at the opening of its purplish head.

She contemplated the uprisen sex thoughtfully. The train clattered over some points. They must be on the outskirts of the city by now.

'It's so big,' she murmured.

With a moment's hesitation, she reached down to the hem of her skirt and pulled it up to her lap. With a rustle of petticoats, she exposed first her buttoned boots, then black silk stockings and finally a pair of close-fitting, lace-trimmed drawers of fine white cotton. She moved her thighs apart, and he could see that the centre seam of the drawers dimpled into the soft outline of her vulva. Almost as if in a trance, the lady's hand stole between her thighs. Her middle finger began gently to stroke the cleft between her legs. Her eyelids fluttered for an instant.

For a moment, both sat silently contemplating each other. The lady cleared her throat. Then she spoke, and her voice was shaking slightly.

'If you are to take me, captain, it must be by force. You must overcome the resistance I will put up, with all the violence you consider necessary. A lady of my breeding cannot consent willingly to such an assault, but must defend herself, even if she suffers injury.'

He could not have been given a clearer invitation. Slowly he stood up, his member seeming to tower over her. She had gone very pale, and her breath was rapid and shallow. Then abruptly he sat down next to her, and reached his hand between her thighs. Violently, she shoved his hand away, and made as if to slap him. He grabbed her wrist and twisted it, seizing a handful of her hair with his other hand. He hauled her towards him, releasing his grip to punch her shoulder. Then he shoved her backwards, sending her sprawling along the carriage seat.

Quickly moving to sit on her stomach, with one hand he held her wrists above her head, while fumbling to unbutton her blouse with the other. He tore it open roughly, sending a button skittering across the carriage. She only wore a corset beneath, which he quickly unclasped to release her breasts. They were quite small but firm to his hand, as she writhed

9

soundlessly under him. He smiled down triumphantly at her helplessness.

Then swinging himself round, he sprawled on top of her, the gold lace and buttons of his tunic digging into her exposed breasts. Forcing his knees between hers, he prised her legs apart. His hand fumbled up between her thighs, feeling through the thin fabric of the drawers for the mound of her sex. Her eyes were screwed tightly shut, but she tried to jerk him off her body. A sudden punch in the stomach made her go limp.

His questing fingers found the cleft they were seeking, and he noted that it was moist beneath the cotton. For a moment he caressed her there, then dug his fingernail into the seam of the undergarment, bursting the stitches. He was able to introduce his finger, and tore the crotch of her drawers open.

With his free hand he introduced the blunt head of his member into her, nudging apart the lips of her sex. She flinched at its touch. Slowly he began to push himself into her. She gave a gasp as the full length of him suddenly rammed into her body. Then he withdrew, so that only the tip of his phallus remained inside her, and then rammed in hard again. Slowly but mercilessly he drove in and out. The woman lay quite still beneath him now, making a little moaning sound at each thrust.

He quickened his pace, slamming his hard shaft into her again and again, as if it were a weapon with which he was beating her. Then, gasping, his orgasm swept over him, his final thrusts pumping his sperm deep into the passive body beneath him.

He lay without moving for a while. The clickety-clack of the train seemed suddenly louder. Then he slowly climbed off her. As he withdrew, semen ran from the swollen lips of her vulva and dribbled onto her petticoats.

He slumped, breathing heavily, onto the seat opposite her. He made no effort to put his sex away, but sat with his legs apart, his wet member hanging out of his breeches. She sat up, and smoothed down her skirts. Matter-of-factly, she refastened her corset and did up her blouse, tutting quietly at the missing button. She reached for her travelling bag. Her face was flushed but she acted nonchalantly. She took out a mirror and checked her hair, tucking it back into place where his rough hands had disarranged it. Without taking her gaze from the mirror, she broke the silence.

'Is this not remarkable? Twenty minutes ago we had not met. Now here I am, full of your semen.' The woman put away the mirror and regarded him.

'Were you not taking a dreadful risk just then? You are young, and a scandal could ruin your career before it has started. What makes you trust me not to report this to the police?'

'Dear lady, I am, as you say, only a young lieutenant, but I flatter myself that I know enough of human nature - indeed, of feminine nature - to know how far I may go.'

'Am I so easily understood, even by a lad?' She smiled sadly to herself.

'No, madam. As I say, I consider myself an acute observer of human character. No, don't think I am boastful - my senior officers think so too, and that is why I am posted to St.Petersburg.' He paused. 'But enough of that. It is better that we remain strangers.'

By now his penis had softened, and he tucked it back into his breeches. She watched closely as he buttoned his flies. Then she took a needle and thread from her bag and began to sew a button onto her blouse to replace the one torn off during the assault. It was rather awkward for her, and he watched her with a lazy interest. He yawned. She sat back in her seat and gazed at him reproachfully.

'Now you've had your pleasure, you want to sleep, I suppose.'

There was a hint of disappointment in her voice, but he could not deny she was right. 'Just a few minutes repose, madam, and I shall be a man renewed.' She tied the thread of the button and trimmed it off.

'Come then, lie along the seat here and lay your head in my lap. I shall be your pillow.'

He came across to her side and stretched himself out. As he laid his head on her lap, he could feel on his cheek the warmth of her thighs through the fabric of her skirt. She gently caressed his hair.

'So young, and so vicious,' she murmured softly. He slept.

When he opened his eyes, he saw she was reading a little novelette which she must have taken from her bag. He got up and stretched himself. They were passing through open country, the empty birchwood landscape beyond the city. She smiled up at him and put her book away. He sat down opposite her.

'Lieutenant, have you ever committed rape before?'

The officer was startled and a little disconcerted by this abrupt question, but tried to recover his poise.

'Rape, madam? Well, I really...'

'Don't be alarmed, lieutenant, I promise I will never betray any confidences. It is just that I think you must have often taken a woman by force.'

The captain hesitated. 'Well, perhaps ... perhaps on occasions it might have been considered rape.'

Her eyes glittered and she sat forward eagerly. 'Tell me about them" Her hands were clasped together tightly in her lap. He swallowed hard, but then decided that this opportunity to brag of his sexual adventures to a well-bred lady was too good to miss.

'Most were only peasant girls or serving maids, you understand. On my family's estate.'

'Where is that?'

'Let us just say it is deep in the country, many days journey from Moscow.'

'Tell me about the first one.'

'Well, I had arrived back home from the academy for the summer vacation. You must know that an all-male boarding school is full of dirty talk and wanking. I was growing less and less satisfied with that. I wanted a real screw, and I wanted it soon.'

'And you didn't much care how you got it?'

He smiled. 'Perhaps. I admit I was hot for sex and to my astonishment, when I got into the house, I met a new housemaid - one of the prettiest I'd ever seen. She was very young, younger than me even, and before she had carried my bags to my room I had made up my mind to fuck her.'

'How long did it take?'

'It was the next evening. I was going upstairs to change for dinner, and I met her on the landing. She stood aside to let me pass, but I stopped in front of her. I praised her beauty and said that such a pretty girl must have many lovers. She blushed, and said she had none.

I pushed my hand against the front of her apron, feeling her crotch through her clothes. She begged me to stop, and said she was afraid someone would come. I told her to come to my room, and that nobody would disturb us there. She was clearly frightened, but I knew she wouldn't dare to disobey the young master. After all, she and her relatives depended on being employed by my family.'

'So she followed you?'

'She had no choice, really. She was pale, though, and looked terrified when I locked the bedroom door behind us. She stood helplessly with her hands by her sides in the middle of the room. I exposed my cock to her - it was the biggest hard-on I'd ever had. Then I told her to lift her skirts. She hesitated, and I had to order her again. She was reluctant, but did as she was told. She began to cry.'

'To cry? Did you pity her?'

'Not at all, in fact I began to feel the spur of cruel pleasure. She was at my mercy, and my prick grew even harder.'

'What did you do?'

'I grabbed her by the hair and forced her down onto the floor. She was sobbing and begging me not to, but that only made me more determined. I pulled up her clothes. She wasn't wearing any drawers - few country girls do. I got my cock to the opening of her cunt and rammed myself into her. She was tight and dry, and it was not easy. She gave a cry as I pushed in, but I told her to be quiet in case anybody heard.

'The actual shagging only lasted a few seconds. I was so keyed up that my orgasm exploded like a bomb, and I must have pumped about half a pint of hot spunk into her.'

The lady smiled at the thought of all that adolescent semen. 'And then?'

'Then I told her to get out, and not to let anyone see she had been crying. I dressed for dinner, and joined the others downstairs. It was pleasant to be served at the table by the red-eyed maid, knowing that my sperm was inside her.'

'You men have no conscience.' She said it sadly, as a fact of life. 'Aren't we women silly to desire you so much?'

'And do you?'

'Alas, too much. It has been the pleasure and the pain of my life. I have always been obsessed by men.'

'And by a particular part of their bodies?'

She nodded. Describing the rape of the servant girl had given him an erection, and her eyes lingered on the long bulge in his breeches. He stood up and slowly undid himself, pulling out his shaft. The head of it bobbed a few inches from her face. She gazed at it admiringly.

14

'It's magnificent.'

She moved forward on her seat to bring herself closer. She reached out with both hands and gently stroked the hard shaft, her fingertips tracing the veins that stood out from its rigid surface. Then she guided it to her mouth. She parted her lips and took the massive erection in. Her soft mouth closed round it and she began to suck. Soon she was working her head back and forth with a rhythmic movement, her cheeks sucked in to grip the shaft. Her soft tongue caressed its hard length. The member nudged the back of her throat and her nostrils flared as she struggled to breathe.

He looked down with a smile of satisfaction: she was certainly an experienced fellatrice. He stroked her hair as she rocked her head back and forth. Soft wetness engulfed his prick. The swollen shaft glistened with her saliva as it slid in and out between her lips. Her free hand slid up the back of his thigh and began to caress his buttocks.

Gradually his muscles began to stiffen and his breathing grew more rapid. She felt his tension rising and quickened her rhythm, her lips gripping his cock just below the head. Her other hand reached up between his legs to squeeze the bulge of his testicles. Just then he groaned, and suddenly jet after jet of hot semen was spurting into her mouth. She coughed and gagged, having to swallow the sticky flood to keep from choking.

Panting, he withdrew his sex from between her wet lips. Expertly, she squeezed the shaft to catch the last dribbles of his sperm in her hand to prevent it dripping on her skirt. Swallowing the last gulp of the semen, she licked her fingers clean.

He slumped back down on the seat opposite, and there was silence for a while as his breathing became slower. She had produced the mirror again and was wiping away a dribble of sperm from the side of her mouth with a tiny lace-trimmed handkerchief.

'There now. I hope you won't consider me rude, lieutenant, if I suck a pastille. I confess after all these years I have never grown used to the taste.'

'Not at all, madam. Please feel free.'

She took a small enamelled box from her bag and popped a lozenge into her mouth.

'Did you find that pleasant, lieutenant?'

'Indeed, I cannot say I have even been more expertly sucked off. I wonder where you came to be so skilful in that ladylike accomplishment.'

'Why, at the Smolny Institute. As you know, it is the most select girls school in the empire. Young ladies of gentle birth are expected to receive a good education, and an important, if unofficial, part of it is how to cope with the demands made upon a young lady by a young gentleman.' She smiled a little mockingly.

'You mean ...'

'But of course. I had not been there a fortnight before the older girls had told me all about those important matters concerning men and women. They told me of the pain and also, I am glad to tell you, of the pleasure. But whatever pleasure we took, we had to ensure that we stayed virgins. Young girls of our class must marry, and marry well.'

'And you had to be able to offer your husbands a maidenhead to force open on the wedding night.'

'Naturally. Without that, or even worse with the scandal of pregnancy, then one's reputation would be ruined.'

'And you avoided that?'

'Ah yes. All the trouble I went to in avoiding pregnancy. And in the end I found I never could become pregnant. No, I am a failure as regards the destiny of women. At least it frees me to take what pleasure I can find in being of the feminine sex.'

The train began to slow down. She looked out of the carriage window at the wooden houses that were beginning to line the track.

'We'll be at Bologoye in a few minutes. I must get my trunk from the luggage van to get some clean underwear.' She smiled. 'It is somewhat uncomfortable to wear drawers that are so thoroughly torn and soaked.'

She stood up and turned round, running her hand over her bottom. 'Please, can you tell me if there is a stain on the back of my skirt. Sometimes it soaks through, and I'd hate people to see.'

'No, madam. There is nothing to tell that anything has happened between us.'

She turned to him and cocked her head on one side with a little smile. 'Let us keep it that way, then.'

The train clanked noisily to a halt at the station of Bologoye. The guard walked along the platform yelling 'Half an hour for lunch, ladies and gentlemen' outside the first class carriages. The lady and the officer climbed stiffly down from the carriage. Together they walked back along the train to the luggage van. The guard was just climbing up into the brake van at the rear, no doubt to eat his own meagre food. At the officer's approach he got down and removed his cap respect-fully.

'Excellency?'

'Get this lady's trunk out from the luggage van at once.'

'But excellency, the lady's luggage is behind all the rest. It was not supposed to be taken out until St.Petersburg.'

The lieutenant flushed with anger. With two quick strides he advanced on the railwayman, raising his stick and bring-ing it down with a vicious blow on the side of the man's head. 'I told you to get it out, damn you. You don't question the order of an officer.'

The man turned pale, except for the red stripe across his cheek where the stick had left its mark. 'Yes, sir. Of course, sir. Apologies.'

The pair of them watched as the guard pulled trunks and bags from the luggage van, until an expensive leather trunk was brought out. The officer silently noted the gold-blocked initials on the lid. The lady bent over it, unlocked it with a small key and began to rummage inside. The railwayman stood by.

'Turn your back, you filth!' the officer screamed. 'How dare you gawp at a lady's private belongings?' He raised his stick again, but the terrified man turned swiftly and smartly as if he had been a soldier on parade.

When the woman had found a new pair of drawers, she quickly rolled them up and transferred them to her travelling bag. Then she re-locked the trunk.

'Thank you, my man.' The nervous guard turned back and saw she was holding out a coin - a silver quarter rouble. Hesitantly he took it and, without looking at the officer, quickly set about reloading the pile of luggage into the van. The lady and the officer strolled back towards the first class restaurant.

'You should not have given that peasant any money.'

'It did no harm, surely.'

'These people have to respect and obey their betters without expecting any reward.'

The lady gave a slight shrug and they entered the restaurant. A large portrait of the Tsar, Nicholas II, hung on one wall. The tables, covered with starched white cloths, were almost empty of travellers.

'You see, lieutenant, there must be many empty compartments.' She spoke teasingly. 'You could easily have travelled alone.'

'I count it my great good fortune that I did not.'

She gave his hand a little squeeze. Then she looked around and spied the door to the ladies' room. 'I will be back in minute.'

He visited the gentlemen's room himself, then took his place at one of the tables. He suddenly realised how thirsty he was and drank two glasses from the water carafe while a waiter hovered ingratiatingly with a menu. He spoke to the waiter in Russian. 'Let's have the damn menu, then.'

He glanced down the list and ordered veal, with a bottle of French wine.

'And for the lady, sir?'

Ah, yes, the lady. The officer had no illusions about how long ladies thought a minute lasted. If he delayed ordering until she returned, they might have to hurry their meal.

'Bring everything on the menu. The lady can choose then.'

'But sir, there are six dishes.'

'Then bring six, blast your soul. Don't you people understand your own language?'

As he expected, it was ten minutes before she returned from the ladies' room. He rose and drew back her chair for her to sit beside him. She thanked him politely. Both gestures had come naturally to people of their class.

Just then the waiter returned with a trolley. He served the officer's veal and the wine, then offered the lady the choice of the dishes, all prepared for her. 'Really, you shouldn't have gone to the trouble. I only wish for a bowl of borscht.'

'Well, have the borscht, then.' The officer tugged a purse from his tunic and paid for everything. The waiter placed the soup bowl in front of the lady and began to wheel the trolley away.

'Hey, you. What are you going to do with that food? I've paid for it, you know.'

'Good sir, it is our custom to give any surplus food to the poor. There are many that are hungry in the town and the villages around, and some come here hoping for scraps.'

'Well they shan't have any of that. Throw it in the bin, do

you understand?'

The waiter looked shocked, but automatically murmured 'Yes, sir. Certainly, sir.' Gloomily he wheeled the trolley away.

'Why did you do that?'

'If the peasants think they can live by sponging off the rich, then they'll never do a stroke of work. Then where will Russia be?'

The lady made no answer. They began to eat. At length she spoke.

'Normally, when a man and woman first eat together, they tell each other about their backgrounds and so on. But I think you understand that would not be wise now.'

'I understand perfectly, my dear madam. The kind of conversation that really would be appropriate for us at this moment would be so indecent that none should overhear it.'

She laughed naughtily. 'You are quite right, of course. Yet I think it would be delicious to shock these dull worthies.' Looking round, the handful of other diners were all solemn men in formal business dress. She leant across him as if to reach for the wine bottle, but her other hand dropped to his lap and squeezed the soft bulge in his crotch. She murmured in his ear.

'My best friend and I used to do this at formal dinners, if we fancied the boys we were sitting next to. If the proceedings were really boring, I would take out his phallus and masturbate him under the tablecloth - all while carrying on polite conversation, of course. We used to take pride in doing it undetected beneath the very eyes of the others. Sometimes the boy would ejaculate, and it was so funny seeing him try to cover his confusion with coughing. It was best, naturally, if you could catch the semen on their napkins. If it got on the front of their trousers, then they had to spill something deliberately to disguise it.'

She giggled mischievously and undid two of his fly buttons. Sliding her cool hand inside, she fondled the sleeping member. 'This has done proud work today.'

'And will again, I trust. I ordered the red wine to restore our vigour - at least, that is what the French say.'

'My vigour is as great as ever, lieutenant.' There was a challenging gleam in her eye.

Just then a handbell on the platform outside announced the train was ready to depart. She quietly slipped her hand out of his breeches and rose from her seat, smiling as he quickly fumbled with his buttons. There was no doubt that they would continue the journey together, and both returned to the same compartment.

They did not speak for some time after the train moved off again. When they began to talk, their conversation was guarded, like two circling fencers. Both wanted to learn more about the other, but without giving anything away about themselves. They discussed foreign travel - he had only been to Paris, but she had travelled widely. He made some observations on the Tsar's determination to crush democracy and maintain Russia as an autocratic empire.

'Oh, sir,' she laughed 'I am a woman and know nothing about politics. Even if I was interested, I wouldn't consider it at all proper for a lady to have political opinions. Here am I, with a good education, but an education that fits me for my position in a man's world. Why should I care that women are not allowed to go to university or work in the civil service? A woman should be content with her natural place in the world.'

'And what is that?'

'A place submissive to her man, of course.' She hesitated ' .... or men.'

The officer nodded thoughtfully. 'So a woman can have several masters, then?'

She looked slightly uneasy. 'Well, from time to time...' The train rumbled past a lake, and the woman took the opportunity to change the subject by drawing his attention to the bright plumage of the waterfowl. He remarked how much he would like to shoot them.

She talked of the shops in St.Petersburg, and the great stores of Vienna and Paris and London. He told her that shopping bored him.

'You must think this is silly female chatter.'

A lifetime of politeness forced him to deny it. 'Not at all, madam. Your talk and your company are an unexpected delight on what could have been a very dreary journey.'

'You are too kind, sir. You have yourself saved me from having to read a very silly and worthless novel. How had you intended to pass the time?'

He unbuttoned the front of his tunic and tugged out a thin, paper-covered book. 'Oh, I bought this French romance in a Moscow bookshop just before I left. It is not a great work of literature, but contains things that may be instructive to both men and women.'

She craned over to look at the cover. It was completely plain.

'What is it about?'

'Come and sit beside me and I'll show you.'

She came over and he opened the book. Every page had photographs of men and women, naked or half-naked, engaged in every sex act imaginable.

She gasped. 'Pornography! I've heard about such books, but I've never seen one before. Show me.'

He began to leaf through the book. The pictures were separated by text, telling a simple sort of story. The photographs were very clear, though. Group sex, orgies, multiple penetration, all were faithfully depicted.

'I suppose the women must be prostitutes.' she murmured.

'Yes, I suppose so.'

'I have sometimes felt that I would make a very good

prostitute myself.'

'You would indeed, dear lady, but is that what you would like?'

'Perhaps not. But I'd love to be photographed like that.' She sighed. 'Of course that's impossible.'

'You mean you might be recognised?'

She nodded. 'That would be very unwelcome, naturally. Come, show me more.'

He turned the pages. The lady suddenly put her finger on a page to study it more closely. A young girl had been kidnapped and was being forced to have sex with her captors. The photograph showed her naked with her hands tied behind her back, bent over and sucking one man, while another took her from behind. The lady's breathing grew faster, and the cruelty of the scene excited him as well. His cock began to stiffen once more.

Without taking her eyes off the book, she felt for his crotch, undid his buttons and pulled out his erection. Gently she began to masturbate him as they both read the story of the abduction, humiliation and violation of the young victim. They came to the end, and he laid the book aside. She continued to work her hand slowly up and down his shaft.

'There was a technique the girls at the Smolny Institute used by which we could make sure we would not get pregnant. The man penetrated one's behind. We called it a l'Italienne.'

'I suppose it sounds more feminine than buggery.' He used the coarse Russian word.

She paused. 'It was a practice to which I became quite accustomed - in fact, I began to develop a taste for it.'

'Indeed? Was it frequently required of you?'

She laughed. 'Oh, regularly. I don't think there was a week during my last year at the college when I wasn't sodomised several times. A cadet came to tea in my room every Thursday during term time. He brought a chocolate gateau and a little tin of lubricant.'

'Didn't it hurt?'

'Yes, of course, at first. I would clench the little hole tightly, but then I learnt how to open my bottom to the men. I began to enjoy it, and even suggested it sometimes to my more bashful suitors.'

'But you can't obtain pleasure that way, surely.'

'My dear sir, a woman can gain pleasure simply from being used by a man. The memory afterwards can sometimes stir her to masturbate to an orgasm. For instance, at our graduation ball - it is called the soiree imperiale, you know - I left the throng and went out onto a balcony for some cool air. I was alone there, leaning on the balustrade and looking down into the garden below. Someone came up behind me and gently lifted my dress. It was a white dress, and I wore my diamonds. I didn't move. Fingers unbuttoned the back flap of my drawers - I always wore drawers like that, because of the repeated buggery I was subjected to. Then I felt the head of a penis push against the crack of my bottom. It was greasy, and I knew what he wanted.

I stuck out my rear and let him push himself into me. I was so used to such penetration that he slid in as easily as you entered my sex just now. I gave a little wriggle of my hips: the men love it. Soon he was finished and pulled out.'

'Who was it?'

'I never found out. He left, and I stayed looking out over the river for a while. I then buttoned up my flap behind and went back to the dancing. It may have been any of the young men I danced with that night, or a complete stranger. Anyway, for several nights afterwards I masturbated to the memory.'

Her free hand rummaged up her clothes and for a moment she fingered herself, while continuing to manipulate his cock.

She cleared her throat. 'I have some lubricant in my bag.'

'You travel well prepared, madam.'

'Yes, a woman never knows when she will be lucky.' She rose and bent over her bag on the opposite seat. He gazed at the back of her skirt thoughtfully. She handed him a beautiful little silver snuff-box, set with black jet jewels. He opened the lid, and saw that it contained a clear grease.

She sat down opposite him. She looked flushed. 'You must think I am a very lewd, dirty woman. And I am. I really am, behaving like a whore.'

'Sinful and wicked, madam.'

'I ought to be punished, don't you think?'

'Undoubtedly, madam. You deserve the harshest punishment for such shameful behaviour.'

'A caning, do you think?' Her eyes fell on his stick.

'A severe caning, on your bare bottom.'

'How many strokes?'

'At least twenty, for such dirty wickedness.'

She nodded, and drew a deep breath. 'I confess I deserve it.'

She got up and turned round, raising her clothes behind to expose the seat of her drawers. She fumbled with the ribbon that tied them in front, then slid them down to her knees. She bent over, her hands on the seat in front, offering him a view of her bottom, framed by the snowy whiteness of her petticoats. Her buttocks were small and firm, and he wasn't surprised to see the faint pinkish lines across them. She was evidently caned and whipped regularly.

He rose and picked up his stick. It was of the kind called a swagger stick, made of cane covered with black leather and topped with a silver knob engraved with the double-headed eagle of the Tsar.

The first blow smacked viciously across her bottom, making her gasp. A red line quickly showed up on the pale flesh. The second and third were harder. She half turned to gaze imploringly at him. Her face was pale.

'Stay still, you filthy bitch!'

Her eyes fell and she turned back, bracing herself to suffer the beating. The callous officer showed her no mercy. The leather-covered cane whistled down and cracked onto her helpless bottom, again and again. At each stroke the erection jutting obscenely out of his breeches grew harder.

After twenty, he tossed the cane onto the seat. She was sobbing now, and her bottom was criss-crossed with angry red stripes. Then he opened the little snuff-box.

He dipped his finger in the grease and applied some to his cock's stiffly-swollen head. Another fingerful was smeared onto the tight pucker of her anus. She flinched as his hands roughly prised apart her sore buttocks.

Slowly, he nudged his erection against the opening of her rear passage. He pushed hard. There was a moment of resistance, then the muscular ring relaxed and allowed the thick head to force itself into her. Inch by inch, he wedged himself deeper into her bottom, stretching the tight passage painfully.

After what seemed an age, the full length of his organ had slid in to fill her rectum. Her ring gripped the root of his shaft. Then he began slowly to drive in and out. She winced at each painful thrust. He went brutally after his pleasure, buggering her mercilessly. He panted in a series of quick, jerky movements. Finally, he grunted deep in his throat and then his sperm was pumping into the tight passage of her behind.

He remained still within her for a minute. The muscles of her violated passage contracted in occasional spasms round the impaling shaft. Then he slowly withdrew from her tortured bottom. Tucking his member away, he sat down heavily, breathing hard.

She rose stiffly, pulled up her drawers and smoothed down her skirts. Painfully, she sat down opposite him. She took out the mirror once more and wiped away the tearstains from her face.

'You are very cruel.' Her voice sounded more respectful than accusing.

'I have been told so.'

She patted a little powder on her face, then put away the mirror and sat back carefully in her seat. She winced with the discomfort.

'We always say that you do not know a man properly until he has taken you in your mouth, your sex and your bottom. You have done all three in eight hours - your youth and vigour do you credit, lieutenant.'

He wondered who the 'we' were. 'You do me too much honour, madam. I have never been so eager to carry out those divine duties.'

The train was already rolling into the squalid industrial suburbs of St.Petersburg. The woman sat forward and gazed at him earnestly.

'If you feel you owe me anything for what has taken place between us, then repay it by being discreet. Please do not tell anybody else, nor try to discover my identity. We shall arrive soon. I will be met at the station. Please do me the favour of staying in the carriage for some time after I have got out.'

'I understand perfectly. No gentleman who has been accorded the favours you have granted me would be so dishonourable as to compromise you .... with your husband.'

The lady blushed. 'Am I so obviously a married woman?'

'I noticed the mark on your finger where you had removed your wedding ring.'

She sighed and, taking a gold ring from her bag, slipped it onto her finger. 'A woman never knows when a wedding ring might be an embarrassment.' She looked keenly at him. 'You are very observant. I think you might be a very dangerous young man.'

'That is exactly what I intend to be, dear lady.'

The train began to slow down. She got up, and automatically he did, too. They faced each other for a moment, then she sank gracefully to her knees to give a lingering kiss to the front of his breeches. Rising, she put on her hat and, as the train squealed to a halt, took her bag and opened the door. He expected a final glance, but she was gone.

True to his word, he waited a full five minutes before the leaving the compartment. Her scent lingered.

## CHAPTER TWO

### The Proposal

The young officer slept badly that night; images of the lady on the train kept returning and prompted his phallus to stir and stiffen as he relived the incidents of the journey. When he awoke, the sunlight was already shining round the blinds of his hotel bedroom. Outside, he could hear the clop of hooves and the rattle of horse-drawn trams. Further away, there was the hooting of steamboats on the river. He got out of the large, comfortable bed and padded across the carpet. He had slept naked, but he felt no shyness in raising the blind and standing at the window, looking down into Znamenskaya Square.

In the centre stood the statue of Tsar Alexander III, a solid giant astride a massive horse. The locals had nicknamed it 'the Hippopotamus', but to him it seemed exactly what it was intended to be: a symbol of the weight of imperial power, crushing any opposition. And he was determined to have part of that power himself.

He opened the window and the familiar horse-dung smell

of St.Petersburg entered the room. The breeze was icy, reminding him that winter had yet to depart. He was used to the cold, of course, and he felt no discomfort as the clammy wind blew over his naked body. Above the clang of the tram bells and the rumble of carriage wheels, he could make out the distant sound of a military band, somewhere down the Nevsky Prospect. The memory of the lady returned once more to his thoughts, and his prick hardened with urgent lust.

There was a tap at the door.

'Come in.'

A young, pleasant-faced maid entered with a glass of tea on a silver tray. She nearly dropped it when she saw a naked man standing in the room, in a state of obvious sexual arousal.

'Oh sir, I beg your pardon, I ...'

'Just put the tea down, girl.'

Flustered, the maid placed the tray on the small table in the middle of the room, trying not to stare at him. She then hurried back to the door.

'Come back!'

'Sir?' She turned, pale-faced.

'Don't you curtsey when you leave?'

'Yes, sir. Sorry, sir.' She bobbed down to raise her skirts slightly.

'No. Higher.'

'Higher, sir?'

'You heard me. Raise your skirts higher.'

She fumbled for the hem of her clothes, pulling the material up. Her starched apron rustled as she gathered the material up to her knees, showing her black woollen stockings.

'Higher. Show me your knickers.'

Pulling the front of her apron, skirts and petticoats up to her chest, she exposed her drawers. The young man stood watching, hands on hips. She felt his hot stare fixed on her crotch. His erection stiffened even more under the girl's horrified gaze. She knew she was not going to get away without sex.

'Half a rouble to suck me off.'

'Oh sir, please...'

'Haven't you been taught to respect and obey your betters?'

'Why yes, sir,' she stammered.

'Then kneel down and suck my prick.'

Her face went pale and she glanced nervously back towards the door.

'Do what I tell you, girl.'

The maid sank to her knees in front of him, and with a shaking hand guided his erection into her mouth. She sucked it awkwardly, without any particular skill. She looked up at him beseechingly, the hard shaft still in her mouth.

'Please, sir,' she mumbled, 'Please don't make me pregnant. I'll lose my job.'

'I'll come in your mouth.'

She returned to her clumsy sucking, but while it interested him, she was obviously not going to bring him to an orgasm that way. After a few minutes, he lost patience with her. He withdrew his sex from her mouth, and slapped her face.

'You'll never make a cocksucker. Put your hands behind your back.'

The frightened girl did as she was told. He walked over to where his dressing gown was hanging. He took the silk cord from it and crouched behind the maid. He tied her wrists together, and then he moved back in front of her, straddling her as she knelt back on her heels. With wide fearful eyes, the young maid gazed up at his huge erection towering over her.

Roughly, he tore open the buttons of her bodice and released her breasts from the corset beneath. Gripping each, he squeezed them together and pushed his hardness into the warm

30

crevice between them. He then began to thrust his hips back and forth, fucking her breasts. The rigid prick slid easily in and out, wet with her saliva. He gripped her breasts harder, making her give a little squeal. He pulled her back and forth, using her body to masturbate himself. Her head jerked backwards and forwards as his thrusts grew more and more rapid. His tension rose.

Then his climax burst upon him. A long jet of hot semen spurted up onto her face, sprinkling her hair and running down her front. Then another and another, splashing her throat and running down between her breasts. He let out a groan. A final dribble of cloudy fluid dripped on to her lap, staining the snowy apron.

He dried the end of his penis on her hair and untied her wrists. Walking over to his purse, he gave her half a rouble. 'Now get out.'

The maid rose shakily to her feet, tucking in her ravaged breasts and trying to wipe the sperm from her face. She left, but not before curtseying to him.

He drank the tea. It had had exactly time enough to cool to the correct temperature. Just then, the factory hooters on the Vyborg side sounded out the beginning of the morning shift. It was time for him to get going as well. He went into the bathroom and took a warm shower. He had only seen shower baths in St.Petersburg and Paris, and considered them one of the few western ideas he really welcomed. Shaved and dressed in a plain civilian suit, he was ready to keep the appointment which had brought him to St.Petersburg.

Outside in the square, he hailed one of the small one-horse cabs. The cabman, in his blue wrap-over smock and shaggy top hat, nodded respectfully as the officer gave him the address: Fontanka 16. They joined the traffic clattering westwards down the Nevsky Prospect - cabs, carriages, carts and horse-trams. The straight, broad avenue was lined with shops and businesses, and thronged with people. About three men to one woman, he noted, and many of the men in uniform - peaked caps and greatcoats were as common as hats and suits. There was still dirty slush lining the gutters of the great street - winter was reluctant to leave.

The building was faced with stone, three stories high, unremarkable. Only the frame on the roof carrying dozens of telegraph wires marked it out as a government building. The young man noticed details like that. In the small hallway there was a reception desk with a clerk, and a heavy man who was probably a Cossack, and obviously the security guard.

'Your name, sir?'

'Lieutenant Markov, of the Tsar's Lifeguard.' He showed his papers.

'Quite so, Lieutenant. You are expected.'

The Cossack led him upstairs. The doors had brass numbers, and the security man tapped at number one. Without waiting for a reply, the Cossack opened the door and stood aside to let Markov enter.

The office window was covered by a net curtain, and in front of it, with his back to the light, sat a middle-aged man behind a desk. He had a heavy moustache and wore gold-rimmed pince-nez glasses. He rose as the officer entered.

'Lieutenant Markov.' It sounded more like a statement than a question.

The young man bowed. 'And you must be Sergei Zubatov, sir.'

The older man stared at him, disconcerted. 'Yes, I am Zubatov, but how ..?'

Markov languidly took a seat. 'I could only imagine I had been sent for by the head of the St.Petersburg secret police. The anonymous instructions to travel to St.Petersburg on a certain day, to stay at a certain hotel, to come next morning in civilian clothes to a certain building - these were not military orders. It had to be the Okhrana.'

Zubatov looked slightly ruffled. He made a point of never using his real name in such interviews, and he felt the young man had robbed him of an advantage.

'Well then, lieutenant, if you know so much, you may well also know why I called you here.'

'I think you intend to recruit me as an agent, having read the report on my loyalty and abilities which my colonel would have submitted at the end of my probationary year in the Lifeguard.'

Zubatov gazed stonily at him. 'Well, lieutenant, there is indeed little I can tell you.'

'Do not be put out, sir. I discovered as much from my colonel - I know these reports are confidential, but if I had no skill in finding out what others wish to keep secret, I would not be of much use to you, would I?'

The older man snorted. This young dog seemed rather too big for his boots.

'You may be aware, then, that the report also describes you as cruel, selfish and obsessed with sex.'

'I can confirm the accuracy of the colonel's opinion.'

Nothing seems to ruffle the infuriating calm of this fellow, thought Zubatov. Well then, let's just get on with it. He took a deep breath.

'You are also aware, as you seem to know everything, that St.Petersburg is the centre of a treacherous web of anarchists and revolutionaries who are seeking to overthrow the autocratic government of Holy Mother Russia entrusted by God to the Tsar.'

Markov nodded politely. Zubatov continued.

'And you are doubtless aware that students at the universities and colleges are amongst the ringleaders of these subversive groups, with their senseless dreams of democracy.'

Again a nod.

'And that it is hard for us to recruit informers within these groups.'

Markov suddenly showed signs of interest. 'You wish me to infiltrate these student groups? Why do you think I can succeed where others failed?'

'Because I have been checking up on you.' Zubatov smiled as he saw surprise on Markov's face. There, you cocky young know-all, I've scored there.

'Yes, I have had enquiries made.' Zubatov picked up a fat file on his desk and leafed through it.

'I note your school report that records you as a brilliant pupil but a vicious bully. I see that you were involved in a duel in your first year at the military academy - over a woman - and that you were nearly expelled for taking a second cut with your sabre when your opponent was already bleeding on the ground. I gather that a prostitute in a Moscow brothel complained that you had beaten her senseless, and only a sizeable sum of money hushed it up. That you are an accomplished liar. And that few women are able to resist your charms.'

'These are my qualifications?'

'Certainly. Many of the subversives are actually young women, who attend semi-legal female colleges in the day, and utterly illegal political meetings in the evening. You have the youth, the looks and the manipulative skill to gain the confidence of these females and to penetrate their organisations - no doubt while penetrating other things as well.'

Markov nodded again, but more reflectively.

The secret police chief continued. 'I don't have to tell you that if the subversives discover that you are an Okhrana agent, they will kill you.'

Markov flicked the suggestion away with a gesture of his hand. 'Sir, do not doubt my courage. Your proposal interests me, I shall carry it out.'

Zubatov looked at him with more approval. 'You know, it is often said that bullies are cowards. However, I employ a large number of bullies, and I cannot see the truth of it.'

They proceeded to details. Markov was to have a free hand, and as much money as he could reasonably require. He was to adopt the character of a student, and pretend to be sympathetic to the reformers. As he had only rarely visited St.Petersburg it was unlikely that anyone would recognise him. Each week he was to report to his case officer, at a restaurant or cafe to be arranged at the previous meeting.

Zubatov took him to a room further along the corridor, full of printing equipment, where a man issued him with a variety of false papers. In another room, an elderly man who looked like a professor gave him a brief outline of what was known of the various revolutionary groups in St.Petersburg. The recent textile strikes had involved female workers organised by the subversives. Their success in obtaining a limit on working hours had encouraged them. The real danger was from the Social Revolutionaries, formerly know as the People's Will, whose campaign of bombing and assassination had killed many tsarist officials. Under their influence, last year there had been student disorders: the Minister of Public Instruction, Bogolepov, was threatening the students with military conscription if there were any more disturbances. The briefing ended, and they returned to Zubatov's office.

'There is one revolutionary in particular I want you to watch out for. His name is Vladimir Ilyich Ulyanov. He was sentenced to a term of exile in Siberia for sedition, but was released last month. He is banned from St.Petersburg, but may be here illegally.. If you can implicate him, we'll arrest him again - this time for good.'

Zubatov signed a formal-looking paper and handed it to Markov. It was an order requiring anyone to assist the bearer in any way they could, or face the harshest punishment the Tsarist state could inflict.

'Another thing, Markov. You will never pass for a student with that military haircut. I will arrange for you to spend a few weeks on one of our country estates, where you will be given some specialised training. By then your hair will be long enough to pass for a socialist intellectual.' Zubatov spoke these last words with a sneer.

He was told to find himself lodgings and be waiting in the back bar of the CafÈ Romanov in five days time, ready for a journey. In the meantime he was to get to know St.Petersburg and stay out of trouble.

The interview was clearly at an end, and Zubatov rose from his desk and shook Markov's hand. They both went to the door.

'By the way, thank you for not screwing the maid at the hotel this morning.'

'One of your agents, I imagine?'

'Well, an informer, anyway. It would have been inconvenient to have to replace her if she got pregnant. It would not be unusual, though. The number of illegitimate births in St.Petersburg is nine times the national average.'

Markov wondered how the maid had reported the incident so quickly. Then he remembered the telephone wires on the roof. If some western inventions could help protect the ancient order of life in Imperial Russia, they were to be welcomed and used.

He left the secret police headquarters in a mood to celebrate. This enterprise offered far greater scope for vicious pleasure than the barracks life of the Lifeguard, with its endless drills and ceremonial parades. Markov's priorities were not the same as Zubatov's. He would certainly find lodgings and go into the country for a while. But before that, he was determined to find the lady on the train.

A cup of strong coffee at an exclusive restaurant on the Nevsky Prospect gave him time to plot his campaign. The first thing was to review all he knew of the woman. She was in her mid to late 20s, perhaps 28 at most, he thought. She was aristocratic, married, and had travelled widely. But, vitally, he knew her initials and that she had graduated from the Smolny Institute. That should be enough for a resourceful secret agent.

Half an hour, a cab to the Institute, and the flourishing of his pass was enough to find him in the headmistress' study. She was a sour-faced, elderly woman with her hair scraped back into a bun. The thick round spectacles glinted icily at Markov.

'And how may I help you?' Markov noted she did not add 'sir'.

'I am a government inspector, charged with that section of the imperial census dealing with average ages of marriage of the different classes. I would like to see the lists of your graduates over the last ten or twelve years, and any records you may have kept of their subsequent marriages - your establishment being, of course, representative of the very highest social class.'

The icy manner of the headmistress melted a little. 'We pride ourselves on the exclusive nature of our school. Last year we had no less than three princesses here, and an average year would see most of the girls coming from the higher aristocracy. Now here ..' She produced a huge, leather-bound ledger, which she thumped onto the desk between them. 'This register shows all the graduates since our foundation, with columns for their husband's name and their date of marriage.'

Markov gazed down the rows of names, arranged by year of graduation. 'This is exactly what I wish, madam.'

'You will notice that almost all girls marry within a few years of graduating, and usually to the very highest in the land. Our girls' reputations are so high that none could doubt their suitability as wives.'

Markov wondered whether the old battleaxe really believed that, or whether she knew that some at least of her young ladies had turned her establishment into a brothel. He merely nodded.

'Thank you, madam. If I may just take a few notes ... the statistics, you understand.'

He quickly turned through the pages. Yes. 1891. The initials were there, matching her husband's surname. She had married in 1895, five years ago. The husband - General Lementov. He had heard the name.

After some aimless scribbling in a notebook, Markov thanked the headmistress and left. Walking across the wide square to the Neva embankment, he leant over the stone parapet and gazed into the river. There were still pieces of floating ice, though not enough to hinder the steamboats puffing busily up and down. He had her name. The army connection was a bonus. It would be easy now.

He turned and signalled for a cab. As one approached from across the square, he looked up at the frontage of the Institute, wondering which balcony it was that she had leant over that night when she was anonymously buggered.

It was not yet noon when the cab dropped Markov back at his hotel, and he went upstairs to his room. As he approached the door, however, his keen eyes noted that another key was already in the lock. He opened the door quietly and slipped inside.

The first thing he saw was the young chambermaid, lying back in the armchair with her legs spread apart and her petticoats up round her waist. Her eyes were tightly closed and her breath was coming in shallow gasps. One hand was between her legs, the middle finger caressing herself. In the other, hanging limply beside her, she held the book of Parisian pornography.

Markov watched silently as she fingered the crotch of her knickers, firmly rubbing the secret nub beneath the cotton. The material was damp in the crevice in which her finger slipped up and down. Her lips were slightly parted, and she held her breath for long moments, letting it go and then taking another quick intake. The book slipped from her fingers. Her body grew stiff, her face became flushed. Then came the orgasm, in long, slow waves as the pent-up breath shuddered out of her. A moan escaped her lips, and her body arched convulsively before relaxing back into the chair. She lay quietly for a moment, her face calm and sleepy. Then her eyes flickered open.

As she focused on Markov, her expression changed to horror. She quickly got up from the chair, smoothing down her petticoats and skirt. She dared not look him in the eyes, but stood like a guilty schoolgirl in front of the headmaster.

'You enjoyed your orgasm?'

She stood silently, pale with shame. He came close to her, his face thrust into hers. 'Answer me!' he hissed. 'Did you enjoy your orgasm?'

'Yes sir.' Her voice was a shaky whisper.

'And you were searching my belongings when you found that book?'

'Yes sir.'

'And you were looking for something to steal.'

'Oh no, sir. Please, no.'

'Then what?'

'I can't say, sir.' She was trembling now. He silently walked round behind her.

'Lying bitch!' His scream made her jump, her eyes widened with terror. 'Do you think anyone would believe you?'

She began to weep silently, tears running down the soft bloom of her young cheeks. Markov grated in her ear.

39

'You realise that if I complain to the manager, I can have you dismissed.'

'No, no. Not the manager, not him" Her eyes gazed round imploringly at Markov. He guessed she was spying on him as well.

'Then I will have to punish you myself."

Her expression changed to one of horror as she realised what he meant. She looked wildly into his eyes like a trapped animal, then her gaze fell. She nodded dumbly.

He gestured towards the bed. She slowly approached it, resigned but fearful.

'Undress.'

The maid began to remove her apron as if in a trance. Markov sat on the edge of the bed and lit a cigarette. With downcast eyes, she unfastened her dress and let it slip to the floor. He could see the dried streaks of his semen from that morning in the cleft between her breasts. Then she fumbled with the side buttons of the petticoats, which fell with a rustle.

'Now your drawers.'

She hesitated, but then nervously undid the cotton draw-string. She lowered her knickers, and stepped out of them. She stood in her corset, black stockings and buttoned boots. Above the cleft where her legs came together, the prominent bump was crested with a little dark hair. Markov stood up.

'That's enough. On the bed.'

She clambered onto the richly embroidered counterpane, which no doubt she had carefully smoothed herself when she had made the bed earlier. She lay on her back, arms at her sides and legs tightly together.

Markov removed his jacket and took something from his trouser pocket. There was a sharp click, and suddenly he was holding a knife with a wicked pointed blade. The girl screamed.

'Be quiet. This isn't for you.'

His cigarette between his teeth, he picked up one of the maid's petticoats. With a few careful slashes of the knife, the cotton was cut into long strips. Folding the flick knife, Markov knotted the strips so he had four lengths. He went to the foot of the bed.

'Open you legs.' Automatically, she parted them.

'Wider'. She spread her legs as far apart as she could, but Markov grabbed a foot, pulling it towards the corner post of the bed. Quickly he tied one end of a strip round her ankle and the other to the bed-knob. He then did the same with the other foot, tugging it to spread her legs painfully apart.

Wordlessly, he repeated the process with her wrists and the posts at the bed head, leaving the maid spreadeagled and helpless. Markov stood at the end of the bed, looking down at her. The slit of her sex was exposed between her thighs, and he eyed it languidly as he smoked. She lay motionless, staring at the ceiling.

Abruptly he turned, grinding out the cigarette in an ashtray and picking up his swagger stick. With a few quick strides he had picked up the girl's drawers, still damp from her sexual excitement, and bunched the material up.

'Open your mouth.' She kept her teeth clenched though, her eyes wide with terror. A sudden hard twist and pull at her left nipple made her open her mouth to cry out. Markov pushed the crumpled fabric between her jaws before she could close them, forcing it in so hard that she could not push it out with her tongue. She was gagged, and the only sound in the room was the rapid and shallow breathing through her nose.

The first blow fell with a crack between her legs, the black leather of the cane striking between the delicate lips of her sex. The maid writhed and tried to shriek, but the only sound was a muffled gurgle. Another hit, and another. Markov stood calmly beside the bed, his arm outstretched to direct each blow carefully and vertically so that it actually struck the opening of her crotch. He used only his wrist and forearm, but there was more than enough force. The sensitive and secret nub of her clitoris, so recently the focus of her pleasure, now sent jolts of unbearable pain through the young girl's body.

The tears flowed in a ceaseless stream now, wetting the material of the drawers stuffed into her mouth and running onto the bedspread below her head. Neither she nor Markov counted the blows. Then he stopped. The maid opened her eyes and saw why. Markov was unbuttoning his flies.

The beating had given him a massive erection, which he slowly pulled out under the maid's horrified gaze. The heavy male organ jutting from his trousers seemed like another instrument of torture. He moved round the bed once more, untying the bonds from the knobs. Roughly, he forced her arms to her sides and bent her legs so that he could tie her ankles, still clad in stockings and boots, to her wrists. He then fetched a pot of ointment from the dressing table and climbed onto the bed, kneeling between her legs. He pushed her knees apart and back and gazed down on her sex, already red and swollen from the beating. He then applied some of the grease to the head of his erection.

For a moment the girl thought he was going to penetrate her cunt, and moaned behind her gag. But Markov had other ideas. He gripped her boots, pushing her knees further back onto her chest. The tight bud of her anus peeped from beneath the cleft of her vulva, and he guided his penis to it. For a few seconds the hard knob probed her there, and then he pushed in. She moaned again as the tiny hole was stretched open by his remorseless pressure. Her anus contracted to resist the violation, but the force was too great. Defeated, she allowed the muscles to relax. The resistance overcome, he was able to push himself into her rectum. The angle was not the best for sodomising her, but nevertheless he began short, stabbing thrusts. The passage was so narrow that the hard shaft did not slide in and out easily, and so tugged the tortured flesh back and forth. The girl's tight ring gripped his cock just below the head, and it was if he was using her young, maltreated body to masturbate himself. The thought quickly brought him to a climax and long spurts of semen jetted into the girl's ravaged bottom.

Markov got off the bed and buttoned up his trousers. Producing the knife once more, he cut the maid's bonds. He then removed the drawers from her mouth. She coughed and sobbed, and burst into a fresh flood of tears as he helped her sit on the edge of the bed.

'Oh, don't cry so, girl. You're wetting my shirt sleeves.'

He lit another cigarette as he watched her dress. She could not meet his gaze as she rubbed the red marks on her wrists and hurriedly put on the clothes which lay crumpled on the carpet. One of her petticoats was in tatters and her drawers were damp. Tying her apron strings, she dabbed at her tear-stained face with a handkerchief. She did her best to hide the effects of the ordeal she had just experienced, but managed to thank him for having only used her bottom. Nor did she forget to curtsey.

Only after the girl had gone did Markov take his own clothes off. Another quick shower and he was ready to dress again. But this time he laid out his uniform. It was time to follow up his plan.

The St.Petersburg Cavalry Club was a grand, almost palatial building with a colonnaded entrance that would have done justice to an opera house or a museum. With 1 1/2 million men and 40,000 aristocratic officers, the army was as important to Imperial Russia as the Orthodox church. Markov knew he belonged to a favoured elite, and was determined to keep it that way. As he came into the great marble entrance hall, the doorman saluted. Markov's uniform was a passport to a privileged world.

He knew his way. He had been to the club once, many years ago, before he had even been enrolled as a cadet. Then he had been a insignificant young visitor, taking in the atmosphere of power and wealth. Now he belonged, and his stride was confident as he made his way up the grand staircase to the smoking room on the first floor.

The room was large and scarlet-carpeted, with glittering chandeliers and heavy, gilt-framed portraits of generals around the walls. Well-upholstered leather armchairs were dotted around, some occupied by officers sipping drinks, reading newspapers or smoking. One tall fellow, in the uniform of a dragoon captain, rose and came over to Markov.

'A Lifeguard, eh what? Well, well, I thought you lot were still in Moscow.'

Markov resented his regiment being called 'you lot', especially by a dragoon, but this was no time to cause trouble. He adopted his most pleasant manner.

'Oh yes, we are - I'm just here waiting for a staff appointment.'

The dragoon looked impressed. 'Imperial Staff, eh? Good show.' He extended his hand. 'Stavrogin's the name, social secretary for the club - better than soldiering, eh what?'

Markov shook his hand. 'I'm Pushkin. Just come to St.Petersburg. Don't know it terribly well. Wonder if you could help me find my feet.'

'Of course, old boy. Delighted. Have a drink.' They sat down in the deep, comfortable armchairs as a waiter brought vodka. Stavrogin chattered brightly about the social scene, the balls, the races, the card parties. Markov paid polite attention to all this froth, eager to win Stavrogin's approval. Then Stavrogin said something that genuinely interested him.

'And tomorrow night, of course, it's General Lementov's farewell party - a lot of the chaps will be going.'

'Lementov? Where's he going?'

'Oh, out east, I believe. Manchuria. Japanese making war-like noises. Don't like this new Trans-Siberian Railway, I hear. Could spell trouble. But he's throwing a hell of a party - hundreds invited. I suppose it'll be a while before he can have anything like that again.'

Markov reflected that, to Stavrogin, an army officer's main purpose was to attend fashionable gatherings. But Lementov, the lady's husband, leaving the city... did this mean she was going as well?

'I dare say. But I suppose he'll be taking his wife with him?'

'Good God, no. What? Take a cultured, well-bred lady to the east? It would be worse than exile. No. Lady Ekaterina will stay in St.Petersburg. Anyway, I've heard tell that Lementov isn't terribly attached to her.' Stavrogin leant towards Markov and murmured confidentially. 'Actually, I'm told he only married her to stop the gossip about him. He's more interested in the young cadets, in fact. But don't say I said so.'

This gave Markov food for thought. 'Stavrogin, I'd like to go to that party, you know, get into the social swing of things and so on. Could you arrange it?'

'Of course, of course. There's an open invitation to any officer staying at the club. Spend the night here and turn up at the party tomorrow. I'll introduce you.'

Just then a booming gong announced the mid-day meal. They went into the splendidly decorated dining room. After dinner the two returned to the smoking room for coffee and cigars. Stavrogin's manner became slightly furtive.

'Look, old boy, why don't you fetch your kit here this afternoon and come out with some of the fellows this evening. We're going to a place I know, to see a moving picture.'

Markov had heard of moving pictures - they had just been demonstrated to an astonished public when he was in Paris.

He hadn't bothered to go and see one, though. Another modern invention to disturb an ordered world. He was about to refuse when Stavrogin continued.

'It's not an ordinary film, you understand - and not an ordinary place, if you see what I mean.' Stavrogin clenched his fist and pushed the thumb between the two middle fingers - the sign for sex. Markov smiled knowingly.

'I'd be pleased to come. Civvy clothes, I suppose?'

'Oh, rather. Must behave like officers and gentlemen, eh what? At least when we're in uniform. Be here at half past eight.'


## CHAPTER THREE

### The Law of Love and the Law of Violence

Entering the breakfast room of the club next morning, Markov saw Stavrogin sitting at a table, his head in his hands. He looked up as Markov approached and it was a grey and haggard social secretary that attempted a hearty greeting. Stavrogin's breakfast was a raw egg beaten in milk, and black coffee. Markov had no remorse in ordering a heavy, cooked meal, which he wolfed under Stavrogin's queasy and reproachful gaze. Nevertheless, despite what was clearly a monstrous hangover, Markov had no doubt that Stavrogin would be ready for the great social event of General Lementov's ball that evening.

Markov spent most of the day assembling a full dress uniform. Belonging to an Élite regiment meant having to pay out for half a dozen different uniforms, depending on the occasion. A round of military tailors, bootmakers and swordsmiths had him superbly kitted out, and the funds that Zubatov had provided came in very useful.

It was late afternoon when Markov, in civilian clothes, made his way to the street where General Lementov's town house stood. It was a grand avenue not far from the Admiralty building, and, as he had hoped, there were a few horse cabs waiting for custom at the corner. He wandered over to the group of cabmen, idly chatting and smoking. He asked for a light, and offered the men cigarettes. They took them gratefully, and his hip flask, they soon agreed, was just the thing to keep out the cold. Markov asked vaguely about the people who lived in the street. Real nobs, they were, apparently. Then what about General Lementov? Oh him. Well, we could tell you a tale or two. But best not. No names, no pack drill, eh? And what about his wife? The Lady Ekaterina? Poor woman. Must be a miserable life. No children, but that's no wonder. She always took a cab to Saint Catherine's cathedral on Sundays, and seemed to devote her life to religious charities. In a thoughtful mood, Markov returned to the club to prepare for the ball.

It was already dark when a cab deposited Markov and Stavrogin outside General Lementov's mansion. It was not as large as the town palaces of the royalty, but grand enough to be among the cream of the aristocratic residences of St. Petersburg. The rows of windows were brightly lit, and the sound of voices and music spilled out into the street. He and Stavrogin went up the flights of steps to the entrance, where a footman bowed them in without any further enquiry.

The spacious hallway was lit by a huge crystal chandelier. There was a roar of conversation, as dozens of guests chattered amongst themselves and waiters carried champagne glasses on silver trays. Behind the balustrade on the first floor landing, a string quartet tried to make themselves heard. Stavrogin steered Markov to the foot of the staircase, where a tall man in a general's uniform was holding forth to a group of young officers.

'General Lementov, may I present Lieutenant Pushkin of the Tsar's Lifeguard?'

'Oh you may, Stavrogin, you may!'

The young officers giggled and joined the general in appraising the newcomer. Lementov was in his late thirties, and wore thick spectacles. He peered intently at Markov, his gaze lingering on the bulge in the crotch of his breeches.

'You are very welcome, Pushkin, very warmly welcome. What brings you to St.Petersburg from Moscow?'

'A staff appointment, sir.'

The general looked keenly at him. 'A staff appointment. Is that what you're after? Look, I'm off to the east in a couple of weeks. That's where reputations are going to be made, you know. Why don't you come with me, as part of my staff? These brave warriors - ' he gestured to the smirking youths '- are going to be my heroes and companions. Why don't you join us?'

'I regret, sir, that my assignment here is already confirmed.'

Lementov shrugged. 'Pity.' He turned away from Markov with an expression of disappointment, and Stavrogin led Markov by the arm up the broad staircase.

'There's someone else you should meet.' At the top of the stairs, a woman in a white lace ball-gown had her back to them. She was talking to a couple of guests, but turned as Markov and Stavrogin approached. It was her.

'Lady Ekaterina, allow me to introduce Lieutenant Pushkin.'

In the instant of recognition, the colour drained from her cheeks and she swayed slightly. My God, she's going to faint, thought Markov. However, she tried to replace her shocked stare with an enquiring smile, and she replied in a steady voice.

'Pushkin, Captain Stavrogin? I don't remember a Lieutenant Pushkin on the invitation list.'

'Oh, staying at the club, don't you know. Arrived yesterday.'

'I see. Well, you are welcome, Lieutenant Pushkin. No doubt we shall meet later in the evening. But for the moment you must excuse me.'

She turned and walked quickly across the landing, rather faster than her composed expression would suggest. She passed through a large door, which closed behind her.

'Come on, Pushkin, old boy. Let's have a drink. Lots of people to meet.'

A succession of introductions followed, which Markov did not trouble himself to remember. He helped himself to champagne and hors-d'oeuvres from the circulating waiters, and kept an eye out for Ekaterina. Eventually a footman in a scarlet tailcoat directed the guests to the ballroom.

There must have been three hundred guests or more standing around the sides of the ballroom, but there was still open space in the centre. General Lementov walked to the middle of the floor and clapped his hands for silence. He then made a speech thanking them for their good wishes, and spoke of Imperial Russia's destiny to bring civilisation to the east. The guests cheered, clapped, and toasted his success. Then the orchestra in the balcony above struck up a waltz, and Lementov led his wife out to begin the dancing.

Markov gazed at the couple as they swung amongst the other dancers that joined them. The general waltzed with style, light and delicate on his feet. The lacy-white figure in his arms seemed almost an attachment to him, or an accessory. The dance finished, Lementov bowed briefly to his wife and left her. She went to a couch against the wall of the ballroom and sat down, fanning herself. When Markov approached her, she gave only the slightest of starts.

'Well now, Lieutenant. I was quite sure I should see you

again this evening.'

'But certainly, madam. Perhaps I may have the honour of a dance? After all, you must agree we have now been formally introduced.'

She took Markov's white-gloved hand and walked out onto the dance floor. They slid into the rhythm of the music effortlessly, both sharing that upbringing in which dancing was a skill expected of everyone. For a while she was silent, accepting his clasp without any sign of intimacy. When she spoke, her voice was low and urgent.

'I thought you were a gentleman, Lieutenant Pushkin. Fate had thrown us together, and I begged you not to pursue me. I was clearly wrong to have put my faith in you.'

'You do me an injustice, my lady. My presence here tonight is pure coincidence, I assure you.'

'Truly? Ah, fate makes fools of us all.' They danced in silence for a few bars of the music.

'So what happens now, Lieutenant? I am no longer an anonymous stranger to you, but a married lady whose reputation is in your hands. Can I trust you?'

'You can trust me by my honour, madam.'

'Your honour as a rapist and a bully? I suppose I have no choice.'

'No, I suppose you haven't,' he agreed. Then he added 'I want to have you tonight.'

'What! Here, tonight? What if we were discovered?'

'You know the house. Just tell me where to be and when.'

She gnawed her lip as they danced. 'Go up the staircase to the third floor. There shouldn't be many guests wandering up there - or servants, either. They're more dangerous. The french windows opposite the top of the stairs lead to a balcony. They'll be open. Be there at eleven. I'll join you.'

The dance ended, and he bowed. She returned it with a graceful curtsey, and a slightly flustered and apprehensive glance.

It was well before eleven that Markov went upstairs and, checking that nobody was around, slipped out onto the balcony. The lights of the street below showed carriages waiting for the guests, the coachmen heavily muffled. At this time of year the night temperature could still fall to freezing. To the north, against the glow of the city lights, he could see the spire of the Admiralty building pushing up into the dark sky.

There was a rustle of skirts and she was beside him. In the dark, the diamonds at her throat sparkled in the distant lights. His cock slowly began to uncoil in his breeches. For a moment neither spoke. Then he gripped her arm, shoving her hard against the wall. She gasped, but did not cry out. He slapped her cheek, with his fist clenched to lessen the sound of the blow.

'Please, mind my earrings. They're very valuable.'

'Never mind your earrings, you dirty slut!' he hissed. 'You deserve the worst I can do to you.'

He grabbed her wrist and forced it up behind her back, unbuttoning his flies with his other hand. He pulled out his erection. Twisting her arm further up, he forced her to bend forward. Stepping round in front of her, he forced her head down to his uprisen member.

'Open your mouth.'

She parted her lips and took in the urgent thickness of his cock. He rammed it as far as he could. The angle of her neck allowed him to push the head of his penis almost down her throat, and she choked, gasping for air as she drew back. He pushed her down again and thrust in and out, her saliva lubricating the softness of her mouth. But he wasn't going to finish that way.

He withdrew from her mouth and pulled her upright, pushing her back once more against the cold stone of the wall. His hand slipped down her cleavage. The white lace dress was

51

low cut, and his fingers soon found a nipple. They gripped and squeezed. She whimpered at the pain.

His sex was nudging the front of her dress, leaving a slimy trail of fluid on the delicate material, and his other hand was roughly dragging her skirts up. His hand rummaged up beneath her petticoats and soon discovered the silken sheen of her stockings. Feeling up further, he found warm, naked flesh.

'You aren't wearing drawers.'

'I took them off before I came. I thought it would make things easier.'

With both hands now, he pulled up her clothes to reveal her white thighs, gleaming dimly in the gloom, and the dusting of dark hair between them.

'Open your legs.'

She moved her feet apart and pushed her hips out to make it easier for him to penetrate her. The swollen head of his cock nudged between the lips of her vulva, and she rose on tiptoe to allow him to penetrate at the correct angle. He pushed slowly in until the full length of his member had invaded her body. He slipped his hands round to her bottom, under her clothes, and gripped her bare buttocks. She held her hands flat against the wall behind her to support his pressure.

Slowly, but with increasing urgency, he began his pelvic thrusts, the force of them almost lifting her off her feet. Her head banged against the stone as he slammed into her repeatedly, faster and faster as he approached his climax. Then his orgasm burst, in great spurting jets, emptying his swollen balls into her body.

Panting, he slipped down and out of her, the last feeble squirt of semen splashing warmly onto her thigh. She produced a large handkerchief from a hidden pocket and wiped his cock. Before she lowered her skirts, she mopped between her own legs.

'So much spunk, Lieutenant. You cannot have had any

other woman today.'

'No. I saved it all for you, Lady Ekaterina. We must meet tomorrow.'

'Not tomorrow. I have so much to do. Anyway, there's nowhere safe. Perhaps the day after, in the evening.' She smoothed down her skirts.

'I am not asking you, dear lady. I am giving you an order. Meet me tomorrow.'

She hesitated. 'Very well. At two o'clock. In the tearoom at the Astoria.'

She hurried back onto the landing but paused as the light revealed his wetness on the front of her dress. She spat on her handkerchief and quickly rubbed the betraying evidence away. A few minutes later, Markov sauntered down to rejoin the party. He was eagerly downing a much-needed drink when he saw her dancing again, this time with a bearded count. On Lady Ekaterina's white satin shoe, Markov noticed, there gleamed a large, pearly drop of his semen.

There were few people in the tea room of the Astoria Hotel the next afternoon. The clock of the nearby cathedral was striking as he took his place at a table and ordered two glasses of tea. They had been brought over, and had begun to cool, before she bustled in. She was dressed in a smart brown jacket, with the puffed upper sleeves that were fashionable and a matching skirt. Her starched collar and brown tie were impeccable, though a little masculine in effect. The straw hat was trimmed with a brown velvet band.

Ekaterina glanced round nervously before sitting down with her back to the door.

'You're late.'

'Yes, I'm sorry. Luncheon party.'

'We haven't much time. Let's go.'

'Go? Go where?'

'Don't argue. Come.'

53

Markov had a carriage waiting outside. He'd hired a large, enclosed one, and as they sat down inside he murmured to her.

'Did you bring a whip?'

She went pale. 'Oh, no, I didn't. Should I have?'

He made no reply, but called out of the window to the coachman to take them to a saddler's shop. The carriage rattled off. They did not talk in the few minutes it took to reach a fashionable saddler's establishment. Telling the driver to wait, he got out and ordered her to follow.

The whip department smelt of leather and polished mahogany. A slim young girl showed Markov the whips and crops on display. Ekaterina stood at one side as he examined them. She seemed afraid to look at them.

'Which would hurt most, do you think?'

The girl looked nervous. 'I'm sure I don't know, sir. One should not actually hurt the horse, you understand.'

'I don't intend to use it on a horse,' he replied evenly. The girl turned a shocked glance to Ekaterina, who stood by silently, her eyes downcast.

He bought a large hunting crop with a stag's horn handle, and the shop assistant's horrified gaze followed the couple as they left.

'I suppose you did bring some lubricant.'

Ekaterina looked as if she might cry. 'No. I didn't think we would...'

His harsh glare cut her short and they got back into the carriage. The chemist's shop was only a few doors away, but he made her accompany him to the counter where a male assistant was on duty. 'Would sir like anything else? Any, er, protective items?' Ekaterina's face was brightly flushed and she sank her chin onto her chest to hide her embarrassment. She followed him out of the shop.

The carriage set off again, this time heading away from

the city centre and out into the less fashionable streets beyond the Fontanka River. After a while, they stopped at a
cheap-looking hotel in a back street. They entered the hotel,
and Markov motioned her to wait while he went over to the
reception desk. An elderly man came and they exchanged a
few words. Markov gave the hotel keeper money, and received
a key in return.

They made their way up a carpeted stair, and down a short
corridor. He unlocked a door and she followed him into a
bedroom. There was a smell of stale cigarette smoke. It contained a double bed with a worn bedspread, and a washstand,
some chairs, a small table. He locked the door behind them.

He turned to the pale and fearful woman. 'Undress.'

He sat and watched as she unbuttoned and removed her
clothes one by one, her fingers fumbling as she did so. Nevertheless, she carefully hung up or folded her garments to
prevent creasing them, and Markov made no attempt to hurry
her. She now stood in her corset, drawers, stockings and boots.

'I said undress.'

She unclasped the corset, releasing small, firm breasts.
The drawers slid down, and she sat on the bed to unbutton
her boots carefully. She stood and faced him, completely naked, although her hair was still carefully gathered into a bun.
Her body was slender, with a firm, flat stomach and a narrow
waist. She had the long, graceful legs of a ballerina. With a
sudden thought, she quickly reached up and removed her
earrings, laying them on the washstand. She then returned
her hands to her side. He slowly walked up to her.

'Filth! How dare you come to me unprepared!'

'Please, I didn't understand ...'

. He grabbed her hair and tugged her across the room
slamming her against the wall. Holding her chin in one hand,
he forcefully slapped her face, first one way, then the other.

'Dirt! You're a disgusting animal! You're not fit to walk

on two legs. Crawl. Go on. On all fours and crawl behind me.' He picked up the whip, its new leather stiff and shiny.

She got down and shuffled awkwardly behind him, the lino of the cheap hotel room cold and hard beneath her knees. He walked quickly, first this way, then that.

' I said follow me! Keep up!'

'I can't, please...'

'You disobedient animal. You need to be disciplined. Kneel by the bed.'

Ekaterina did what she was told.

'Bend over it'. She leant forward and stretched her arms out on the rough and discoloured bedspread.

Markov stood over her and surveyed the pale expanse of shoulders, back and buttocks offered to him. He picked his target and put all the strength of his body into the first lash. She arched as the leather cracked loudly across her shoulders but no sound escaped her clenched teeth. There was a pause and he struck again, angling the next one so that the welts would cross. Again and again he lashed her, always giving her plenty of time between strokes so she could savour the intensity of the heat as the leather seared her. As the beating continued and the full expanse of her buttocks became striped to match her back, she began to writhe in almost orgasmic fashion, her hips swaying and wagging at each kiss of the crop, her hands clawing at the coarse fabric.

After what seemed an age, he stopped, gazing down on the skin he had criss-crossed with welts. Her breath was coming in shuddering sobs and her tears had made a damp patch on the bedspread below her head. Then Markov slowly undressed and he noted how Ekaterina's tear-filled eyes widened as they gazed at his massive erection. He laid down the whip and picked up the pot of lubricant.

'On the bed. On all fours.'

She climbed painfully onto the bed and Markov got up behind, kneeling so that the tip of his hardness prodded between the cheeks of her bottom. He applied some of the grease first to the tip of his cock, then to the pucker of her anus. He felt her wince as the blunt head began to push into the tight opening, but then the muscles that were clenched against the intruder relaxed. His shaft slowly entered her, filling the passage with its thickness and length. He began to sodomise her, driving mercilessly after his own pleasure. Soon his fluid spurted into the tight confines of her rectum.

After a pause, his penis slid out of her sorely-stretched behind, and he lay down, gasping, on the bed. He gestured her to lie beside him and, careful of her sore back, she gingerly stretched out on her side facing him.

'That was most enjoyable, madam. I am very glad I was able to make your acquaintance again.'

'Yes, I am glad, too. You seem to understand women like me.'

'In my business I need to know what makes people what they are, how they think. How did you come to be like this?'

Ekaterina began to toy thoughtfully with Markov's penis, lying limp and soft now.

'I cannot tell. I have often wondered, but I can never remember a time when such things did not excite me. When a child, I longed to be tied up in our games, and I adored the boys who treated me roughly. It was in my mid teens, though, when I understood it was a sexual thing. I saw a peasant woman being whipped for stealing in the market square of our town. She was stripped to the waist and the town bailiff had a horsewhip. The square was full of men, but many women were watching in the background. I felt my pulse quicken and my nipples stiffen as he lashed her, and I felt myself becoming moist down there.

'I couldn't get the image out of my mind, and I even began to steal things myself in order to be punished like that. Of course, an aristocrat's daughter would never have been flogged, but I made a thorough nuisance of myself. Nobody could understand why I, who could buy anything I wished, should steal stupid little things and get so easily caught. I worshipped the town bailiff and even confessed imaginary crimes to him, but he was afraid of my father and sent me away. My parents were glad to pack me off to boarding school.'

'Did you not think your feelings were unusual?'

'Of course not. The only natural relationship between the sexes is one of dominance and submission. Men have traditionally dominated women, and women have assented to it. A woman is weak, small and inferior, and needs and wants a master to rule over her. She naturally subjugates herself to the stronger and superior male. She can only expect her master to love her as long as she is passive and obedient.'

Ekaterina cradled his slumbering penis in her hands and gave it a tender kiss.

'I share the contempt that men feel for women. After all, what have women achieved compared with men? We are inferior to the male, and the accepting of this inferiority is the essence of femininity.'

'And the beatings?'

'The association between femininity and suffering is an ancient one. From the earliest times, pain has been the focus of a woman's sexuality, and her pleasure is to be passive and receptive. After all, every sex act has something of the character of a violent assault or rape.'

She lay musing for a minute, then suddenly sat up. 'It's cold in here, and you're naked.'

She opened an old wardrobe in the corner and took out the cleanest blanket she could find. She softly settled it round him. He slept.

When he awoke, she was already dressed, and she had

carefully picked up and arranged his clothes which he had torn off in his haste to sodomise her.

'We must go, Lieutenant. I am taking tea with the Bishop in ten minutes.'

They walked to the end of the street, where they were able to hail two cabs. They parted, agreeing to meet the following evening.

Markov spent the next day shopping and packing for his trip to the country. At the appointed time in the evening he was waiting at a corner in the business district. Night was falling, and only a couple of the offices had any lights showing. A few clerks and officials hurried past on their way home, then she came round the corner and gestured to him to follow.

Another corner led to a smaller street, and she entered the doorway of what seemed like an office building. He followed into a lobby with a stone staircase lit by a single electric bulb. She mounted the stairs, past doors with signs of accountancy firms and brokers. At the top, she turned a key in a door with a brass plate engraved with an Orthodox cross and the inscription The Ladies' Guild of St.Dionysia. One of her religious charities, evidently. She held the door open for him, then locked it behind them.

They were in a small hallway or lobby, with coathooks and an icon with the gilded image of a saint on the wall. A candle in a red glass bowl glimmered in front of it. She took off her coat and hung it up - two or three others were already there. Markov followed her example. Then she opened a small cupboard and took out two black masks. One she put on herself, and the other she handed to Markov.

'Elastic loops round the ears,' she said quietly. 'Much more secure than tying behind the head.' He put on the mask, made of stiffened black leather, and followed her through a heavy curtain and a doorway beyond it.

They were in a large, high-ceilinged room with velvet drapes obscuring what must have been the windows. The plasterwork of the ceiling was gilded, and the walls were hung, not with paintings, but ornate mirrors. The room was lit by a large electric chandelier, and wall lights with angled shades. Well-upholstered couches and chairs were arranged round the room, with small tables between them. Two women, similarly masked, were sitting at a table, and rose as they entered.

'Ladies, I have brought a friend.' The women regarded him warily, their eyes glittering behind the masks. Ekaterina turned to Markov. 'Here we are known only by our guild names. This is Penosugia -' the older of the two women, perhaps 35 and with red hair, offered her hand, which Markov kissed politely '-and this is Coitolimia.' The other raised her hand, which he carried to his lips. Ekaterina turned to him. 'And you must call me Anometia.'

'And by what name does your friend go?' asked Penosugia.

'I have given it much thought, and consider that he is Hermes.'

'Well, let us not keep Hermes standing. Pray be seated, my lord, and we shall bring you refreshments.'

Penosugia hurried to a cabinet while the others sat down. She brought over a cut-glass decanter of wine and some small glasses. She poured his drink first, then the others. He offered a toast to Saint Dionysia, and the ladies laughed politely. Nevertheless, he could feel the tension. Another woman came in with a man, and the women stood up. Then another woman entered on her own. Markov noticed they did not stand up for a mere woman, but gave her reassuring smiles. Yet another masked woman bustled in, apologising for her lateness. Ekaterina - 'Anometia'- sat by Markov, but the other man wandered away and took a seat on the other side of the room, lighting a cigar. The other five ladies gathered round a table, talking in an undertone and casting nervous glances at

Markov.

'Don't worry, my Hermes. You are the first man I have introduced to this society, and of course you are a matter of interest. We all depend on secrecy and confidence, naturally, and they need to know that you can be trusted to be discreet.'

'Madam, you may depend on me, as sure as my name is Pushkin,' replied Markov.

'Hush. You are Lord Hermes, and nothing else.'

He looked round. 'Well, what happens now?'

'The men usually arrive by another door, which leads to a building in the next street. In a moment the ladies will go into the withdrawing room to remove our outer clothes. And most will insert diaphragms.'

'Diaphragms?'

'Yes, little rubber domes we push up inside us, covered with a special jelly to prevent any risk of pregnancy. It protects us for a whole night's activity. Of course, I don't bother.' Markov raised an eyebrow, but changed the subject.

'You remove your outer clothes? Then you appear in your underwear?'

'Oh, very special underwear.' She giggled mischievously and pulled up her skirt to show a leg. Markov was astonished to see that her black boots did not stop at her ankles, but continued up over her knee to end at mid thigh. 'And the corset I'm wearing is made of the same leather.'

She rose and followed the other women out. Markov and the other man were not alone for long. A man entered by a door on the far side of the room, soon followed by two more, all masked like the others. Several more arrived together, and then a final man came in just as the women filed back from the next room. They were naked except for the long boots and corsets of soft leather which ended just beneath the breasts, pushing them up provocatively. Buckled on their wrists, like bracelets, were broad straps with iron clasps attached.

Penosugia went to a crank mounted on the wall and began to turn it. Looking up, Markov could see four gilded chains being lowered through carefully concealed openings in the ceiling around the chandelier. Two other women opened a large cupboard built into the wall and carried out a narrow but heavy table with a padded leather top. Inside the cupboard Markov glimpsed whips, chains and other equipment neatly hanging from hooks.

The women then drew aside the drapes, revealing not windows but a wooden frame about seven feet high and hinged to the wall. The women unfolded it, forming a heavy and rigid square frame. There were various rings and hooks fixed to the framework. While they were doing this, the other women, Ekaterina included, served drinks. As they bent to their task, the men fingered their breasts, bottoms and crotches as they pleased.

The women then went to take seats, and 'Anometia' sat beside Markov once more. She poured herself some wine with shaking hands and took a gulp.

'Nervous?'

She smiled weakly. 'A bit. It hurts, you know. And I've still got the bruises from yesterday.'

Penosugia rose and cleared her throat. 'Gentlemen, you are welcome to this meeting of the Ladies' Guild of St. Dionysia. Before we proceed, we have a new guest to welcome. Lord Hermes, please come forward.'

Markov stepped out into the centre of the room. Penosugia continued.

'You have been brought here, as all guests are at first, by one of our sisterhood, to whom you have proved yourself worthy to be admitted. Within this room you may do whatever you wish with any of the ladies here gathered, save that you must not actually injure them. Outside this room, you must keep all secret and make no effort to contact either the ladies or their guests.'

At this point, one of the men, a heavily-built, black-haired fellow in evening dress, stood up. 'Yes. You must know, Hermes; and the rest of you better remember, too -' his sinister masked gaze took in the men '-that anyone who betrays this gathering will pay the highest penalty. I can give you my personal word on that.'

Penosugia smiled nervously. 'Thank you, Lord Corvus. But, of course, we all trust each other completely, and I'm confident nothing will spoil our activities. Come, let us drink and the god of wine will inspire us.' She raised her glass and downed it in a single draught.

Two or three of the women rose, and began to refill the men's glasses. A murmur of conversation arose. One woman, young and freckled beneath her mask, poured red wine into Markov's glass. 'Thank you.'

'Oh, do not thank me, my lord. It is my honour and privilege. If I can serve you in any other way, please use me as you wish.'

She passed on. Ekaterina glared after her, her cheeks red with anger.

'Come, Anometia, surely you cannot be jealous here?'

'No, I suppose not. But ...' She squeezed Markov's hand. 'If you hurt anyone here tonight, I want it to be me. Or anyone except Nymphia. Promise me?'

Markov sighed resignedly. Women will always be women, he thought, no matter what the circumstances. 'Yes, my lady, as you wish.'

The talk was noisier now, and one of the men had a woman on his knee - it might have been Nymphia. He seemed have his hand between her legs, and she was squealing and wriggling. A man with a goatee beard next to Markov was smoking a cigar, and he clicked his fingers. Coitolimia came over immediately and bent towards him, holding out her hands.

63

He tapped the hot ash into her hand, and she barely flinched. Another man, passing behind her, found her jutting bottom too tempting a target and pinched it hard. Coitolimia's eyes screwed shut behind her mask, but she made no protest.

Penosugia went over to Corvus and murmured something to him and another man. The three returned to the centre of the room, where the gilded chains were hanging almost to the floor. Penosugia laid herself face down on the polished wood, and the two men grabbed her ankles and wrists, forcing them together behind her back. Markov then realised that the boots the women wore had a thick strap round the ankle, with an iron ring at the back rather as a spur is worn. A few deft clicks, and the woman's ankles and wrists were securely fastened together. Then the four chains were brought together, and attached to the central point. Corvus strode to the wall winch and began to crank.

The conversation died down as the company watched. A rapid clicking sound could be heard. First the chains tautened and Penosugia's limbs were pulled up as they took the strain. Then, with her body now flexed backwards, she was slowly lifted from the floor. She twisted and swayed a little, but the four chains kept her in position as she rose a couple of feet in the air.

The shorter man was watching intently. 'That's enough, Corvus. Your cock is higher from the ground than mine.' There was a snigger from the onlookers. Corvus locked the winch, came over to the suspended figure, and snapped his fingers. Two women came up to the men and, falling to their knees, undid the fronts of their trousers. Reaching inside, they carefully drew out the men's erections. The women rose to their feet and stood aside as the men approached the helpless figure; one to her head, the other behind her.

Almost simultaneously they entered her, Corvus in her mouth, the other deep into her sex. The hanging body quivered as they rammed into her, the chains rattling slightly as they began their pumping action. Markov felt his own cock stirring and took a pull at his wine. He glanced at Ekaterina. She was staring fixedly at the scene, her breathing shallow and rapid.

Corvus was gripping Penosugia's hair now, holding her head still as he raped her mouth. The other man was quickening his thrusts and reached his orgasm with a groan. There were a few derisive cheers as he pulled out, his female attendant wiping his prick and buttoning him up. Corvus was still pumping, with Penosugia's lips tightly gripping his shaft. Then his tensed body relaxed as his climax swept over him. He kept his cock in her mouth, however, until the bobbing of her throat showed that she had swallowed all his semen.

Corvus unlatched the winch, and lowered Penosugia to the floor rather roughly. The two men sat down to drink, leaving the women to release their victim from her chains. She got stiffly to her feet, rubbing her wrists and shrugging her shoulders to restore the circulation. Her eyes were bright behind her mask as she took a seat, smiling round at the others.

One of the women rose from where she was kneeling beside a man's chair and went into the cupboard. She reappeared carrying a cushion on which lay a long whip and a leather collar and lead. She sank to her knees in front of the man, who, rising, fastened the collar around her neck and took the lead in one hand. In the other he held the whip.

The crack of the first lash was like a pistol shot, and all heads turned toward the woman, cowering at the end of her lead. The second lash had her shuffling on all fours away from her tormentor, but he savagely yanked her back for a third blow full across her back. She half crawled and he half dragged her round the room, her pale, exposed skin marked by cruel red stripes as the whip fell mercilessly. Finally, she lay hunched on her side and weeping in the centre of the floor. Her torturer produced his rigid erection, and stood astride her. A few rapid movements of his wrist brought him off, and he ejaculated over her sobbing form.

Ekaterina and Coitolimia went across to help her to her feet, and supported her to a couch. Penosugia bent over her and, looking up, quietly called ' Lord Caduceus'. A bearded man came over to inspect the whip marks. He snorted and made a dismissive gesture. Nothing serious, clearly.

Next two men escorted Coitolimia to the padded table. They instructed her to climb up and stretcth out, while Ekaterina and Nymphia were beckoned over. Coitolimia's hands were secured to the table above her head, and a broad leather belt was brought up under the table and buckled firmly over her stomach. Her bottom was on the edge of the table, with her legs hanging down. Ekaterina and Nymphia were ordered to take an ankle each and hold it straight up, raising and parting the victim's legs and opening the cleft of her sex for all to see.

The first man exposed his erection and moved up to them. He ordered Ekaterina to guide his cock into Coitolimia's cunt with her free hand. Nymphia was told to part the lips of the vulva with hers. The man sank himself in, and the attendant women dropped their free hands to their sides as they watched him screw their friend. The other man had moved round to Coitolimia's head, and was stroking her hair. There was silence in the room, and the wet noises of the fucking were clearly audible.

The first man finished with a grunt, and abruptly turned away, doing up his flies. The other now took his place. When he had inserted himself, though, his hands felt for Ekaterina's and Nymphia's crotches. He pushed his fingers up their vulvas, as he thrust himself rhythmically to the peak of his pleasure. Breathing heavily, he withdrew from Coitolimia's body. The men's sperm dripped wetly from her open sex and made a small puddle on the floor.

Suddenly Markov realised that Penosugia was kneeling beside him, with the tall bulk of Corvus standing beside her. She laid her hand where the pressure of his erection was pushing out the material of his trousers. Her gaze was direct, but her voice respectful.

'Lord Hermes. I would like to serve your penis with my mouth. Will you grant me that distinction, unworthy though I am?'

Markov, only a little startled, nodded and made to undo his flies.

'No, my lord, in the arena, if you would be so gracious.'

Markov rose and walked into the middle of the room. Penosugia knelt before him and her cool, slender fingers quickly unbuttoned and freed his erection. It was harder than he could ever remember, and Penosugia's eyes seemed to darken as she clasped it reverently between her hands. Only then did Markov notice that Corvus had followed them out. He was standing behind her, and carrying a whip.

Wetting her lips, she guided his hardness into her mouth. As her lips closed on his sex, the first whiplash struck her back. She groaned and jerked a little but began to suck. The whip fell again and again as she worked her mouth back and forth along his shaft. Sometimes she allowed a gasp to escape her lips, but did not pause in her fellatio. Her soft tongue slid along the underside of his erection, sending soft shivers of excitement up his body. Gazing down at her with satisfaction, Markov saw her hand creep between her legs and start to caress herself. The whip rose and fell with a harsh regularity, Corvus' masked eyes glittering. Penosugia's head began to move back and forth to the rhythm of the whip, as did the hand working between her legs, the fingers sunk deep into her and fetching damp sucking noises from the flooding vagina. Soon her breathing became irregular, and sweat broke out on her forehead. Her orgasmic moan was muffled by his penis.

Corvus coiled the whip, and Penosugia opened her eyes. With reluctance, she allowed his still-rigid cock to slip out of her mouth. She stood up, shakily.

'Well, Lord Hermes, did you not wish to fill my mouth with your precious fluid?'

'Dear Penosugia, I intend my outpourings for Anometia.'

She seemed a little put out by this, but turned and took Corvus' hand as they made their way back to their seats.

Nymphia had no less than five men around her as they led her to the chains. She lay on the floor, but face up. Deftly, four men attached the chains, one to each ankle and wrist, and the fifth began to hoist her up. This time the chains drew out the woman's body in an X-shape, her whole weight hanging from the straps. She was raised until her gaping sex was at the men's shoulder height, and they clustered round between her outstretched legs.

She let out a little scream, and Markov could see one had fixed some sort of spring-loaded clamp to her clitoris. Another was pulling her breasts and attaching similar clips to her nipples. She writhed in the chains. Another man was pushing some sort of rubber plug or dildo into her bottom from below. The other two had gone to the cupboard, and brought out a large rod of black ebony, as thick as a man's arm and carved in the shape of a huge uprisen male sex. They guided the head of it between the widely splayed lips of Nymphia's vulva, and pushed.

She screamed loudly now, arching her back as the massive object was pushed into her. The soft membranes of her sex were painfully stretched, but the men continued to force it into her. When it could go no further, they lowered the agonised body down to crotch level. A wide leather funnel was produced, and the narrow end was pushed into her gasping mouth. The five men then gathered round her head, their cocks in their hands. They began to masturbate, their wrists flickering back and forth as they strained to position their pricks above the opening of the funnel.

First one, then the others ejaculated, the spurts of warm liquid squirting into the funnel. Man followed man in emptying himself into the helpless and tortured girl's mouth. The last finished, and the group of men left her hanging there.

Ekaterina and the other women hurried round the suspended victim. Penosugia issued quiet instructions, and the funnel was taken out of Nymphia's mouth. She coughed and gasped for breath as rivulets of sperm ran down her face. Then two of the women gently eased the massive phallus out of her vagina, while the others unclipped the clamps. Ekaterina went to the hoist and released it. Nymphia fell with a bump onto the floor and let out a yell. She glared round at Ekaterina.

'They haven't taken the thing out of my bottom yet, Anometia.'

Ekaterina apologised sweetly, with a pleasant smile.

Nymphia hobbled back to the couch, and bent over so that Penosugia could gently remove the rubber plug, now driven hard up her anus. The man with the goatee beard next to Markov watched with amusement.

'Well, Hermes, it's just you and me now. I'm Satyr, by the way. Let's have Anometia, she's had an easy time so far, and deserves to be punished, don't you think?'

Before she could sit down, the two men took her by the arms and led her across to the wooden frame.

'What do you think, Hermes? Facing the wall?'

'Yes, that will give us more room to swing the whips.' Ekaterina allowed herself to be attached to the frame; her arms upraised to the crossbar, her feet forced apart and clipped to the bar that ran along the base. Markov was fastening one of her wrists in place when she whispered to him.

'I'm strong. Show me no mercy, I beg you.'

The two men gestured to the women, who brought a selection of whips for them to choose from. Both took thick, stiff whips of plaited leather, and turned to the woman, held rigidly with her back towards them.

They took it in turns, first one then the other striking her helpless back and buttocks. The pale flesh, already marked by her ordeals at Markov's hands, was soon disfigured by vicious scarlet lines, patterned by the diamond weave of the whips. Her tensed body showed that she was in agony, but no sound escaped her as the regular cracks echoed through the room. At one point, Lord Caduceus came forward and signalled a halt. He felt Ekaterina's carotid pulse. He turned to the men and nodded them to continue. They lashed her with the full force of their arms.

Satyr had pulled out his cock as he started the whipping, and each blow seemed to make it grow harder and longer. Eventually he stopped his flogging. 'I'm sorry, Hermes, I've just got to have her. Will you join me?'

'What do you mean?'

'Well, you take one hole, I'll take the other.' Satyr signalled for lubricant, which Coitolimia brought across.

'Well, Satyr, you have the narrower entrance, I'll take the broader.'

The bearded man gestured to Coitolimia, who anointed his erection and parted the red-chequered cheeks of Ekaterina's bottom to allow him to penetrate her anus. He pushed in. Markov stepped round in front of her and introduced the head of his cock into her sex. It was soft and wet inside, and he had no difficulty driving up into her body. He began his in and out motion, answering the thrusts of Satyr as he buggered her from behind. His orgasm rose in him. Her eyes were closed, but as he pushed up close to her, they flickered open.

'My lord.'

He came.

70

# CHAPTER FOUR

## A Month in the Country

It took both of them to half-carry Ekaterina back to a couch. The masked ladies were now serving brandy and coffee. Ekaterina was too weak to stand, and a coffee was brought to her. The bearded man called Caduceus came over and offered her a white pill from a tiny round box.

'What is that?' asked Markov suspiciously.

When Caduceus replied, it was with a distinct German accent. 'Aspirin, a mild analgesic. Recently introduced by a German firm. I am interested in its effects.' He wandered off to see if any of the other victims wished to try his new painkiller.

Ekaterina swallowed the pill with her coffee. She smiled weakly at Markov.

'Well, what do think of our Ladies' Guild of St.Dionysia?'

'I am enchanted, madam.'

'I hope you will be a frequent visitor. It would be safer for us to meet here than elsewhere.'

'Alas, my lady, I must leave St.Petersburg tomorrow, for some time.'

Ekaterina started. 'But you have just arrived. Surely you stay longer.' She gave his hand a gentle squeeze.

'We shall meet again, I give you my vow.'

The following day saw Markov, carrying a Gladstone bag, keep his appointment at the Cafè Romanov. A man in his mid-twenties, with a small goatee beard and moustache, was sitting at a table for two. He returned the secret gesture Markov had been instructed to give. Markov took the other chair and the two men appraised each other for a moment.

'You'll never pass for a student in that smart suit.' said the stranger, with perhaps a touch of the condescending attitude his extra years and experience might entitle him to. 'Anyway, we'll kit you out before your return.'

A waiter appeared, and Markov ordered vodka. The stranger pursed his lips disapprovingly: he was toying with a glass of tea.

'And have you been settling in?' It sounded as if the stranger was not in the least interested in the answer.

'Oh, certainly. I have made some interesting contacts.'

'Good. Well, drink your vodka quickly. This isn't the place to talk.'

Soon they were in a cab hurrying south-east. They crossed the Obvodniy Canal, and soon were among the factories and tenements of the industrial quarter. They travelled in silence. Now they were deep in the suburbs, with trees and glimpses of open countryside. Eventually the stranger indicated a house to the cabman. They got out and the stranger paid the fare.

Markov turned to approach the house, but a grip on his sleeve stopped him.

'Wait 'til the cab's out of sight.' came a murmur.

When the cab had disappeared around a bend in the sub-urban street, the stranger gestured him to follow. Not to the house they stood outside, Markov noted with surprise, but across the street, down a side-alley and into the stable-yard of a mansion which must have stood in the next street. They entered a back door, and Markov followed up a narrow stair to a bedroom on the first floor.

On a table under the window, a samovar was steaming, with silver-mounted glasses in attendance. The stranger poured them both tea.

'My name is Ignatiev, by the way. I already know yours. I am your case officer, and during operations you will call me by code names that will change from time to time.'

Markov wondered if anybody in St.Petersburg used his or her real names.

'Your transfer from the Tsar's Lifeguard has been approved. Though still technically in the army, you will now take your orders from us.'

Markov's eyes flashed for an instant. He strongly disliked taking orders of any kind. Still, it was unavoidable.

'As a cover, for the next few weeks you will wear the uniform of the Interior Ministry mounted police.' Ignatiev went a large, elaborately carved wardrobe and took out a black tunic, black leather breeches, riding boots and a peaked cap with the imperial cockade. 'I will wear the same as I accompany you through your training. You had better change now while I go and arrange for our carriage.'

'Our carriage? Is there further to travel?'

'Of course. It will take two days, perhaps more, to get to the Institute. We must start as soon as possible.'

He left, and Markov changed. The uniform fitted well - they must have checked such details. A good sign: it meant they were thorough. When Ignatiev returned, he was dressed in the same uniform.

'Ready? Well, let's go.'

In the yard a large travelling carriage was waiting, and the coachman was adjusting the buckles on the harness of four excellent horses. They were getting in when Markov noticed a door of one of the sheds was open. In the gloom inside, he could make out the shape of several coffins.

It was not long before they were rolling eastwards through open country. Dusk was falling, but the coachman simply stopped for a minute to light the lamps. Ignatiev explained they were to stay at an inn that night. His manner became friendlier as the journey progressed, but did not offer any information about his background.

The country inn was hardly more than a farmhouse, and any fantasies of chambermaids soon vanished when Markov realised the staff consisted of the innkeeper and his mother.

In fact, of the two, the elderly innkeeper was the more attractive. Markov slept badly.

The following afternoon found them at the iron gates of a country estate. A painted wooden sign proclaimed in modest letters Institute of Investigative Research, but their entry was denied until the gatekeeper had consulted Ignatiev's pass and swung the heavy gates open. A twisting drive led to a large, three-storey manor house, sheltered by trees. The carriage deposited the uniformed men at the main door, at which Ignatiev knocked. A man in a similar uniform armed with a pistol and carrying a whip, immediately opened it. They entered a large hallway, paved with marble, in which their voices echoed.

'Welcome, Captain Ignatiev - and this must be Lieutenant Markov.'

'It is indeed, Kreisky. I want you to show him to his room, give him a tour of the house, and then give him tea. Has Dr Konigsberg returned?'

'No, sir. The Director is still in St.Petersburg. We expect him to arrive during the night.'

'Very well. I must write some reports. I will see you for tea, Markov.'

Kreisky led Markov to a room on the top floor of one wing, overlooking the front of the house. It was more like a hotel than a secret police base. There was a double bed and, as he laid his bag on it, he realised there was a chain and leg iron attached to one of the corner posts at the foot of it.

He was given a guided tour of the staff areas, the dining room, the bath-house for the regular social sweat-baths, and finished in what was half a lounge and half a library. Tea was ready, served by a bald-headed steward wearing a grey shirt and black breeches.        Ignatiev joined them, and soon other staff members drifted in. Some were recruits under training, like himself. Others, usually in civilian clothes, were specialists of one kind or another. Chemists, photographers, code experts were all introduced to Markov, and he was to come to know them well. Ignatiev outlined the programme of his training, following a tough timetable with little leisure.

'In any case, you are not permitted to leave the grounds during your stay here. I prefer to spend my free time in the cellars.'

Markov thought this an odd remark, as he had never seen Ignatiev touch any alcoholic drink. His attention was diverted, though, by the entrance of a woman. She was over forty, with a hard face that had already begun to wrinkle. She wore a plain blouse with a starched collar and a black tie with a silver double-headed eagle brooch. Her skirt was of the same soft leather as the men's breeches, and it buttoned all the way up the front.

'Markov, this is Miss Stolypin. She has charge of the female prisoners.' Markov clicked his heels and bowed, and to his astonishment Miss Stolypin did the same.

'Well, Lieutenant, you will be pleased to hear a new consignment of volunteers has arrived this morning. They are being bathed and issued with their clothing now. They will be paraded at dawn tomorrow in the entrance hall. I have no doubt you young men will wish to be present.' She spoke coldly, but there was a strange glint in her eye as she turned away.

'What's all this about volunteers?' he asked Ignatiev.

'Well, inmates of civilian prisons are offered reduced sentences if they will volunteer for interrogation experiments. Many do. In fact, so many that we ask the prison authorities only to send us the most sexually attractive.'

'Do they know what's store for them?'

'Oh, certainly. Beating and sexual molestation are common in prisons anyway. At least here they gain some benefit from it.'

'Are all the prisoners female?'

'Not all, but only one or two of the staff prefer men, and they are kept separately. It is best not to enquire too closely.' Markov nodded thoughtfully.

The following morning, as he had asked, the steward woke him at dawn. Markov hurriedly put on his uniform and hurried down to the entrance hall. The grey light was already filling it, and Ignatiev and many of the others were lounging about.

The door on the far side was unlocked, and Kreisky appeared, whip in hand. Behind him followed a silent file of girls. They were mostly under twenty five or so, their hair pulled tightly back into buns. All were slim, and some actually skinny from their prison diet. Each wore only a white singlet of the stretch cotton that men's underwear was usually made of, and navy-blue briefs or shorts of the same material. They were bare-footed on the freezing marble floor.

There were about three dozen of them, and Miss Stolypin followed at the rear. She began ordering the girls into lines facing the staircase. As she screamed and shoved them into place, the terrified girls stood at attention like parading soldiers. Markov noticed that their singlets were stencilled with prison numbers. Their navy-blue briefs were so tightly fitting that the soft bulge of their crotches was clearly outlined, with the fabric dimpling into the cleft between their legs.

Having smacked the last girl into line, Miss Stolypin screamed for silence. Just at that moment, a bearded man in civilian clothes came down the central staircase. He paused on the bottom step. When he spoke, it was with a distinct German accent.

'Well, young women. You are here because you chose a month as an experimental subject above several years of imprisonment. You made the right choice. You will not die here, nor will you be permanently injured. You will, however, aban-

76

don all rights you ever had to your bodies for the time you are within these walls. You cannot refuse any demand made of you, whether it is shameful, painful or degrading. If you do, you will be returned to your prisons. This moment is your last chance. You can be sent back now, and nothing more will be done to you. If you stay, you will be freed in four weeks' time. Does any wish to leave?'

There was a deathly silence in the hall. After a moment, the Director nodded. 'Good. Continue, Miss Stolypin.' He turned and went back up the stairs. The wardress stepped forward.

'Stand at ease!' The girls parted their legs and clasped their hands behind their backs.

'Gentlemen, you may inspect this latest consignment from the dross and rubbish of our nation. What do you think?' The men moved up and down the ranks, fondling the girls between the legs, stroking their bottoms and feeling their breasts. The girls stood still and stiff. With some enthusiasm, Markov joined in this cross between a parade and a slave market.

'Well what do you think Markov?' smirked Ignatiev, idly tweaking a nipple beneath the snowy cotton material.

'Hmm,' replied Markov, as he slipped down a pair of elasticated briefs and pried open a vulva, he was impressed by how slick it was. Clearly the thought of being the helpless plaything of all these men was not entirely displeasing to some of the girls. 'These have been carefully selected.'

'Yes they have, Lieutenant' cut in Miss Stolypin, who gave a violent slap to a tightly-knickered bottom, 'and you do not have to inspect them for disease. That has already been done.'

Markov, faintly irritated, gestured to the girl to pull up her pants. Ignatiev came close and murmured.

'Avoid the ones with pink ribbons in their hair. They're the ones Miss Stolypin has chosen for herself. There are usually only two or three.' Markov nodded, and finally selected a tall, brown-haired girl with remarkably fine features. He beckoned over to Ignatiev again.

'Can I have this one now?' he whispered.

'Of course. You can have any of them whenever you wish. We use them to practice interrogation techniques. They are kept in their cells until required for use, unless somebody wants them overnight, when they are chained to his bed.'

'Well, it's been nearly forty eight hours since my last screw, so I think I'll have this one now.'

The other men paused in their inspection to watch as Markov stood behind the tall, brown-haired girl and undid his breeches. His cock stuck out stiffly, and as he nudged it against the soft material tightly stretched over the girl's bottom, he left a wet stain on the navy-blue material.

'Bend over.' Without leaving her place in the rank, she bent forward, her hands on her knees. Markov contemplated the smooth roundness of her buttocks for a moment, then eased down her knickers until they were half-way down her thighs. Guiding his erection, he pushed it into her sex from behind. It was wet and ready for him, he noted, and it was an easy matter to slide into her sexual passage until the front of his leather breeches met her naked bottom.

Hands on his own hips, Markov thrust back and forth. There was silence in the hall now, and the slippery wet sounds of his copulation echoed around it. Then he increased his speed as his orgasm began to rise in him. He gripped the girl's hips and savagely hauled her back each time he thrust forward. Her head nodded at each impact, and she kept her feet with difficulty. Then came his climax, and he felt as if pints of semen were pumping into her body. Buttoning his breeches, he ordered her to pull her pants back up.

After that, he left the hall to take his breakfast. As he crossed the hallway after breakfast, he saw the girl he had fucked with her hands tied behind her back, following Miss

Stolypin. The crotch of the girl's knickers was dark and wet with his sperm, and he stopped her for a moment to feel her there.

The working day began with codes and ciphers - Markov hadn't realised they were different things - and the chemistry of secret inks. He was not particularly interested in either, but he knew his life might depend on his professional skills, and he was determined to acquire them. After lunch, an electrician in a laboratory festooned with wires and mysterious boxes tried to make him understand about microphones. Markov disliked this even more. Such inventions were all from Western Europe and America, the source of all the modernity he so hated. As far as he was concerned, messages were carried by men on fast horses and that was that.

Then, in mid afternoon, he was told to report to Dr Konigsberg in the cellars. He went down the stone steps and through a guarded door. Dr Konigsberg, wearing a white coat, welcomed him. A stone-vaulted chamber was brightly lit by electricity, and around the rough walls were benches with equipment, including whips, chains and handcuffs. In the centre of the room was a leather-topped table, on which one of the female prisoners lay. Her arms and legs were stretched out towards the ceiling by chains, and she was blindfolded. Electric wires emerged from her singlet and shorts. What caught Markov's attention, though, was the rubber mask over her mouth, connected to a corrugated tube that looped over to some glassware on a bench.

'Here we approach the matter of interrogation scientifically, Markov. Pain and fear are the commodities in which we deal, and we need to be in control of them.' He gestured to the helpless figure. 'For example, this subject is connected to apparatus which measures her breathing and the amount of carbon dioxide she produces, which varies according to stress.' He walked over and closed a switch on the workbench.

The girl's body arched, but her scream was muffled by the rubber mask. Konigsberg watched with satisfaction as the indicator on the equipment started to rise.

That voice, thought Markov. Why was it familiar? Konigsberg ushered him into the next chamber, leaving the tortured girl alone. The chamber was a mixture of workshop and study, but two comfortable chairs flanked a desk covered with papers. The doctor motioned him to take a seat.

'You see, for the interrogator, pain must be controllable pain. Our contract with the subject ...' Markov noticed he used the scientific word for 'victim' '... our contract with the subject is that when she confesses, the pain will cease. We must be able to withdraw it at will. A gross injury would not be withdrawable, and so is not part of a credible contract. You follow?'

Markov nodded. This German accent... 'Take burns, for example.' There was genuine disgust in the doctor's voice. 'The threat of them is very effective, of course, but actually to use them is to relinquish control. The pain continues without cease, unless opiates are used - at which point the subject is beyond our questioning. Any fool can knock out a subject, but a professional will maintain consciousness.'

Markov suddenly realised where he had heard his voice before. He kept the recognition to himself. It would probably prove useful later. Konigsberg was talking now about his experiments with electric shocks, but Markov was glad to hear that these were still under development and that he would be taught traditional techniques. He was told to report the following day to the cellar under the other wing to begin this training.

That evening he walked along the corridors of the girls' cellblock, peeping through the spyhole at each. He found one which attracted him, and unlocked her door with his pass key. He beckoned and she followed him meekly up to his room. He chained her ankle to the bedpost, and used her all night in every way he could think of, finding her co-operative and enthusiastic. At some time deep in the night he smiled to himself as the girl's head bobbed up and down in energetic fellatio after her most recent shafting and buggering. He was obviously a better screw than her previous jailers had been. His opinion was reinforced by the muffled but satisfied moan which came from the girl as his sperm pumped out into her mouth and was eagerly swallowed.

In the training cellar next day, Markov found the doctor waiting. A girl was standing in the centre of the chamber, her wrists bound and stretched up to the ceiling. Her eyes were wide with terror as Markov approached her. Another female prisoner stood motionless by the wall, staring straight in front of her. Beside her sat Miss Stolypin, severe in her black leather skirt.

'The art of flogging, Markov, is to hurt without injuring.' The doctor brandished a short, whippy crop. 'You must avoid the head, of course, but also the stomach - for fear of the spleen- and the lower back - to protect the kidneys.' With the whip he indicated each part on the girl's quivering body. 'But elsewhere as you please, bearing in mind that the muscles are better able to take the blows than the joints. Like this.'

He began a slow, heavy beating of the girl's shoulders, buttocks and thighs. She squealed at each blow and writhed in her bonds.

'From time to time, check the circulation, if the wrists are bound. Loosen the bonds if necessary to bring the colour back to the fingers. If she faints, let her down until she recovers, then begin again.' He recommenced his heavy, deliberate flogging. The girl was howling now, her tears running down into her open mouth.

Miss Stolypin stood up and gestured to the other female prisoner. The girl knelt in front of her and Markov could see the pink ribbon that bound her bun. From the hem, she began to unbutton Miss Stolypin's skirt, and when only the top button remained, Miss Stolypin drew the two halves apart. Underneath were boots and stockings, but no drawers. Markov could see that her pubic hair was flecked with grey. Miss Stolypin parted her legs slightly, and the girl's head bent towards her mistress's crotch.

As the regular lashes fell, Miss Stolypin's eyes never left the crying victim, twisting in her chains. At her feet, the kneeling girl licked her clitoris. Markov watched the scene with interest, and was impressed how soon it was that Miss Stolypin began to sway, close her eyes and moan. Soon the shuddering gasps announced her orgasm.

Konigsberg continued beating his young woman for a while, then tossed Markov the whip. 'Now you try.'

Miss Stolypin had sat down now, and the girl who had performed the cunnilingus curled up at her feet. The older woman caressed her hair and both watched Markov being instructed in the art. To begin with his natural excitement at having a comely enough girl strung up before him made him wield the crop rather too quickly and Konigsberg advised him to slow the cadence of his delivery, and also to moderate the force he put into the lashes. His own pleasure was not, after all, the point at issue here. He ignored the thrust of his erection against his breeches and tried to concentrate instead on working the crop on the girl's body as an artist might brush paint onto a canvas. Carefully he applied the livid lines onto the twisting and

leaping body in front of him. And at last when Konigsberg called a halt, Markov was deeply impressed both by the technique and its recipient. The subject had taken a much more prolonged and thorough beating than she would have if he had been left to his own devices. In fact he was perversely proud of her; a Russian girl could take a flogging like no other, but then it was what they were used to, he reflected. He moved round to stand in front of her and roughly grasped a quivering breast.

'Do you regret your volunteering now girl?' he asked.

She shook her head and Markov laughed aloud as he felt the nipple harden under his hand.

Day followed day, and something of a routine developed. In the day, he carried out his formal training, in the evening he talked with the others, played chess or cards, read books. At night he would select a prisoner to share his bed. Apart from a few strolls in the park around the house, however, he hardly left the building. The weather was getting warmer now, and he felt like a good ride to take the air and leave the secret world of the Institute behind. He approached the Director about it.

'Yes, Markov, we do have saddle horses here, but they are for despatch riders. Besides, the park is too small for a good gallop and you are not permitted to leave it.' Dr Konigsberg smiled regretfully.

'I'm sure you could arrange it, Dr Konigsberg - or should I say Lord Caduceus?'

'What did you say?' The doctor's eyes were wide with astonishment. 'What do you mean?'

'I mean, if I have a horse at my disposal and freedom to leave the grounds, then Lord Caduceus will be forgotten.' The doctor sat down heavily behind his desk, staring pale-faced at Markov.

'Very well. I'll see to it. But not a word to anyone, you understand?'

'It is a poor secret agent who cannot keep a secret, sir.'

So it was that the next Sunday saw Markov mounted on a black mare and leaving the park by a back gate in the cherry orchard. He trotted up onto a ridge, and saw stretched out in front of him a long, grassy slope down to a distant river. Just

83

the place for a gallop.

He began to walk his horse down the slope and then urged her into a trot. Suddenly, from behind a rise to right, another horseman appeared, riding hard. He was a youth in khaki breeches and a lighter shirt, vaguely military looking but without a cap. About fifty yards from Markov, he rose in his saddle and gave a rude gesture in his direction. Damn the little sod, he was challenging him to a race!

Markov sat down and squeezed his mare into a canter. The boy's horse was not much more than a pony, and Markov was sure of an easy victory. To make sure, he tickled her with his spurs and then they were in a magnificent flat gallop. The distance was closing when the youth disappeared over a shallow rise. When Markov reached the crest, however, he couldn't see the boy at all. What was suddenly revealed, though, was a deep, sunken road right across his path, only a few yards away.

My God, the bastard's led me into a trap. Markov realised he couldn't stop his horse in time. 'Jump, you whore, or we're both done for.'

Only two or three strides to gather for the jump, then horse and rider were in the air, the gravel track ten feet below them. The mare made it across as if she could fly, and Markov reined her in to pat her in thanks for his life.

There was a high-pitched laugh behind him. Turning, he saw the youth leading his pony down into the lane and up the bank towards him. As the figure approached, Markov realised with a shock that it was a girl. Her hair was cut short in the style of a pageboy, but despite her flat chest, there was no mistaking that wide-hipped walk.

'You did well there, Mr Policeman. I thought I'd got you.' She seemed more amused than anything. 'I suppose you'll arrest me now.'

Markov gazed at her boyish face, with its defiant stare.

'No, I won't arrest you. Just come and sit down with me under that tree while I get my breath back.'

The girl's expression changed to panic. 'You won't do anything to me?'

'Nothing you don't want me to.' She followed uncertainly, leading her pony.

They tethered their horses by their head-ropes to the tree, and watched them crop the grass. Markov produced his flask and offered it to the girl. She hesitated, but took a swig - then burst into pink-faced coughing.

'Oh God, I wish I were a man and could drink brandy properly. And fight. And live with a woman.'

'Is that what you'd like?'

'All my life I've wanted to be a boy. I was christened Karolina, but I make everybody call me Karl. I've never felt attracted to boys, only girls. I got into trouble over it when I was at boarding school.'

Markov nodded sympathetically. She continued. 'You were at a boy's school. What was that like?'

'Rough. Cruel. A lot of sport. A lot of sex talk. There were no girls, of course. We used to toss each other off a lot.'

'Toss off?'

'Yes, mutual masturbation. You know, wanking your hand up and down the other boy's cock until he came off.'

Karl was silent for a while. 'What's it like to have a cock?'

'Oh it's great fun. Here, just feel. Why don't you get it out?'

He took her hand and guided it to the front of his breeches, distended by the stiffness of his erection. Hesitantly, she gripped the hard length of his phallus beneath the leather. She let out a little gasp as she felt the size of it.

The man said nothing, letting her proceed in her own time. After gnawing her lip a little, she fumbled with his fly buttons, and slipped her hand inside. It felt cool against the hot

85

shaft within. Awkwardly, she drew it out, and it sprang upright. She gazed down at it for a moment and then cleared her throat.

'What did you say the boys do?'

'Masturbate each other. Let me show you.'

He took her hand and folded it around his hard, uprisen sex. Then he squeezed her fingers together to grip it, and began the slow up and down motion. When she was copying his rhythm, he released his grip and let her continue on her own. As he gave her gentle instructions as to her grip and her wrist action, his own hand fell to the crotch of her breeches. For a moment she stiffened and stopped wanking.

'It's all right. This is what the boys do.'

She resumed her masturbation of his shaft, and Markov began to rub between her legs, his fingertip seeking out the little nub beneath the thin cotton drill. She sighed and shifted her position to enable him to touch her there more easily. He slid his fingers up from the warm fork of her breeches, and started to unbutton her flies. He slowly inserted his hand, and felt down inside for the damp crevice. He found the hard little clitoris and started to caress it.

The girl moaned, but did not stop wanking him. Markov felt the great wave of his climax about to sweep over him.

'Faster, Karl, faster. Grip it just under the head.'

Then a long, hot jet of liquid jetted up from his cock, causing Karl to squeak with surprise. Some drops splattered onto her breeches. It ran down in rivulets over her fingers as she instinctively slowed her movement. Markov withdrew his hand from inside her fly, and sat back against the tree.

Karl, blushing now, examined the sticky fluid on her fingers. She licked it and pulled a face.

'What's this?'

'Semen, dear Karl. Have you never seen it?'

She shook her head. 'At least girls don't make such a mess.

Is that what you used to do?'

'Yes, though some of the boys used to bugger each other. You know, boys don't have cunts, and they had to use the tighter hole that everyone has.'

Karl nodded reflectively.

It was with a friendly smile that she did up her breeches and untethered her pony. 'That wasn't so bad. It's hard to meet interesting people in this dump. Look, why don't you come and meet my girlfriend, Tatiana. She doesn't know much about boys - her mother won't even let her talk to them. To-morrow afternoon at half past four in the boathouse in that clump of trees by the river. See you.'

With that, she mounted and rode off.

Markov used his hold over the Director to leave the Insti-tute early the next afternoon, and half past four saw him lead-ing his mare through the riverside trees. A two-storey boat-house built of wood, with a balcony overlooking the river, stood shaded by the trees. There was real warmth in the spring sun now, and smell of waterweeds and rushes filled the air. Leaving his horse tethered, he entered the rear door. Several skiffs and other boats floated inside, and a flight of stairs rose to his right. He climbed up and opened the door.

The upper room was decorated in the manner of some eastern palace, with exotic printed hangings on the walls, and piles of heavy cushions. Karl and a young girl were sprawled on the cushions, and both rose to greet him.

'This is my friend Tatiana, Mr Policeman.' The girl grinned and giggled. She was petite, with bubbly fair hair, and wore a fussy dress trimmed with lace hanging down from the short sleeves.

'Do you like Tatiana's dress? I ordered it for her from Paris.' Tatiana dropped a pert little curtsey and giggled again. Karl invited him to sit, or rather lie, and she took a bottle of white wine and some glasses from a cupboard. She served

87

Tatiana first, then Markov.

'This boathouse belongs to my father. He owns all this land round here. We come here so nobody can see what we get up to.'

Tatiana giggled again, and when she spoke it was with a slight lisp. 'I wouldn't mind if they did see.'

'What sort of things do you get up to?'

Tatiana simpered, 'If Karl has enough wine, you'll see for yourself.'

Karl frowned. 'Are you saying I need drink to pluck up courage?'

'Don't be so silly.'

'I'm not silly, you...'

Tatiana stood up and stuck her tongue out at Karl, who rose to her feet and began to chase her round the room. Tatiana giggled constantly, and Karl's face was flushed with pleasure. With a lunge, Karl caught her round the waist and the two girls fell and rolled on the cushions. Tatiana struggled a little, but Karl's hand felt up her clothes, pulling up her skirts to expose her shiny silk stockings. Tatiana lay still now, panting, as Karl knelt between her legs and tossed her skirts up almost to her chin. Tatiana was wearing tiny drawers of white silk, trimmed with lace, and Karl was able to pull aside the gusset between her legs, revealing the pink lips of her sex. Karl lay down on the cushions; her head buried between Tatiana's outspread thighs, and began to lick.

Soon Tatiana was sighing and wriggling, her body lifting to her lover's caresses. She began to let out little cries, arching her back rigidly. Then with a long, drawn-out 'Ooooh!' she went limp, sweat beading her carefully powdered face.

Karl rose to her feet, wiping her mouth and smiling triumphantly at Markov. 'There, you see. Who needs a penis?'

'Oh Karl, you know I like the thing up inside me.' Tatiana stretched luxuriously on the cushions.

'Which thing would this be?' Markov enquired. In answer, Karl went to a loose floorboard in the corner and, lifting it, took out a box of polished wood. She opened it, and showed the contents to Markov. It was a dildo of ivory, perfectly shaped like a phallus and fitted with straps of soft leather.

'Shall I show you how it works?' Without waiting for a reply, she unbuttoned her breeches, letting them slip down to her knees. Then she deftly buckled the dildo to her waist, passing other straps round the tops of her thighs to keep it firmly in place. With hands on hips, she proudly flaunted the hard shaft that arose from her crotch.

'Why don't you push it into Tatiana when she's on all fours,' suggested Markov, 'while I bugger you from behind?'

'Bugger me? Push your penis up my bottom? But it's too big. Won't it hurt?'

'Yes, but that's what boys do.'

'Well then, I suppose so.'

So it was arranged. Tatiana went down on her hands and knees, slipping down her panties wet with her lover's saliva. Karl positioned herself behind her, and gently guided the dildo into her cunt. Markov exposed his own erection, and produced the small jar of grease he had brought for this eventuality. Karl flinched as he lubricated her anus, but when Markov began to penetrate, she manfully bit her lip to prevent herself crying out. He was gentle, and it took several minutes to push into her virgin rectum. Tatiana kept demanding to know what was going on, but Karl could only answer between clenched teeth.

Soon Markov started to drive in and out, which forced Karl forward and back against Tatiana's bottom, thrusting the dildo at the same time. Karl was hissing between her teeth now, but Markov's frenzy was on him, and he was not going to stop short of his climax. It burst like a broken dam, filling

89

the girl's rear passage with hot sperm, and causing Tatiana to laugh out loud.

He withdrew carefully from Karl's bottom, and she in turn pulled the dildo from her lover's vagina. Karl got up stiffly and unstrapped the ivory phallus. She pulled up her breeches and sat down carefully, her face pale. Markov poured her more wine.

'Well, I least I know now what some boys feel.' she murmured philosophically.

Tatiana was all-agog, having missed the details by having to face away from the other two. She was intrigued by the whole thing, and delighted that boys had sex with boys, as well as girls with girls. She cuddled Karl, and hoped she was not badly hurt. Markov dozed a little as the two girls kissed tenderly.

They talked and drank for a while, and Markov offered them cigars. Only Karl took one, but it was clear she wasn't a real smoker. Tatiana steered the conversation around to boys' cocks.

'Karl told me about what you did together, and I'd just like to see one. I've never been allowed anywhere near boys, you know. Karl said it was big and hard, but I've often looked at the front of men's trousers and there can't be anything like that inside.'

'Well, come over here and I'll show you,' answered Markov, undoing his breeches and raising his hips to slide them down to his knees. Tatiana sprawled by his side and stared at his half-stiffened sex, then gingerly reached out her hand.

'May I?'

'Of course.'

Tatiana first stroked his pubic hair, and then tentatively touched his slumbering penis with her slender fingers. Plucking up courage, she gently held it.

90

'Ooh! It's getting bigger!'

In the girl's hand, his penis stiffened and straightened, growing fully erect under her astonished gaze.

'I really don't want to have it up inside me. But I would like to do what Karl did, you know, make the white stuff come out with my hand.'

Markov considered. 'What about in your mouth? It would be easier, and just like Karl's licking you, really.'

Tatiana looked doubtful. Karl spoke up. 'Why not, Butterfly? I'd be interested to see it myself.'

Tatiana was nothing if not adventurous, and knelt beside Markov as he stretched out on the cushions. He unbuttoned his tunic and drew up his shirt, so he was naked from stomach to thighs. His cock stood stiffly up from its bush of dark hair, the opening in the purple head glistening with a drop of clear fluid.

Bowing her head, Tatiana parted her lips and took the swollen knob into her mouth. Markov quietly instructed the young lesbian in the art of fellatio. Karl watched intently. Once Tatiana had got used to the idea, she was sucking him expertly, her head bobbing up and down, faster and faster. His tension rose.

Markov's orgasm caught her by surprise, flooding her mouth with his foul-tasting semen. Tatiana squealed and spat it out, dabbing at her lips with a tiny handkerchief.

'It tastes so horrid! You beast, Karl, you knew it would.'

Tatiana began to throw cushions at Karl, who cheerfully threw them back. It soon developed into a pillow fight, and Markov quietly withdrew, adjusting his clothes. He could still hear shrill voices as he rode back through the woods.

# CHAPTER FIVE

Sketches from a Hunter's Album.

The spring sunshine flooded across the bedroom and struck sparks from the blonde hair spread in a golden fan on the pillow beside Markov. He gazed down for a moment at the peacefully sleeping woman, her face calm in repose. He slapped her cheek suddenly. Her eyes flew open in terror, but before she could speak he had grabbed her hair and forced her head down under the bedclothes towards his crotch. She knew what was required, and her questing mouth quickly found his penis, iron hard with a morning erection, and began to suck.

Markov lay back on the pillow, his hands behind his head, and idly pondered the events of the last month. This was his last morning at the Institute, and he felt he had spent his time well. Whatever his dislike of modern inventions, he could now install a hidden microphone to eavesdrop on secret conversations, he could write reports which nobody but the authorities could read, he could take photographs with a camera so small it could be hidden in a pocket, and many other skills a government spy might need. Especially, though, he had perfected the art of the torturer, and many evenings had been spent in the cellars practising his techniques. The sessions had always terminated by him forcing himself into one of the orifices of the volunteer's body and filling her with his semen. He possessed a degree of self-discipline, and had limited himself to one, or at the most two, orgasms each day.

He remembered the girl hidden beneath the bedclothes. He flung back the covers, and she gazed up at him fearfully.

'Up.'

She swung her naked body to the edge of the bed, standing up carefully. There was a rattle as the chain from the bed end slipped to the floor. Markov got up and unfastened it from her ankle. Without another word, she began to help him dress. Pulling up his breeches, however, his erection was so hard that he chose to leave it jutting stiffly from his open flies. As he adjusted his uniform, the prisoner quickly pulled on the singlet and knickers that were her only clothes. Then Markov handcuffed her wrists behind her back and shoved her out into the corridor. They went down the stairs into the hall, where Miss Stolypin was bullying the girls into line for the morning roll call. The girls were supposed to keep their eyes on the ground, but several peeped furtively at the up-risen sex protruding from Markov's breeches. Men who had taken prisoners for use during the night were sleepily leading them to their places in the lines. Ignatiev was one, and he smiled as he saw Markov's erection.

'You're insatiable. A night with blondie and you look ready to fuck the whole lot of them.'

'Of course I could, if I wished.'

Ignatiev paused and looked hard at him. 'Are you seri-ous? All of them? All thirty-four? '

'I mean what I said. I could screw all thirty-four and leave some my semen inside each one at the end.'

'Impossible! A hundred roubles says you couldn't'.

'Very well. You shall see.'

Markov went over to Kreisky, who was checking that all the girls were present. He was startled by the proposal, but nodded his agreement. Miss Stolypin was informed, and while she looked sour, she acknowledged the man's right to do whatever he wished. As rumour of the challenge went round, other staff and trainees appeared to watch. Kreisky stood on the bottom step of the stairs and barked instructions. Two of the girls brought a table and stood to attention in front of it, facing the lines of silent prisoners. A third girl stood by with a jar of the lubricating grease widely used in the Institute when sodomising the female prisoners. Kreisky pulled out a watch and called out the first name from his list. The girl stepped forward and at a brusque command pulled her knickers down and off. Naked except for her singlet, she was helped to lie back on the table by the assistants. They raised and parted her legs, each holding an ankle high to expose the victim's cunt wide and open to the gaze of the watching men.

Markov stepped forward and the attendant prisoner smeared a little grease gently on his cock. He lodged the head of his cock between the parted lips of the victim's vulva, and rammed into her. A gasp escaped her lips, but Markov gave a few pelvic thrusts and withdrew.

'Next.'

Another girl was called forward and the actions were repeated. Knickers off. On the table. Legs high and wide. Penis lubricated. Penetration. A few quick in and out thrusts.

'Next.'

And so it went on. Kreisky, his eye on his watch, ticked off each name as the girl was penetrated and returned to her place in the line. She had hardly pulled up her knickers before Markov was into one of her fellow prisoners. Doctor Konigsberg appeared at the top of the stairs. He did not interrupt but paused to observe the scene silently. Ignatiev watched with increasing alarm as ten, then twenty girls were used and discarded without any sign that Markov was reaching a climax. The grease had long since been discarded, the sight of Markov's indefatigable sex plunging in and out of girl after girl had had its inevitable effect on those who still waited their turn and he was now able to slide into slickly lubricated vaginas. In fact, Markov had one of those hard but almost numb morning erections and felt he could continue forever.

The thirty-first was violated, then the three serving girls took turns on the table themselves. Triumphant, Markov pulled out of the last one, his phallus glistening with the girls' vaginal fluids, but as rock hard as before.

'Seventeen minutes.' cried Kreisky. 'A little over half a minute each. Bravo!'

Kreisky was about to dismiss the girls when Markov interrupted him. 'One moment, Kreisky. I have not finished.'

He beckoned the three serving girls from their place in the rear rank and gave them their orders. One stood on either side of him and the third knelt in front of his still massive cock, her hands raised and cupped in front of her. Markov fondled the bottoms of the attendants beside him, tracing the cleft of their buttocks through the warm stretch fabric of their pants. The one on his right made a ring of her finger and thumb and gripped his shaft just below the swollen knob. She began to wank him.

There was silence again in the hall as Markov's tension rose. The hand of the masturbatrix flew up and down, faster and faster. He stopped groping the girls' bottoms, and closed his eyes as his climax drew nearer and nearer. His breathing was loud now, rapid and irregular. Every eye in the room was fixed on his cock and the blur of the girl's wrist.

A loud gasp and a moan and a hot jet of thick, cloudy fluid splashed out of the opening of his penis and into the cupped hands of the kneeling girl. Another spurt, then another not quite so powerful, then a final trickle. Markov stood panting for a moment, then a jerk of his head ordered the kneeling attendant to rise. She got to her feet, carefully cradling the pool of semen in her hands, and approached the first girl in the line. A quick whisper and the girl bowed her head, sticking out her tongue and licking a little of the sperm from the cupped hands of the attendant. She passed along the ranks, and each prisoner tasted of Markov's outpouring and then returned to attention. The attendant then came back to Markov and the other two. He was leaning back against the table, mopping his brow. The other girls each lapped up a little of the remaining fluid and the attendant finished it, licking her fingers clean. All three returned quietly to their places.

'Well, Ignatiev, you must admit I have fulfilled the terms of our wager.'

Ignatiev, half annoyed and half amused, nodded and promised to pay him later. Markov guessed that Ignatiev was going to use some of the lavish funds that the government gave to secret agents to pay his debt.

After breakfast, Markov reported to Doctor Konigsberg's study for his final interview. He was greeted warily. The doctor was aware that Markov knew the secret of his membership of the Guild of St.Dionysia and it was a guilty secret. Nevertheless, the review of Markov's training was encouraging, with good reports in the technical subjects. It was in the doctor's own field of torture and interrogation that he had distinguished himself, however. Konigsberg had been impressed and had discussed his talents with the authorities, and with Zubatov himself. They had agreed that, as well as his undercover work with subversive student groups, he was to set up and command a new interrogation centre based at the fortress of St.Peter and St.Paul.

Markov had much to think about on the journey back to St.Petersburg. Seasonal flooding in the low-lying areas slowed his journey and he had plenty of time to plan the personnel, the accommodation and the equipment such an interrogation unit would require. He had a calculating mind, as much at ease with staffing structures as with whips and chains.

Back in the city, a couple of hours visiting the cheaper shops and stalls provided suitable clothes for a lower middle-class student. His hair had grown long enough for him to pass as an intellectual, the effect heightened by a pair of gold-rimmed spectacles - which had plain lenses. He had resisted the advice to grow a beard or wear a false one: the first would have taken too long to grow, and the last would have been too easily detected at the close quarters he intended to operate. He found lodgings on Vasilevsky Island, in the university district. They were shabby rooms on the top floor of a boarding house for which the landlady demanded rent in advance. She had known too many students.

The next morning he reported to secret police headquarters, where he was given a pass and an introductory letter to the commandant of the fortress. He was to report there at noon. A cab was soon trotting over the Trinity Bridge, the spire of the Peter and Paul cathedral rising like an unsheathed sword over the water to his left. As he entered the fortress by the Peter Gate, the noonday gun sounded from the Naryshkin Bastion. The smoke still hung in the spring air as he arrived at the commandant's house, a long two-storey building, the upper storey painted a delicate pink.

The commandant received Markov coolly, and invited him into his office. Vodka was offered and did not go amiss, and the men warily eyed each other as they raised their glasses to the Tsar. The letter Markov carried from Zubatov impressed the commandant, and grudgingly he agreed that Markov should have whatever he required. It was clear that the commandant resented this young lieutenant - in a bad suit, not even a uniform- who seemed to have authority which rivalled his own. The Okhrana was a civilian secret police and the Corps of Gendarmes a military one. Both were dedicated to defending the Tsar, but each hated the other and co-operation was rare and reluctant. Nevertheless, the commandant led Markov out of the house and past the Mint buildings.

'Interrogations are normally carried out in my house. Of course, the political prisoners are kept in the Trubetskoy Bastion.' The commandant gestured to the grim bulk ahead and Markov nodded. His training course had included such details.

'Sixty-nine solitary confinement cells, I believe, and two

97

punishment cells below the water line, commandant?'

The commandant nodded curtly, and they continued to walk in silence until they paused by a flight of steps that led down under a rampart to a wide, double door.

'The Alexeyevsky Ravelin beyond used to be the site of the Secret House, lieutenant.' The commandant stressed Markov's lowly rank. 'It has now been demolished, but the cellars remain below the Ministry buildings. They are sealed off except for this entrance and used only for storage now. I think they would suit your purpose.'

The name of the Secret House, the notorious torture centre of the last century, still had the power to evoke fear. Intrigued, Markov followed the commandant down the steps and paused as the door was unlocked. The gloom inside was only a little illuminated by the lantern the commandant lit. A large vestibule or entrance hall had doorways leading from it. Their footsteps echoed on damp flagstones as they passed through corridors and chambers, mostly empty, but some piled with old military equipment. Markov noted everything. These would be the cells, this the guardroom, this large vault the main interrogation chamber.

'And what about my own quarters, commandant?'

'Your own quarters? I assumed you would live outside the fortress.'

'Sometimes. But I must have comfortable accommodation here.'

'Very well. There are some furnished lodgings belonging to the Mint that are empty at present. You may use them for a time.'

The rooms, with their own separate entrance, were adequate and Markov settled in to begin the carefully planned procedures that would create his interrogation centre. He would need Ignatiev as his second in command, with a hand picked staff of jailers and interrogators. At least twelve, to cover a twenty-four hour watch with staff absences to be taken into account. A secretary was needed for administration and the typing of confessions. The cellars must be cleared, cleaned, and electric light installed. Stonemasons, carpenters and locksmiths must prepare cells. Ironworkers must make cages, chains, spreader bars and racks. Leather workers must produce cuffs, collars, gags, and harnesses. No detail was omitted.

Markov slept in his student digs that night and saw Zubatov the following morning to approve his staff levels and authorise the expenditure. There was so much to do, but Markov was determined and clear as to how he was going to do it. He even found time to visit the horse harness shop to make his personal selection of whips.

Coming out of the shop, Markov was lost in thought as he made his way along the crowded street, and they almost collided before he recognised Ekaterina. She was wearing a short jacket trimmed at the neck and wrists with fur, a high starched collar to her blouse and a grey skirt. A squarish, flat bag hung from her shoulder and she was carrying an umbrella. A hat adorned with a feather crowned her face, which was pale with surprise.

He raised his hat. 'Madam, how pleasant to meet you again. It seems so long since our last meeting, but my memories of it are still fresh. Allow me.'

He took her hand and delicately kissed the tips of her fingers. The serpent of his lust began to uncoil slowly behind the front of his trousers. She looked around nervously. He glanced down. The toecaps peeping from the hem of her skirt were grey. 'I see that you are not wearing those delightful boots I saw on that occasion. You are not on your way to a meeting, then?'

'No. Not today.' She looked into his eyes and saw the desire in them.

' Well then, madam. Shall we take tea together?'

Ekaterina nodded dumbly and he took her arm. He steered her towards a little cafe further down the street. She murmured confidentially as they walked.

'I didn't know what had happened to you. You vanished and nobody seemed to know where you had gone. Some even insisted there was no Lieutenant Pushkin in the Tsar's Lifeguard.'

Well, thought Markov, she appears to have gone to a lot of trouble to trace me. I seem to have made a hit.

'My dear lady, you should never believe anything a soldier tells a beautiful woman.'

They entered the cafe and took a small table in a secluded corner. There was an angled bench seat in the corner, and they sat down. His left knee brushed her right. They ordered tea.

'What news of your husband?'

'Very little. All I received was a note telling me to forward the silk knit underwear he had ordered from Paris when it arrives. Apparently such things are hard to find in Manchuria.'

'And how is life without him?'

'I notice little difference. I have sent most of the servants to our country estate, and only live in a small part of the house here. I have my charities..... and the Guild, of course.'

She seemed slightly flustered and opened the squarish bag. She drew out a few sheets of typewritten paper - in Roman, not Cyrillic, lettering, Markov noted. 'Soon I am going to give a lecture to a missionary society. These are the notes I have prepared.'

'You typed them yourself? Is that not an unusual accomplishment for a lady?'

'Oh yes. There was a time when my family thought the only way to stop me causing scandal was to send me to Paris to work as a secretary. They spared no expense in my training. However, I was not prepared to waste my life in such a way.'

She paused. 'Lieutenant, life has suddenly become very much more interesting.' Her eyes met his with an unmistakable message.

'But what about your reputation? Aren't you afraid to be seen with a younger man while your gallant husband is away fighting for Mother Russia and the Tsar?'

'My reputation? Perhaps I'm less sensitive about that after what happened the night before he left.'

Markov said nothing. He knew she would tell him everything without prompting.

'A young boy, a first-year cadet came to the house, begging to be taken to the East as part of my husband's entourage. The General was out, at a private party given by the closest circle of his men friends. The boy wept and beseeched me to intercede with my husband.'

Ekaterina took a sip of tea. 'He told me of their intimacy together. Every detail. The kissing, the buggery, the oral sex. To show how close they had been, I imagine. He was mad with grief that his love should desert him. Anyway, the General returned. The boy threw himself at his feet and hugged his boots. My husband was drunk, and just kicked him away. He told him brutally that he couldn't imagine that a pathetic runt like him would be worth taking on campaign, and anyway, he had better company than his going with him.'

She drained her glass and sat toying with it on her saucer. 'The boy rose without a word, saluted and walked out. As the street door closed behind him, he pulled out his pistol and shot himself in the head.'

Markov pursed his lips. 'Most inconsiderate of the lad. What happened next?'

'My husband told the butler and the first footman, who were both in the entrance hall at the time, to take the body to

101

the Neva and throw it in. There was nobody about at that hour, thank God, and they returned without raising suspicion. My husband told me to wash the blood from the front steps.'

'And he left the next morning?'

'As if nothing had happened. His only comment was that the campaign in the East had claimed its first casualty already. There has been no scandal yet, and maybe there never will be. I feel that if my own reputation has survived that incident, then it will survive anything.'

Markov nodded thoughtfully and laid his left hand on her thigh. He felt the warmth of her body through the material of her skirt. 'I'm sure you're right.'

Still keeping his left hand on her thigh, he half turned to her and fumbled towards the hem of her skirts with his right.

'What are you doing?' she whispered.

'Only what you did to me at the railway station.' He got his hand under the hem and began feeling up under the petticoats till he came to the smooth sheen of her stockings. Ekaterina glanced round apprehensively, but the other customers were ignoring them. The table hid everything.

Sliding his hand up her silk-clad leg, he came to her knee and the soft lace that trimmed the leg of her drawers. He reached further, his fingers slipping in between her thighs until they came to the warm mound at the centre seam of her crotch. He stroked her there, and she parted her legs a little to let the teasing fingers probe deeper.

'Where can we go?' he muttered.

'Not to the house. Besides, I am expected to address the missionary society in ten minutes.'

'Then there's not much time. I'll have to have you standing up in an alley, like a cheap prostitute.'

Ekaterina smiled. 'I've always wanted to be a cheap prostitute.'

'Come on then.'

They paid and left. Out in the street she paused, looking left and right. 'I know. There's the market building in the next street. We could go to the upper promenade. Few people go up there.'

They were soon mounting the steps to the upper storey of the market. At this late hour the stalls that opened onto the gallery were mostly closed and shuttered. There was still some business going on in the courtyard below, however, and Ekaterina leant with her forearms on the balustrade to watch.

Markov moved fast but with careful deliberation. He unbuttoned his flies and drew out his erection. It jutted stiffly, at a steep angle. Stooping, he lifted Ekaterina's skirts from behind, the white, rustling petticoats covering her back like a fall of snow. The seat of her drawers was exposed to his gaze, with two linen-covered buttons that secured the rear flap. His fingers deftly undid them and he lowered the flap, revealing the paleness of her buttocks. He guided his cock down into the crevice between them, slipping past the pucker of her anus and into the moist opening of her cunt.

His thrusts were rapid and urgent. Ekaterina had to grip the edge of the stone balustrade to avoid being shoved back and forth, though all the while gazing mildly at the peaceful scene of commerce below. Markov's eyes closed and his orgasm rose rapidly in him. He had the self-control to make no sound as his hot sperm jetted in long, satisfying spurts into the gentlewoman's body.

In a moment he was doing up his trousers and her fingers reached behind to fasten the flap of her drawers with practised ease. A quick toss of her skirts and there was nothing to show for their escapade.

He let out a sigh. 'About twenty seconds at the most, I imagine.'

'I hope the next time will be more ... unhurried, lieutenant.'

'Well, I need a drink. Will you come?'

'I really cannot. If I hurry, I might just be in time to give my missionary lecture. I shall, of course, have to talk to the ladies with your spunk soaking my drawers and dribbling down my leg. Ah me, what it is to be a woman.'

'I would like to meet you regularly, madam, but it is I who must contact you. I would be glad, naturally, to attend Guild meetings.'

'You have missed one meeting since the one you came to. There is not another until next month, but I hope to hear from you before then. When you summon me, you will not find me reluctant.'

Markov returned to his student lodgings and spent the evening in tedious but necessary paperwork. The following morning he visited the fortress to check the progress of the work. After this he felt ready for an early dinner and then to embark on his campaign against the subversives who would destroy the nation he loved. A good meal in a good hotel and then ... then what? He would see.

The ImpÈriale had a facade in the swirling Style Moderne. A waiter met him in the lobby and led the way into a large dining room, decorated with palm trees in heavy pots. It was fairly busy, mostly with groups of two or three women drinking coffee and eating cakes. Markov was shown to a table near the back, and the waiter hurried off with his order.

The nearby tables were empty, but beyond them two middle-aged women were discussing servants, while at another table three girls were loudly advising each other about fashion.

Markov looked round. A waitress had approached from a door behind him, and he was immediately struck by her good looks. She was fair-haired, not so unusual in St.Petersburg, and with attractive Scandinavian features. She looked tired, though, even so early in the day. She was carrying his order: wine, caviar, and steak tartar.

She poured his wine, conscious of his hot eyes on her. She turned to leave.

'No, stay. I would like to talk to you.'

'But sir, there are other tables.'

'They can wait.'

She stood beside the table, nervously twisting her hands in front of her starched apron as he ate.

'This is a rather grand restaurant.'

'Yes, sir. I am lucky to work here.'

'Do they pay you much?'

'Pay me, sir? I have to pay them in order to work here.'

Markov was genuinely surprised, a feeling he found unpleasant. 'Pay them?'

'Yes, I must pay them, and hope that my tips each week amount to more.'

'And do they?'

'Usually, sir. I am a student, and I must work to pay for my evening classes.'

'I see.'

He surprised the waitress by asking for the bill, when he had scarcely half finished the meal. She went off while Markov poured another glass of wine. She was not long in returning, with an elaborately engraved bill for a quite shocking price.

'Surely this bill is incorrect, miss.'

The girl turned pale. 'Oh sir, in what way?'

'Come and see.'

The waitress moved to stand beside his chair and as she did so, he slipped his hand below the hem of her skirt from behind. Slowly, to avoid making any rustling sound, he thrust his hand up under her clothes until he was caressing the outline of her buttocks through the thin cotton of her knickers.

'You see, there is nothing added for the service.'

She stood motionless, her hands by her sides, as she submitted to his groping. The women at the nearby tables seemed not to notice anything.

'Oh no, sir. You leave only what you wish as a tip.'

His hand pushed between her legs from behind. Instinctively, she shifted a little, parting her legs. His finger traced the cleft of her vulva, and found the tiny bud of her clitoris beneath the thin material. She closed her eyes as he caressed it.

'How much I give will depend on the service I get.'

She breathed deeply and opened her eyes. 'Would you like to come with me, sir?'

Without waiting for an answer, she turned and walked towards the kitchen door. Screwing up his napkin, he rose and followed her.

Beyond the swing door was a short, tiled corridor. Through an open door at the end, he could hear the clatter and shouting of a large kitchen in action. To the left, another corridor led off, and it was down this that the waitress turned. He followed her, and she turned the handle of a door. She went in, and stood aside to let him enter. She carefully closed the door and turned on an electric light.

It was a tiny closet; smelling of soap and polish, with hardly room enough for the two of them. A large white sink took up most of the space, and mops and brooms hung in rows. For a moment they stood and looked at each other, the girl pale.

He moved close to her. Slipping his hands behind her back, he quickly untied the bow of her apron and pulled the starched white material from her chest. Then his fingers went to her buttons: first the ones down the front of her black silk bodice, and then the white blouse beneath. He unfastened the corset beneath and let her small, firm breasts thrust out, their nipples erect. He cupped them in his hands for a moment.

106

'Will anyone disturb us here?'

'No, it's quite safe.'

Shakily, she fumbled at his fly buttons. Her fingers slid into his trousers, gently pulling out his erection. She gazed down at it in her hand, hot and hard, with the veins on its surface prominent. A bead of clear fluid glistened at the opening in the purple, plum-shaped head. She stroked it for a few seconds. Then she knelt down in front of him. The space was cramped and her button boots creaked as she squatted on her heels.

His cock stood stiffly out, its head almost nudging her face. She parted her lips, and took it into her mouth. Her lips closed around it and she began to suck, working her head slowly back and forth along it. He moaned with pleasure, but did not want it to end that way.

Bending, he grabbed her elbows and hauled her to her feet, pushing her back against the sink. His hands were urgent as they pushed her skirts up over her hips and tugged at the drawstring of her knickers. Roughly, he dragged them down her thighs, the cotton material ripping slightly.

His erection nudged between her legs, and she tried to open them as wide as she could, hampered as she was by the drawers round her knees. She leant back against the sink and thrust her hips forward to make it easier for him to penetrate her. He slipped his hands round her naked bottom, grabbing each cheek and pulling her onto the head of his erection. It was difficult, but he was able to push his maleness into the opening of her sex. Tugging her towards him, he rammed himself in. She gasped as his hard length filled her secret place and then gave a little cry as his grip on her buttocks tightened painfully. He began to thrust.

She gazed down, watching his penis slide in and out of her body. She only had a little, fair pubic hair, and they could both clearly see the lips of her vulva drawn out and pushed

107

back around his shaft as his thrusts quickened. He released his grip from her behind and held her hips. Now he was screwing her violently, his hips grinding powerfully into her crotch with savage force. Her bottom was crushed painfully onto the hard edge of the sink.

He shuddered and groaned deep in his throat, his hot sperm jetting up into the young waitress's body. His breath came in loud, relieved gasps as he slipped his phallus out of her. For a few moments they both gazed down at his wet and softening organ. A large drop of semen dripped from the parted lips of her sex and trickled wetly down the inside of her thighs, leaving a stain on her black stocking tops.

She straightened up and pulled a handkerchief from her sleeve. Carefully, she dried his cock and slid it back into his trousers, buttoning up his flies.

'Now that was excellent service' murmured Markov, and gave her a rouble.

She bent down and hauled up her knickers, fumbling under her petticoats to tie the drawstring. Her fingers then fled to her exposed breasts, quickly doing up her clothes.

'Aren't you afraid of pregnancy?'

'The other girls say you can't get pregnant if you do it standing up. So I always do, if I can.'

'The other girls?'

'The other female students. Many of us have to do this from time to time. Just to afford food, let alone lodgings and books.'

Just then an angry male voice could be heard in the corridor outside. 'Ingrid! Ingrid! Where is the blasted girl?'

Markov grabbed her wrist. 'I must meet you again.'

Ingrid paused. 'Very well. Outside the back door of the restaurant at six.'

She quickly grabbed a mop and hurriedly left the closet. Markov heard her quiet voice explaining that she had to fetch a mop, and the man's harsh voice cursing her. When they had gone, Markov made his way back to his table. As he languidly poured out another glass of wine, he reflected that things were already looking promising.

At six Ingrid was waiting in the squalid alley behind the luxurious hotel. She had removed her apron, and was wearing a thin, badly-worn coat. She had no hat.

'Well, Ingrid, what would you like to do?'

'Sir...' She paused. 'Sir, would you take me somewhere to eat?'

'To eat? But you work in a restaurant. Surely...'

Ingrid shook her head abruptly. 'Oh no. If any of us are seen eating even the scraps from the plates we are dismissed on the spot. There are many waiting to take our places.' She stared at the ground. 'If you take me somewhere for dinner, you can take me anywhere else after that.'

Markov nodded. 'Where would you like to go?'

'Nowhere near here. Somewhere cheap, of course. I'm not fit to be seen anywhere you would normally go.' There was no bitterness in her voice, just resignation.

The cafÈ near the docks smelt of boiled cabbage and tobacco, but at least it was clean and the helpings of food were generous. Goulash and rye bread washed down with thin beer seemed the basic menu. Markov watched with detached interest as Ingrid wolfed down two platefuls. It must be hard to serve food all day with hunger a constant companion.

'Where now?' he asked the girl as she wiped her plate clean with a crust.

'There's the park. We could do it up against a tree. Or the stairway of an office block. Sometimes the street doors are open and one of the landings will do. If you don't mind, I'd like to do it quickly, so I can get to the meeting tonight.'

'A meeting? One of your evening classes?'

'No. It's some sort of political meeting, I don't know exactly what it's about. A friend of mine asked me to come along. He said there were people, many people, who cared about social justice and that if we all ...' She suddenly halted. 'He said I wasn't to tell just anyone. Only people that could be trusted.. I hope you can be trusted,'she finished quietly

'Of course. I see how the present society is wrong, fundamentally wrong. I too hope to build a fairer future, where everyone is free to make a better life for themselves.' Markov gripped her hand firmly across the table. 'I'd rather go to the meeting with you than to the park.'

Ingrid sighed with relief. 'I'm glad. I liked the look of you and I'm pleased you don't just want to use me like most men do.'

He took her to a wine shop, and a glass or two soon had her relaxed and talking. Markov quickly discovered that she really did know nothing of the group organising the meeting that night. Her friend was a male student to whom she gave sex for nothing, he apparently not being able to pay for it. In return he promised her a future in which no woman would need to sell her body, and everyone would be free to live and love as they chose. A reasonable bargain, thought Markov.

The meeting was in what had once been a rather grand apartment near the university but was now distinctly neglected. A knock on the door, a brief perusal by a young man with a beard and Markov and Ingrid were directed upstairs. It was a large room, packed with cheap wooden chairs, most of which were already occupied. In fact, many people were already standing at the back of the room or perching on the furniture which had been pushed back against the walls. While most seemed of the student type, a surprising number wore working clothes as if they had come straight from the factories. Many were women. There was a buzz of excitement as if something important was about to happen.

Markov helped Ingrid to squeeze her way to an empty

seat. He himself had to make his way to the back wall. He had a good view of the room until a slim young woman in a grey dress slipped in at the last moment and stood right in front of him. A door at the end of the room opened and a student type with thick-lensed spectacles entered. The room fell silent.

'Comrades!' Markov had never heard this form of address before. 'Comrades! We are privileged to have here with us tonight one who has sacrificed much for acting as a herald for the inevitable march of history, one who has tasted the bitterness of exile for the future of mankind, one who carries the flag of justice forward regardless of the burden to himself. Comrades, welcome our brother Lenin.'

A gasp and then earnest applause greeted a neatly dressed man of about thirty with a virile face and a well-trimmed beard. When silence fell, he began to speak in a firm, clear voice that reached everyone in the room. Russian society, he said, was like a wedding cake. The lower layer was the peasantry and workers, supporting everybody. Above them was the crushing weight of the parasitic classes: 200,000 priests, 40,000 army officers - all of them noblemen. Then the Tsar, the greatest landowner of all, answerable to no one.

'His government oppresses the people: Witte, the Minister of Finance, overtaxes the peasants. What is to be done? If we all act together, how can they resist us? The strikes by female textile workers in St Petersburg three years ago succeeded in obtaining a reduction in working hours. The exploiters fear us, they fear our united strength. Last year's student protests similarly shook the authorities.'

A voice near Markov interrupted. 'Yes, and now Bogolepov, the Minister of Public Instruction, threatens us with conscription into the army.'

Lenin paused and glared coldly at the heckler. 'Perhaps it is no bad thing, young man, to learn how to use a gun.'

111

Markov gave an involuntary snort and the young woman in front of him turned. She was pretty in a thin-faced way and her eyes met his. She maintained eye contact rather longer than Markov thought necessary before turning back with a half smile.

The speaker continued, outlining the necessity, the inevitability of a revolution. He was clear, logical and persuasive, but Markov's attention wandered, studying the figures in the room. He could mostly see the backs of their heads, but he attempted to memorise distinctive characteristics so that he might recognise them again. Absorbed with this, he was suddenly jolted by the realisation that somebody was fingering his crotch.

The girl in front of him had her hands behind her back, and her fingers were gently tracing the bulge in the fork of his trousers. She seemed unaware of what she was doing, but Markov knew she was quite deliberately touching him up. Glancing to right and left, he noted that the students around him were concentrating on Lenin's oratory. His penis began to respond to the gentle feminine stimulation and he thrust his hips forward slightly to meet the questing fingers.

Without betraying any reaction, the girl changed her technique. Now she was gripping his hardening shaft beneath the material of his trousers, gently working her hand up and down its length. Markov's erection was full and stiff, and glancing down he saw her delicate fingertip circling the wet spot in the fabric where the fluid was seeping from the tip of his cock.

The applause and eager shouts of the audience abruptly drew his attention back to the speaker. Lenin was clenching his right fist, and some of the audience began a song he did not recognise. It soon petered out, however, as the bearded figure left the room as suddenly as he had entered it. The students and workers turned to each other with a hubbub of eager discussion. One or two began to make their way to the exit, and the girl in front of Markov made a move to follow them. He grabbed her arm.

'Not so fast, young lady. You can't imagine I'll allow you to leave me in this state.'

'Well now, I suppose it would be not be comradely. You may walk me home if you wish.' Her voice was cultured in a middle-class fashion, and her glinting eyes betrayed a wicked amusement.

He took her arm and escorted her out into the dark and windy street. She lived in a residential block only a few streets away, and soon they were climbing the stairs. They were carpeted, he noticed, and if it was an old and worn carpet, at least it was better than most student lodgings.

Her rooms were small but neatly furnished. Markov allowed her time to light the oil lamp before seizing her round the waist and pushing her down on the sofa. She giggled.

'Comrade, not so hasty! Let me light the fire, then we can take our clothes off.'

He was left on the sofa as she lit the fire in the small, enclosed grate and then turned to him. Her undressing was quick and practised, with a certain nonchalant grace as she folded her garments onto the fireside chair. After a moment watching her, he rose and tore off his clothes with hurried fingers, leaving them in a crumpled heap at his feet. The soft lamplight and the flickering flames illuminated her pale, slender body and his hard nakedness, his prick jutting rigidly upwards. She stepped up to him and clasped his shaft with both hands, one above the other. The purple head was still uncovered.

'A two-hand cock. I thought so. Mmmm...'

She sank to her knees and, parting her lips, took his hardness into her mouth. Rather than sucking, though, she ran her tongue up and down the underside of his shaft, teasing the

113

opening at the tip. Markov let her take her time. There was no doubt he was going to have her, and this time at least he was prepared to let the woman set the pace.

The chill was leaving the room and the girl rose to her feet. Gathering cushions and the embroidered cloth draped over the sofa, she made a soft pile in front of the fire. She lay down on it, opened her legs and reached out her arms to him. Markov knelt over her, and her hand guided his phallus to the entrance of her sex. Restraining his urge to ram himself in, he gradually slid the length of his hardness into her moist but tight opening. She sighed and arched her hips to welcome the male intruder into her body.

Markov began his pelvic thrusts, but was a little surprised when she thrust back against him. He had fornicated a thousand times or more and was used to the women lying passively as he took his pleasure. Only once or twice before he had met this response. He pushed himself in and out of her, but she seemed more interested in grinding her body as hard against his as she could. It was his intention that she should enjoy this sex and he tried to sense what she wanted. Quickly he realised that instead of sliding his cock in and out, he should ram himself fully into her and force the root of his shaft hard against the soft opening of her sex. That was where the clitoris was located, he recalled, the little sensitive bud to which he had paid particular attention during his interrogation sessions in the Institute.

The girl's body was damp with perspiration now, her face flushed and she held her breath as the tension of her body focused on the single point of feeling. Then she came, a long shuddering groan and rapid panting as the relief flooded through her. Her body relaxed and Markov knew the time had come for his orgasm. After a moment he began those rapid, repeated thrusts that soon had his semen spurting deep into the cunt of the dreamy, contented girl.

Markov rolled off her and lay still, getting his breath back. Her eyes were closed and he turned on his side. His gaze wandered round the small room. The walls were hung with dozens of pictures, mostly watercolours and sketches. One he recognised was a fairly good copy of the Mona Lisa, which he had seen in Paris.

A cool finger began tracing down from the point of his shoulder, outlining his waist and then slowing to caress his buttock.

'You have a beautiful body, comrade.'

Markov grunted and turned to her. Her eyes had regained their mischievous gleam. 'My name's Anastasia. What's yours?'

Markov suddenly realised he did not know.

# CHAPTER SIX

## Lunch on the Grass

The question had caught Markov unprepared, and for a moment his mind went blank. Who was he? He covered his confusion with an enquiring grunt.

'What is you name, comrade?'

Then mercifully his cover identity came rushing back.

'I'm Ilya Ivanovich, my dear, but you may call me Ilyusha.' He hoped that by allowing her to address him by an intimate form of his name, she might not ask his family name. This would give him some anonymity.

'And I'm Anastasia,' she repeated. She did not offer to be known as Astia, which hinted that he had been too familiar. After all, their acquaintance was only an hour old and was limited to a grope and a fuck.

'I'm an art student. My parents can afford to keep me in

reasonable comfort, but all around me I see poverty and deprivation. I'm only a woman, but I intend to do what I can to bring about reform.'

Markov turned to her and met her level gaze. 'And what can you do?'

'Not much at the moment. Attend meetings, distribute pamphlets. The time will come, though, when all of us, men and women alike, will rise up and turn this rotten society upside down.'

She stroked his chest with the back of her hand. 'And if I can bring comfort to fellow comrades in the struggle, then that is something only a woman can offer the revolution.'

Markov nodded gravely. A great sacrifice, to be sure.

'You see, I've always been a rebel. A very naughty little girl, and a very defiant teenager. I hated the narrow, middle-class conventions of my family and longed to be an artist, free and creative - like the Bohemians of Paris. I was barely in my teens when I realised that sex was the perfect way for a girl to reject convention. Even when I had been in short skirts I had noticed how some men would gaze at me in a funny way. I used to tease them by sitting or lying so that they could look up my dress. I knew I wasn't supposed to let men see my drawers and that men wanted to, but I didn't know why. I just knew it was wrong and I got a thrill from it.

'Then one day I was in a crowded tram. Everyone was packed together, and suddenly I felt something pressing against my bottom. A man was right behind me, and I knew he was pushing his thing against me. Of course I knew a bit about sex at that age, but no more than girls' gossip. I felt a rush of excitement that I was part of something that ordinary society considered shameful. That evening I masturbated for the first time.'

'I don't imagine it was very long before you found a lover.'

'A lover? Several! The first was the schoolmaster, then

116

when that liaison began to be known, half the town seemed to want to make my acquaintance. I didn't take just anyone, you understand, but I had schoolboys, businessmen, soldiers, even the chairman of the zemstvo.'

'And you became pregnant.'

Anastasia paused. 'Yes, of course. Quite soon. They say that semen can remain active in a woman's body for three days or more. I calculated that I must have had the sperm of at least five men inside me at the time. So I did the only thing I could.'

'Which was?'

'Went to the richest of them, said it was his, and demanded he pay for an abortion. It was dangerous, I knew, and illegal. If anything that made it more attractive. Anyway, he paid up without a murmur, I came to St.Petersburg and found an obliging doctor.'

She lay on her back, staring at the ceiling for a time before continuing.

'The operation was a success in preventing me having a child. Unfortunately it prevented me from ever having a child. I don't care about that now, but I'm told I will when I'm older.'

She sighed and turned back to Markov. 'Still, comrade Ilyusha, it means I can screw any young man that takes my fancy. And you do, naturally.'

'Really? But you don't know me.'

'I know you are a supporter of the revolution, or you would not have been at the meeting tonight. It was rare and exciting to see Vladimir Ilyich address a public meeting. He has the reputation of a conspirator rather than a rabble rouser.'

The name struck Markov like a hammer blow. Lenin was Vladimir Ilyich Ulyanov! A new cover name! And to think he had been in the same room as the most wanted agitator in St.Petersburg and had left without taking any action. Anastasia was still talking.

' ... and of course I could see you had a beautiful body under that suit. Why are men's clothes so drab? Why can't they wear the tights and codpiece of the Renaissance period? That really was elegant.'

Markov grunted, his mind racing with the possibility of trapping Lenin.

'You see, I understand what is artistic, what is natural and beautiful. When I saw you naked just now, I realised what a perfect life model you would make. Will you come to the art school with me and act as a model?'

'Certainly, yes, of course.' He was thinking how to get a report to Zubatov as soon as possible. She chattered on about her course, combining art history with practical technique.

'And what about you? What courses are you taking?'

With an effort, Markov recalled his cover story. 'I'm doing postgraduate work with Dr Popov. It concerns the wireless propagation of electromagnetic waves.'

Anastasia's eyes glazed slightly. 'Oh. Science. I don't really understand all that.'

Of course not, you're a woman, thought Markov. The subject was chosen carefully so that no female contact would be likely to have any knowledge of the people and the research he was supposed to be involved with. Markov himself thought Alexander Popov's wireless waves were verging on black magic, but had acquired enough knowledge not to give himself away.

A mantelpiece clock chimed eleven with a thin, silvery sound. Anastasia got to her knees and added some more wood to the fire. Markov was slightly apprehensive that she might question him about his revolutionary contacts: there at least they could be expected to have friends in common. However, she merely yawned and stretched.

'You'll spend the night here, comrade Ilyusha?'

118

'I'd be glad to.'

The bedroom was small and it was a single bed. With rapid movements that spoke of long experience, though, Anastasia pulled the bed a few inches from the wall and packed the space with large cushions. It was not the most comfortable bed he had shared with a woman, but it was large enough and the warmth from the fireplace that backed onto the bedroom wall allowed them to sleep naked.

It must have been around four in the morning when the questing fingertips on his genitals woke Markov. Really, the girl was insatiable. This time he took Anastasia his own way, hard and roughly. They slept until the bell of the nearby church roused them.

Markov left with a promise to meet Anastasia at her art school that afternoon. After calling at his lodgings for a shave, fresh clothes and a coffee, he went first to one of the secret contact points to leave a report for Zubatov, then in a closed carriage to the fortress to check progress. The work there was proceeding rapidly. The labourers seemed anxious to complete their task and get out of the dungeons as quickly as they could. The specialist equipment had been made to his designs and was being installed. On the organisational side, Ignatiev had agreed to act as his deputy and would arrive in a few days. His letter of acceptance betrayed just a little resentment that the younger and less experienced man had suddenly been promoted over him. A brief but not unfriendly meeting with the commandant showed that there was at least a measure of co-operation to be expected. The guards were being selected from the elite 'Specials', with their distinctive green cloaks. One of them, Nickolai, held the equivalent rank of sergeant and Markov delegated to him the routine business of duty rosters and so on. In fact, it would not be long before the interrogation centre was ready to open for business.

A light and hasty lunch, and it was time to take a cab to keep his appointment with Anastasia. The art school was in one of the grand buildings which lined the Fontanka canal. The entrance hall was paved with marble and, though large, seemed cluttered by the statues and sculptures that were stuck in every possible nook and corner. Anastasia was already waiting and squeezed his hand as they exchanged a kiss.

She led the way up a staircase, dominated by a huge oil painting of Tsar Alexander freeing the serfs. Bloody fool, he thought. If the peasants were still slaves, there would be none of this revolutionary nonsense.

Along a top floor corridor, Anastasia tapped on a door.
'Come in.'

The mistress who taught life drawing had a small office with a high ceiling and a window looking out over the Fontanka. The walls were covered with drawings and sketches, mostly of nudes. She herself was in her late thirties, her beauty beginning to fade. She wore her grey-flecked hair in a bun, and her gold-rimmed spectacles would have given her a forbidding air if she hadn't smiled at the couple so warmly.

'Anastasia! And who's this?'

'Miss Katskaya, may I introduce my friend Ilya Ivanovich .'

Markov bowed, and the teacher, rising from behind her desk, inclined her head graciously.

'I wanted you to meet him, Miss Katskaya, because I think he would make a wonderful model for our life class.'

At this the teacher raised an eyebrow and asked mockingly 'What makes you think so, Anastasia?'

She blushed, and mumbled 'You were speaking about the importance of proportion in the human form, Miss Katskaya.'

The teacher nodded absently, her gaze never leaving the young man. She looked him up and down slowly, like a connoisseur examining a work of art.

'Yes, indeed, Anastasia. You understood the lesson well.'

The art teacher looked him in the face.

'You understand that I will need to see you naked, young man. You are not shy?'

'Not in the least, madam. I will be happy to undress for you - in the interests of art.'

'Then go down the corridor to the small studio, Anastasia will show you. Go behind the screen and get undressed. Put these on.'

She had opened a cupboard and handed him a pair of small cotton briefs.

'When you have shown your friend the studio, Anastasia, you will go straight to the students' common room. Wait for your friend there - do you understand?'

'Yes, Miss Katskaya.'

Then to Markov she smiled politely. 'I will join you in five minutes.' The young man bowed, and clutching the briefs, followed Anastasia back into the corridor.

The studio was a bare room about twenty feet square, with the windows boarded up. It was lit only by a skylight. Some easels were stacked against the wall, and a few wooden chairs. An old horsehair couch and a tall folding screen were the only other furniture.

Anastasia left him alone, and he went behind the screen. Behind it stood a chair and a washstand, with a rather grubby towel. A full-length mirror, its silvering mottled, was fixed to the wall. He removed his clothes, putting them on the chair. With difficulty, he pulled on the briefs. They were at least a size too small for him, but the front was shaped to the bulge of his genitals. He contemplated his reflection. He had never considered his body as anything more than functional, and it was a strange feeling to have others consider it artistic.

He stood waiting behind the screen. The room was colder than he had first thought, and smelt of chalk and dampness. He wondered idly if his body would gain the art teacher's approval.

He heard the door open and shut, then a sharp snap as it was locked. There was the creak of the floorboards as someone moved across the room. He expected someone to come round the screen, but all he heard was a rustling sound.

Then the teacher's voice. 'Come out, then, and show yourself.' He stepped from behind the screen.

She was stark naked, standing with one hand on her hip and gazing at him. Her body was firm, with none of the plumpness of youth. She had removed her glasses, and let down her hair. Her eyes had a sharp gleam as she coolly looked him up and down.

'Well, Anastasia has chosen well. The proportions are absolutely classic. And the modelling of the muscles very firm, very prominent.' She spoke with a sort of detachment, as if she were talking to herself. Miss Katskaya came over to him and began feeling his muscles, his arms, his buttocks and his calves. Markov half expected her fingers to stray to the bulge in his briefs, but instead she gripped his upper arm.

'You are strong, young man.' She was staring into his eyes at uncomfortably close range: she must be fairly short-sighted. 'A man like you could force any woman, no matter how hard she fought.' Her hand slipped to his wrist and tried to push it back. Very well, then.

His free hand slapped her across the cheek. She did not release her grip on his wrist, however, until he punched her hard in the shoulder. As Markov drew back his hand for another blow, she raised both hers to protect her face, but this left her stomach open to a swift jab. She staggered back gasping, but then lunged to grab both his hands. He quickly broke her grip and now it was her turn to have her wrists grasped. He forced them behind her back and then twisted them upwards. She did not cry out, but a hiss of pain escaped her lips. She was forced to her knees in front of Markov, her face level with the front of his briefs, which were now straining under the pressure of his erection. The helpless art teacher contemplated the tumescence beneath the white cotton for a moment, then with a swift movement of her head bit it.

The blow to the side of her head sent her sprawling onto the floor and Markov followed her down. Their naked bodies wrestled on the cold linoleum until she ceased to struggle and lay gasping. Getting up, Markov eased down his briefs, his rigid cock springing upright when released from the constricting material.

'I can't take any more,' panted the woman. ' You are the conqueror. Take me as you will.'

Markov gazed down on the pleading figure beneath him. Straddling her, he lowered himself so he was sitting on her stomach, his erection jutting over her breasts.

'Now toss me off.'

Forming her thumb and forefinger into a ring, she gripped his shaft just below the head, and began to wank him. She judged the tightness of her grip and the speed of her wrist to his response; light and slow at first, then firmer and quicker. At the same time she was doing this, her other hand reached behind Markov. He realised that she was seeking her own pleasure, and he shifted his position slightly to allow her to reach her clitoris.

Her breathing, rapid but with long pauses, showed that it was almost a race to see which would come to a climax first. As Markov's sperm began to rise, Miss Katskaya lost a little of her rhythm as her own orgasm approached. Her body stiffened under him, but she did not stop her wanking, even as her own fingertip was stroking herself to ecstasy.

His semen boiled up and spurted from his penis, long odorous jets that splashed onto her face and breasts. Hardly had the last dribble run out than she also was in the throes of orgasm, moaning and quivering as if in a fever. For a minute or so they remained still, while their breathing gradually slowed to normal.

He rose from the sperm-sprinkled woman. She quickly got up and went to the washstand, returning with the towel to dry his prick. Then she wiped the spunk from her face and breasts.

'You are more than satisfactory, young man. You will attend the life class here tomorrow at two in the afternoon. The rates are 15 kopecks for each class, with more for evening work.' She went to her purse and pressed something into his hand. It was a silver 15 kopeck piece.

'Consider this afternoon your first session.' Markov nodded and they both began to dress in silence. He was ready first, of course, and he left Miss Katskaya without another word. Asking for the common room, he found Anastasia waiting.

'How did the interview go?'

'Very well. I start tomorrow.'

'Marvellous. Look, would you like to come on a picnic on Friday? The weather's getting warmer. There'll be some others- all comrades, you understand. I thought we might go out to the Duderhof Heights.' Markov agreed and was making a note of the arrangements when a young man came up to them. He ignored Markov.

'All right for this evening, Anastasia? The ballet, then back to my place for supper?'

'Of course, Volodya. I'm really looking forward to it. Come on, it's time for the Impressionist class.'

They left together and Markov shrugged. Outside, the canal was busy with cargo boats and he paused on the embankment to consider. Was it worth keeping the appointment as a life model? There was much in the fortress needing his attention. But Anastasia was his only contact so far with the revolutionaries. Better to cultivate her, for a time at least.

A visit to another secret drop - a bar near the Finland station - revealed a note from headquarters acknowledging his report that morning and stating that 'Lenin' must be arrested at once. Addressing meetings such as the one reported was an offence and it was clear that his time in Siberia had not modified Ulyanov's revolutionary attitudes. Markov was to discover if and when 'Lenin' was to speak again, with enough notice to have the venue staked out by the Okhrana. He need not be involved directly. He was to write immediately he had a lead, or even better, telephone.

Being so close to the fortress, he spent the night at his quarters there. The morning was taken up with paperwork for the interrogation centre, and there was the welcome information that Ignatiev would arrive from the Institute on Saturday. Perhaps it was professionalism that made Markov bathe and shave carefully before leaving for the art school, or perhaps it was vanity. He adopted the usual technique of changing cabs once or twice on each journey to make it hard for anyone who might be following. He walked the last few hundred yards and reported to Miss Katskaya's office.

To his surprise, the teacher was not in, but a young girl was. She blushed nervously when she saw Markov.

'Miss Katskaya asked me to show you to the life studio. She is already with the class. You are to... um, prepare yourself in the dressing room and come in when you are called.'

'Must I undress completely, or am I to wear those ridiculous pants?'

Her blush deepened. 'The class discussed the matter this morning, and we agreed you... that is, the subject should be completely undressed.'

He followed her down a narrow backstairs and into a small windowless room. Historic costumes hung from hooks, and there was a simple dressing table and a chair.

'You will be sent for, um, sir.' The red-faced girl left

125

quickly by the second door. Markov undressed methodically and sat waiting. He idly examined the costumes. One appeared to date from the time of the Teutonic Knights. Another seemed to be a tsarina's coronation robes.

The inner door opened and Miss Katskaya entered. 'The girls are ready for you now.'

The girls? Was this an entirely female class? It was. The large studio had a glass roof and there were about a dozen girls sitting at drawing boards on low easels. The art teacher led him onto a small stage or podium midway down one wall, and he turned to face the class.

The first thing he noted was that Anastasia was not among them. For some reason he had assumed she would be there. The girls were all younger, perhaps first-year students. They wore white pinafores to protect their dresses, though it seemed only pencil and charcoal was being used. One or two were gazing hard at the floor, but most were regarding him with expressions that ranged from shy curiosity to frank inspection. Several were attractive, one or two even pretty, and there was nothing he could do to stop his body responding. The frisson of lust that flooded through him converged at its natural focus, and his member began to stiffen under the students' gaze.

Nobody spoke, but one of the girls coughed nervously and others swallowed hard. Hands loosely on his hips, Markov faced them with his sex rigidly uprisen. Miss Katskaya broke the silence.

'Come closer, girls.' The students left their easels and clustered round the podium, the more embarrassed ones folding their arms protectively across their chests or twisting their hands together.

'I will make the assumption that most of you will not have seen an erect male penis before. If you wish to know the human body, you must understand all its secrets. I want you

126

study the male genitals closely.'

Some girls craned closer as the teacher indicated the parts of Markov's sex with a fingertip that did not quite touch him. 'You will have noticed when the subject entered that his organ was hanging limp, with the foreskin or prepuce covering the head. When a man becomes sexually excited, as in this case, his pulse quickens and blood causes his penis to stiffen. Note how the scrotum contracts during sexual arousal, pulling the testes close under the base of the penis. The testes themselves enlarge, and a clear fluid is secreted from the meatus, which is the opening at the tip.'

The girls nodded as the bead of liquid overflowed and dripped down from Markov's cock. Miss Katskaya continued in a level, academic tone. 'The glans or head is purplish-grey in colour and has a shiny appearance when engorged during erection. Beneath it is the corona, which is the rim where that part of the foreskin not stretched back terminates. Do not be surprised, girls, if you do not see this so well marked in some men. They may be circumcised. The ligament which separates the two sides of the glans in front is the frênulum, and below it, along the shaft, you may see the ridge of the urethra, through which the seminal fluid is ejaculated at orgasm.'

Some students were jotting down the technical terms, and one craned over her neighbour's notebook to copy a difficult spelling. 'There is as much variation in the penis as in any other part of the anatomy. Some are curved, most are smaller than this one, and as a man grows older the angle at which his erection sticks up becomes less. This, though, is a fine example. I want you to draw the genitals in detail, then the whole body with the erect member.'

The girls returned to their easels and began sketching. Miss Katskaya murmured to Markov. 'Please stay in that posture for as long as you can. Are you able to maintain your tumescence without, er, stimulation?'

'Certainly. For as long as you wish.'

She was clearly impressed, but bustled off to tour the class, advising, criticising and encouraging the young female artists. From time to time, a girl would come up and peer closely at Markov's erection, but all avoided meeting his eyes.

After what seemed an age, the teacher returned to the podium. 'Well done, girls. I have never seen you work so quickly and with such observation. You have all finished satisfactorily and there is still half an hour of the class remaining.'

One of the students put up her hand. 'Yes, Sophya?'

'Could we sketch the organ in its soft state, then?'

Miss Katskaya looked a little flustered and turned to Markov. 'Could you, er, allow yourself to ...?' She seemed uncertain of the correct terminology.

'Not just like that. I must come to a climax first. After all, that is what my body has been preparing for.'

The teacher looked nonplussed. 'Well, I really don't see how that can be achieved.' One of the prettier girls spoke up. 'Miss Katskaya, I don't mind bringing the subject to a climax if that would help. I know how to do it.'

There was a gasp, and the first giggle the girls had let out during the session. The teacher's glare soon silenced it. Miss Katskaya opened her mouth and Markov thought she was about to explode at the girl. Whatever she was going to say, she thought better of it and closed her mouth with a snap. She paused.

'Very well. I am sure we will all find it most instructive.'

The young student was only blushing a little as she joined Markov on the podium. She stood beside him. Her cool, artist's fingers encircled his cock and she began to masturbate him.

Markov abandoned himself to the sensuous stroking of the slender fingers gripping his phallus. The sperm, pent up for so long, was soon rising like a boiling tide. The first gush splashed onto the polished wood of the podium, causing a murmur of surprise from some of the girls. The masturbatrix knew to continue her wanking until the final squirt had left a wet stain on her pinafore.

Markov turned to her. Their eyes met and he smiled.

'That was a clever trick. Where did you learn that?'

She spoke confidentially, but everyone was listening. 'I've been doing it for years. The stable boy at home made me do it; he still does when he can.'

The obliging art student returned to her place, and Markov's softening phallus became the centre of attention for scratching pencils and pursed-lip study. Eventually, the silent and moody art teacher dismissed the girls. Before leaving, two or three came to the podium and stared down at the puddle of semen as if at some sacred mystery. Miss Katskaya shooed them away and curtly handed Markov his 15 kopecks before leaving him to dress and leave in his own time. She did not give him another appointment for modelling, nor even asked for a contact address. Markov got the impression that his career as a male model was probably over.

The next day was Thursday, and Markov spent it at the fortress. Care was needed to keep his two identities as student revolutionary and secret policeman separate. Making sure he was not followed came almost as second nature, as did the coded reports that kept his superiors informed. If anything happened to him, at least they would know how far he had penetrated the subversives' organisation. As Friday dawned, he knew that he had done everything necessary to prepare his interrogation centre for action. All he needed now were the prisoners on which to practice his art.

The day could hardly have begun more innocently. The wicker hamper he had bought was filled with food, and a separate basket held champagne. A carriage hired for the day

129

rolled out of the city in the weak spring sunshine. Markov drove, with Anastasia beside him on the driving bench and two other student couples in the carriage behind. They passed through the dreary suburbs where the paved sidewalks beside the street gave way to wooden duckboards and then to gravel paths. Soon houses were replaced by farmland and open country. The road climbed and at the crest the travellers turned off the highway onto a track. At a grove of trees that gave them seclusion and a good view, they halted. The horses were unharnessed and allowed to graze in their head collars.

The season was still young, and the grass was damp and chilly. One of the male undergraduates had brought a patent paraffin stove, and after some trouble he was able to get a kettle boiling. Tea and fresh mint were stirred in the glasses and the three couples settled down on rugs. The others had been introduced to Markov only by first names, so he was no wiser about their surnames than they were of his. Perhaps this gave them a certain freedom of expression, for it was not long before the conversation had progressed to politics of the most radical kind. There was no doubt that none would have spoken the treason they did if they had suspected Markov to be an informer. With an easy manner he agreed with all they said, rephrasing and repeating their own opinions to reassure them he was not only trustworthy, but a true comrade.

It was time for lunch. Each produced their contribution to the feast: sausages, ham, vodka, black bread. Markov had been careful not to bring food that was too sumptuous for a poor student, although the champagne he considered might loosen tongues. They ate and discussed political philosophy as if words alone would change the world around them.

Then came the payoff. One of the young men casually remarked that Lenin was going to talk at a meeting of textile workers on Sunday evening, in the warehouse of a certain factory. The student himself would not be going, for he had seen him speak only two nights before - at the meeting where he remembered seeing Markov.

Markov was curious as to the lack of security this implied. 'But is he not afraid that the secret police will not be there too? After all, if ordinary workers know, why not traitors?'

'Indeed there is a risk, but modern science comes to our aid. The Okhrana extensively uses the telephone now, especially when notifying the uniformed agencies to act against us. One of our number is employed as a telephone operator, and contrives to handle all the calls from their headquarters. She lets us know immediately of any danger.'

He betrayed none of his excitement. With careful handling, this information was enough to break their organisation wide open. He relaxed and opened the champagne. Six glasses were soon filled and soon emptied. The talk turned to the organisation of society and the subservient role of women.

'Surely marriage is nothing but slavery for women,' suggested one of the young men. 'Would it not be better for each woman to take whatever man she wished without becoming his possession?'

Sonia, one of the other girls, seemed doubtful. 'Marriage, comrade, is necessary where there are children. What is needed is not no marriage, but marriage which is fairer and more equal.' Anastasia was oddly silent, though usually eager to offer her opinions. Markov spoke up.

'Yes, for children, to be sure. But a man and a woman can enjoy their sexuality without being forced unwillingly to become parents.'

'You mean the diaphragm, comrade?' the female student called Anna interjected. 'It cannot be trusted. One of the girls in my residence used it, indeed recommended it to us. Nevertheless, she became pregnant and had to leave her studies. She is now just another housewife. We can't all be like you,

131

Anastasia.' Markov sensed a tension between the two women. He hastily continued.

'But there are many ways of enjoyment other than straightforward screwing.'

Anna spoke again. 'Yes, true. All give pleasure to the man, and some give pleasure to the woman.' She smiled at her boyfriend. 'And if a woman is in love, then her man's pleasure is her own.'

'And which method do you two use?' Markov asked. He looked at the boyfriend, but it was Anna who answered, self-consciously tracing a circle on the turf with her foot.

'If a man may not enter by the front door, he is welcome to come in the back way.'

Markov smiled encouragingly. 'Yes indeed, we have all done that.' He addressed the other couple. 'What about you two?'

This time the boy, sharp-featured and with a glossy beard, answered. 'Sonia has a beautiful mouth. She is a singer, you know. Perhaps her vocal skills contribute to her ability to pleasure me with her lips.' Two red spots of embarrassment appeared on Sonia's cheeks, but she did not look offended. She threw the question back at Markov.

'And you, Ilya Ivanovich? How do you find satisfaction?' She addressed him in the singular, as if excluding Anastasia from the question.

'Oh any way I can, you know.' There were smiles all round. The third bottle was already empty, and with a loud pop the cork of the fourth flew in a graceful arc. Markov refilled their glasses.

'Sex is important to all people. It is one of the few things common to all levels of society. Why should we be ashamed of it?'

The boyfriend spoke up. 'We are not ashamed, as such, but society has taught us to be secretive.'

'But we here are dedicated to the overthrow of everything that society forces on us. Why should friends like us be reluctant to enjoy sex in each other's company, in the same way we have enjoyed our food?'

As he spoke, he slipped his hand up Anastasia's thigh as she lay beside him, his fingers stopping on the front of her skirt above her sex. She languidly stroked his hair, then dropped her hand to his crotch. She began that delicate groping which he had experienced that first night at the meeting, and the swelling beneath his trousers was soon obvious to the onlookers. The boyfriend moved beside Anna and slipped his arm round her waist. His eyes never left Anastasia's fingers.

Then the bearded youth ran a finger along Sonia's lips. 'Well, dear Sonia, what do you think? I wouldn't mind.'

She hesitated and then half turned to him, so she could get both hands to his fly buttons. She began to undo them, then suddenly looked up at Anna.

'Annushka, you don't mind me getting it out?'

Anna was lying on one elbow by now, as her boyfriend rummaged up her skirts. From where Markov lay half-sprawled he could see the whiteness of her petticoats and the creamy paleness of her thighs. The glimpse of dark hair confirmed she wore no drawers.

'Oh no, Sonia. I don't mind in the least.' Neither seemed to think Anastasia would object.

Sonia opened the youth's trousers and gently disentangled his erection from his clothing. He lay back as she knelt beside him, her head bent over his member. Wetting her lips, she took the hardened shaft into her mouth. One hand gripped it, while the other slipped into his open flies to cup his balls. She began to suck, and at the same time pumped her hand up and down his phallus. A wisp of her hair fell from her bun, and the bearded youth gently swept it back from her face so he could see her better.

Anna's boyfriend tugged open his own trousers and pulled out his cock. He guided her hand to it, and returned to fumbling up her clothes. There was silence except for the wet sounds of the penis jiggling between Sonia's lips as she pumped and sucked. The bearded youth lay still, but his body grew rigid. Then a cough and a sigh, and from Sonia a muffled grunt. She sat back on her heels, wiping her mouth with the back of her hand.

'Do you always swallow it, Sonia?' asked Markov pleasantly.

'Oh yes. It makes such a mess if you don't.'

Markov turned to Anna. 'Would you like to show us, as well?'

Her boyfriend eagerly assented, and made Anna go on all fours. Pushing up her skirts, he revealed her naked bottom. A smear of grease and he was pushing into her anus. Anna's face winced with pain. 'Please, not so hasty,' she whispered.

The boy was too hot to heed her, though, and his vigorous buggering of her was soon over with a muttered blasphemy. Anna smoothed down her clothes with tears in her eyes, but gave her boyfriend's hand a squeeze as he hugged her. Then all eyes turned to Anastasia.

She murmured to Markov. 'Lie down, comrade.' Unfastening his trousers, she skilfully unbuttoned the tabs of his braces. 'Raise your hips.' He did so, and she slid his trousers down to his knees. His erection stuck straight up from the small bush of his pubic hair.

Markov resented being ordered about by a woman in this fashion, but even more so by what she did next. Hoisting up her skirts, she straddled him and lowered herself carefully, impaling herself on his cock. She closed her eyes and sighed as the full length slid into her. Then, gnawing her lip a little, she began to thrust her hips forward and back. Her movements grew less regular and more urgent as her face became flushed. The other couples watched; the men eager, the women a little enviously. Anastasia's tension rose and rose until her orgasm burst upon her. A gasping rattle in her throat and she slumped forward onto Markov's chest. She lay limply, panting.

Markov wasn't going to take that lying down. Without withdrawing his penis from her body, he rolled her over so he was on top. His pelvic thrusts were hard and rapid, and Anastasia murmured for him not to be so rough. He ignored her, however, and drove mercilessly after his pleasure. It came with sudden force, like a flow of lava, and he pulled out of Anastasia's body at the first hot spurt. He was able to get the rest of his sperm to dribble onto her rumpled skirt. She squealed, but Anna gave a short laugh.

The champagne was finished now, and the girls became more subdued. Perhaps it was time to go back. The picnic was packed away as Anastasia crossly tried to wipe the semen stains from her skirt. The horses were harnessed up, and the party made their way back into the city.

Markov dropped the others off and was free at last to contact headquarters. He took the risk of going there in person, though entering by a side door in case the front entrance was watched. There could be no doubt that the building's identity was well known.

Zubatov was not in his office, but the underlings to whom he reported were at first unbelieving, then shocked, then anxious to avoid blame for a massive breach of security. Markov soon pointed out that they could turn the situation to their advantage. All that was necessary was to send a few misleading calls which suggested, for example, that the Okhrana had information that Ulyanov had left St.Petersburg. This would set the revolutionaries at ease, and they would proceed with their meeting with confidence. The rest was just good old-fashioned police work, without any of this modern bloody machinery.

He returned to his quarters in the fortress to await developments, changing into the black leather uniform he now routinely wore when on official duty.

The commandant had issued a standing invitation to supper at the officers' mess, and so later Markov strolled across there. He found the master of the Mint holding court to a group of well-dressed ladies in the salon. The master knew Markov slightly and broke off to hail him.

'Lieutenant. These ladies are wives of the army, and wish to have a medallion struck to celebrate our progress in the east. Very patriotic, don't you agree?'

The group turned to look at him. One of them was Ekaterina.

She had been shocked once before by his unexpected appearance. This time she concealed her astonishment very well, and only the widened eyes that took in his leather uniform betrayed her surprise.

The group was served drinks, and Markov took the opportunity to take Ekaterina's arm and lead her aside. His cover was blown, that much was certain.

She spoke first. 'Well, lieutenant. Your present uniform becomes you as much or better than the Lifeguard's. Who are you really?'

He had expected to be safe in the fortress and had no glib explanation ready. She was an intelligent woman, and not likely to be deceived by any story he invented on the spur of the moment. He had to have time.

'Not here. Come back to my rooms.'

She followed obediently to the suite of rooms behind the Mint. He lit the gas. She took off her cape and laid a paper on the side table as she turned to face him. He strode up to her and the first slap to her cheek raised a red mark on the pale flesh.

His voice was heavy with menace. 'You are not to tell anyone. Anyone, you understand?'

She nodded meekly, and Markov felt lust rising hotly inside him as he realised she was as much at his mercy as he was at hers. Two could play at blackmail, if necessary, but only he could threaten force. The second slap was purely for his own pleasure.

'Who would believe you, anyway? A whore, a liar, an adulteress, a hypocrite who conceals a degenerate secret life beneath an outward show of pious charity.'

Ekaterina nodded and tears filled her eyes, but this only urged on his cruelty. 'You're filth! Wicked filth! No punishment is too bad for you.'

The whips he had bought were still lying in their wrapping paper. With feverish force he tore it open and brandished a long, flexible dog whip.

She stood, head bowed, hands limply at her sides and her meekness made him too urgent to bother with stripping her. He flogged her where she stood and she made no move to avoid the blows he rained down on her shoulders, her back, her breasts. Satisfied at last, Markov undid his breeches and produced his erection. A hard shove sent her down onto the carpet and a few swift movements had her skirts pushed up, her legs forced apart and his cock rammed home. He scarcely registered the ease with which he penetrated her, he was coming to expect the pleasure she took in being whipped. Flushed and excited, Markov was soon thrusting his way to an explosive orgasm.

He got off her, and she painfully rose, only to sit heavily down in an armchair. He poured himself a stiff vodka, and one for her. She took it wordlessly, but after a moment she spoke.

'Lieutenant, you said you would answer my question. Just who are you?'

In the seconds it took him to drain his glass, he decided to tell her the truth. He trusted nobody, but he was going to trust her. Names, dates, places he concealed or distorted. Nevertheless, as she sat in his best armchair sipping vodka and rubbing her sore limbs, she learnt the essentials of the story. 'Lieutenant, thank you. You have done me the honour of taking me into your confidence. I'm sure you have disobeyed orders in doing so.'

Markov nodded carelessly. Orders didn't mean much. She continued 'I want you to know I admire you. I too hate the revolutionaries, and their politics of envy and violence. I wish I myself were in a position to protect our motherland against them.'

Markov's eyes fell to the paper she had put on the side table. It was a typed sheet, in French. A thought struck him. 'What's this?'

'Oh, I jotted down some thoughts I had on the design of the medal and its inscription. A habit from my secretarial days.'

Her secretarial days? He poured himself another drink and refilled her glass.

'I need a typist, someone to take dictation. Not full-time, you understand. Will you be my secretary, here at the fortress?'

Her hand shook as she raised her glass to her lips. She set the empty glass down and rose, pale-faced, to her feet. Then she sank to her knees, hugged his boots and then bent down to kiss them.

'Thank God,' she whispered. 'Thank God. I will be with you now.'

# CHAPTER SEVEN

## Crime & Punishment

There would have been inconvenient questions to answer if Ekaterina had stayed the night. It was arranged that she should return the next morning for further instruction, and Markov wrote her out a pass. It was not long after sunrise that she put in an appearance, and he shared his breakfast coffee with her.

'You had no difficulties over coming here?'

'No. The medallion is a perfect excuse for visits to the Mint.'

He showed her the apartment. It had been intended for a high official, and was fairly luxurious. The present postholder had a much finer residence in the city, however. The stairs up from the private entrance led to a landing with two doors. One opened into a large sitting room. Off this lay two bedrooms, a small but well-appointed bathroom, and an even smaller kitchen. The other door led to a grand office, with a large desk and a smaller one with a typewriter.

'You will work here. You will type reports, confessions - anything I tell you. You will send letters by the official messenger, and open any letters delivered to the tray inside the door. All paperwork is to be kept in this safe, and any waste paper is to be burned in the fireplace. You are to take no documents of any kind out of this room. You understand?'

Ekaterina nodded. Markov continued, 'you are to tell nobody of what goes on here. You are aware, I am sure, that you will suffer the most serious consequences if you disobey.'

She nodded again, and brushed the keys of the typewriter with her fingertips. 'I am less experienced in typing with the Russian script, Lieutenant. However, I am confident I can give satisfaction.'

She knelt and kissed his hand, as if in token of submis-

139

sion. Rising, she smiled brightly at him. 'Now will you show me the dungeon? It sounded so interesting as you described it.'

Markov was a little surprised. He had not intended she would ever go there, but on reflection thought it no bad thing if she were familiar with the whole operation. He led her downstairs and outside, across to the steps that led to the doorway below the rampart. He produced the key and inside the gloomy interior he snapped on an electric switch. He locked the door behind them.

The vault, now clean and bare, had a singular contraption in the centre. It was an iron framework like a couch with adjustable extensions. Parts were padded in leather, but clamps and straps did not suggest comfort. Ekaterina approached it slowly, then ran her fingers over the cold metal as if meditating.

'I see,' she said at last 'that you understand your business well.' Then she looked up at him. 'Show me the rest.'

Through one doorway was the guard chamber, and through another the passageway with the cells on either side. Markov opened one, and ushered her in. The bed was wider than usual, almost a double, but upholstered with black leather like a couch. Chains were fixed to the head of the bed. The cell was otherwise bare.

She lay on the bed and stretched her hands up until they touched the chains. Then, at her request, Markov left the cell and locked the door. He turned the electric light off from outside.

When he went in again, Ekaterina was still lying with her hands stretched up. She sighed and then got briskly up. 'What else is there?'

'The main interrogation chamber. This way.' The end door of the passage opened into a large vault whose arched ceiling gave it the appearance of a short, wide tunnel.

Chains hung from the ceiling; some in pairs, one heavier, with a winch to raise it. The walls were hung with whips and other instruments. A padded shelf held stainless steel castings made in the shape of an uprisen male member. They were graded according to size. A long wooden bed with rollers at either end was clearly a rack. A massive leather-covered block, about waist high, was fitted with clamps. Ekaterina regarded it with her head on one side.

'What's this?'

Markov hesitated. 'A flogging block. The ankles are clamped down here, the subject is bent over and the arms hang down the other side. The wrists are then fastened. The back and buttocks are thus available.'

'Your subjects will all be women, won't they?'

He had not said so, but the equipment was undeniable. 'Indeed. The prisoners here will be quite separate from those held in the Trubetskoy Bastion. They will be given special treatment.'

Ekaterina sighed and stroked his upper arm. 'I knew it, of course. It was too much to expect I could have you to myself.' She looked back at the flogging block.

'That's too big for most women. It needs to be adjustable. Let me show you.' She stood at the block. 'Fasten my ankles.'

He squatted down and clipped home the clamps. Then Ekaterina bent forward. 'See? The block is too high. It catches me in the middle of the stomach and I cannot reach down the other side to have my wrists held.'

Markov noted that both the height of the block and the clamps must be adjustable. Ekaterina then inspected the rest of the equipment. Most of it met her approval, though some of the fixed ceiling chains needed to be lengthened. 'No doubt the contractors thought they were for male prisoners,' she remarked.

The steel phalluses caught her attention and she examined each one. They had been brightly polished, and she admired the craftsmanship with which the balls and even the veins were depicted. She picked up the largest of all and weighed it in her hand.

'I know someone who would really appreciate this. May I have it?'

Markov shrugged. 'Take it. I can get another made.'

She put it into the velvet bag she was carrying. Only with difficulty could she close the bag when the heavy metal phallus was inside. Markov then escorted her back to the entrance hall. There Ekaterina swung round to face him. She gripped his hand.

'You will do as you will, I know. But I want you to make me one promise.'

'What's that?'

'That everything you do to these women, you will do the same to me.'

He raised an eyebrow. 'Everything?'

'Yes, everything. I couldn't bear the thought ...' She broke off, and looked away. Markov placed a hand on her shoulder. She smiled weakly at him, and then abruptly turned to the framework.

'This is for rape, isn't it?'

'Of course. Each prisoner will be given a choice: to tell us all she knows, or suffer whatever violation, torment or indignity we can inflict on her. Her fate will be in her own hands. This rack will be used on all who refuse to talk.'

'Show me how it works.'

He consulted his watch. 'Very well. We have a few minutes. You will have to undress, though. Come to the guard room.'

She followed him to the chamber off the vault and quickly began to remove her clothes. Markov opened a cupboard, revealing piles of brand-new black gym knickers and singlets. He threw a couple to her. Half-naked, she held them up for inspection. Without a word she continued her undressing, then pulled the prison garments on. She was unfamiliar with the stretch fabric, and he had to help her. She then followed him back to the rack. Markov released a catch and the padded top swung up until it was vertical.

'The subject is made to stand with her back to this, arms at her sides. Usually two men are needed to hold her. They first clamp her wrists and upper arms to the sides, then pass this strap across her stomach, just below the breasts.' Markov demonstrated as Ekaterina stood passively against the rack. More than her nakedness, it was her patient compliance which made the lust begin to stir in his breeches.

'Next her ankles are clamped.' He crouched, adjusted and clicked shut the clamps at the end of the two extensions that now reached to the floor. 'I trust you notice that this device can be altered for different sized prisoners. I designed it myself.' She nodded quietly.

'And then..' With a swift push, Markov pivoted the frame backwards. With an involuntary cry, Ekaterina found herself helpless on her back, her legs held out on the iron extensions. There was a click as the frame locked in its horizontal position.

Markov released catches in the leg extensions beneath her buttocks and knees. He began to turn the first of a series of cranks.

'The legs can then be forced open, raised, the knees bent at any angle.'

Ekaterina now lay with her legs high, splayed wide apart and her knees flexed. The fabric of her knickers was strained tight where it covered her crotch, dimpled by the lips of the sex beneath. Markov smiled down at her triumphantly. She raised her head from the leather pad and smiled back. 'There's just one thing I don't understand.'

143

'What's that?'

'Why did you make me wear these pants? Surely it makes it harder for you to get into me?'

Markov was slightly taken aback. He hadn't imagined she wanted him to screw her there and then. Still, there was no question that he was ready.

'There is little difficulty. Allow me to show you.' Markov stood between her legs and pulled out his erection. With a finger he then hooked aside the tightly-stretched material between her legs. It gave way enough to expose the lips of her vulva, and he guided the head of his cock between them.

She was wet and open to his member as he pushed into her, and she closed her eyes with a moan. Standing up as he was, it was easy for him to thrust his hips back and forth. The vaulted hallway echoed the quiet, moist sounds as his shaft slid in and out.

Then a deep groan from Markov and his hot sperm spouted into her. He pulled out, and breathlessly tucked his cock away. Ekaterina still lay with her eyes shut, but after a moment they flicked open.

'An excellent invention, lieutenant. Now if you would be so kind as to release me...'

Wiping perspiration from his forehead with the back of his hand, Markov straightened the leg extensions and returned the rack to its vertical position. He undid the restraints and Ekaterina stepped out. She was slightly flushed, and the crotch of her knickers glistened wetly. Her voice, though, was as cool as ever.

'These clothes are all very well, lieutenant, but don't you think that on occasion your prisoners might look to better advantage in leather?'

'Leather? Well, I suppose so. What had you in mind?'

'Something like the costume of the ladies' guild.'

'But I have no idea where to get such things.'

'I do. When we have both changed, I will take you'.

Thus it was that Markov, in a civilian suit, accompanied Ekaterina to a small but expensive-looking shoemaker's shop off the Nevsky Prospekt. Just before entering, she took two black masks from her bag and slipped one on. Markov quickly followed suit. A middle-aged man came forward as they entered.

'My dearest Lady Anometia! How pleasant to see you once more. And your friend?'

'My friend Lord Hermes wishes to place an order for those garments you make so well.'

Markov nodded curtly. 'Yes, a large order. And it had better be completed in record time, or I promise there'll be trouble.'

The man seemed to catch the hint of danger in Markov's voice, and the order was jotted in a small black notebook with a shaking hand.

'Three dozen leather corsets,' the shoemaker repeated ' three dozen long boots, in a variety of sizes. The wrist straps you say you have. You understand that these are costly items and that we have never taken so large an order. Normally they are made individually ..'

Markov cut him short. 'I expect the first dozen the day after tomorrow, the rest in a week. I will pay in gold when I collect.'

The shoemaker bowed. 'Of course, sir. We will take on extra workers, sir. Please be assured of our best endeavours.'

They parted outside the shop, Markov telling Ekaterina to come to his quarters in the fortress that evening. A call at one of the pre-arranged contact points yielded no messages. Blast headquarters! They demanded to know everything, but told him nothing. How was he supposed to know what was going on?

Returning to the fortress, he found Ignatiev already comfortably at home. There was genuine warmth in their greeting, and not a little respect from the older towards the younger agent. Markov must have impressed the authorities immensely to be given what was virtually a free hand. They ate and drank- Ignatiev only mineral water- as the two secret policemen brought each other up to date. Ignatiev was able to tell him a little about the political background. Ulyanov's return from Siberia was conditional on not entering St.Petersburg: he had broken this condition. Of those in power, some wished to see Ulyanov executed; some exiled again; others simply wanted him out of the country. Anyway, it was essential to arrest him without delay. In return, Markov told Ignatiev of his arrangements. They came to an agreement over Ekaterina.

She came exactly at the appointed hour, and Markov introduced Ignatiev to her. She acknowledged his bow graciously, and sat on the sofa covered with French damask. The men remained standing.

'You must know, dearest lady,' began Markov in a formal tone, ' that Captain Ignatiev and I share not only these quarters, but also responsibility for the operation of which you yourself form a part. Accordingly you will work for him exactly as you would for me.'

Ekaterina cleared her throat. 'I would be happy to carry out secretarial tasks for the Captain.'

'I mean exactly as you would for me. In every respect. If he wishes to use you personally, you must obey. If you require punishment, you must receive it at his hands also. I think I make myself clear.'

Ekaterina gazed up at Markov with panic in her eyes. He smiled evenly. 'Do this for me. I will measure the nature of your obedience by this.'

Her head fell, then she rose. Stepping up to Ignatiev, she knelt and kissed his hand. The men exchanged glances. They undid their breeches and exposed themselves to her,

'Undress.' It was Ignatiev who gave the order. For the second time that day, Ekaterina took off her clothes in male company.

'As confirmation of your submission, you will now receive both of us into your body. To symbolise the fact that you are common property, you will be blindfolded so you cannot tell who is penetrating you.' Markov produced a black silk scarf and bound it round her eyes. She stood perfectly still.

Ekaterina was then ordered onto all fours. Dutifully, she went down on the carpet. The men then proceeded to use her as they wished. First Markov knelt in front of her and pushed his cock into her mouth. When he withdrew, he went behind her and entered her sex. At the same time, Ignatiev was using her mouth. Markov gave way to him, and then when Ignatiev pulled out of her cunt, Markov immediately forced his hardened shaft into her anus. He buggered her until he reached his orgasm, then Ignatiev returned to her vagina, discharging his sperm deep into her body. The woman was told to rise, and her blindfold was removed. Before she was allowed to dress, she was told to make and serve them coffee. This she did without hesitation.

She requested that she might be allowed to wash before dressing, and she emerged from the bathroom fully clothed. She was told when she would be needed again, and both men kissed her hand as she left.

Church bells heralded the dawn of Sunday, but the day passed without incident. Neither Markov nor Ignatiev attended any service. While they both approved of the church as a vital pillar of the nation, its morality was entirely irrelevant to them. They spent the evening gambling with some of the fortress officers.

The next morning Markov noted an air of tension in the fortress. There were more guards than usual and he was asked for his pass when he called at the commandant's house. The commandant was triumphant.

'We've got him, we've got Ulyanov.'

'How was it done?'

'A tip-off from someone, I dare say, then a simple raid. Traditional methods. No need for special interrogation centres, you know.' Markov was irritated by his smugness, but knew better than to reveal his own part in the affair. Just then a messenger entered, but it was with a letter for Markov, not the commandant. The man wore the large top hat and blue smock of a cab driver, but without doubt he drew his pay from the Okhrana.

'I called at your quarters and was told you was here, sir. I was to give it into your own hand myself, personally.'

Markov nodded, and slipped the man a coin. He waited until he had left before opening the envelope. It was from headquarters. Their plan had succeeded. Markov was now free to act against the telephone operator who had been eavesdropping on the secret police line. The address of the exchange through which the calls passed was given. It employed twelve girls. She must be one of them. He was to proceed at his own discretion.

'Well, what is it?' The commandant was understandably curious.

'Oh, I must go and arrest a young girl. Can you let me have twelve soldiers?'

'Twelve men to arrest one girl?' The commandant's tone was half astonished, half contemptuous.

'Not to arrest her. To find out which one she is.'

An hour later Markov, in Cossack uniform and wearing a false moustache, rode out at the head of a squad of Cossack cavalry. With Markov, they made thirteen. When he had explained his plan to them, they had eagerly agreed to volunteer. He had taken care to ensure that the men were certified

148

free from venereal infection.

They clattered across the Trinity Bridge and past the Summer Garden, already green with the fresh season's growth. Then among the high buildings of the streets beyond the Engineer's Castle, until their goal came in view. High above, a dark spider's web of telephone cables converged on a wooden frame on the roof of an office block. They dismounted and entered the building at a run.

Markov led them up the stairs, their boots thumping and sabres rattling in the echoing stairwell. Scared faces peeped out of office doors, but quickly closed them as the Cossacks rushed past. At the top, a glass-panelled door was etched with the name of the telephone company. Markov did not bother to turn the handle, but kicked the door open.

There were feminine shrieks as the soldiers jostled through a lobby into a large room beyond. The opposite wall was entirely filled with the switchboards, mahogany frames with hundreds of plug sockets in neat rows. In front of them sat a dozen girls, wearing skirts and the full-sleeved blouses that were fashionable. They wore telephone headsets, and some were in the act of plugging leads into the sockets to make connections. They had all frozen in horror as the men burst in.

Markov stood in the centre of the room, weighing up the frightened women. The Cossacks lined up against the wall facing the operators, who instinctively rose to their feet to face them. Markov was absurdly reminded of a peasant dance in the country, the village youths along one wall, the maidens along the other.

The silence was broken by a bespectacled, middle-aged man, presumably a manager, who must have been in a front office and who now followed them in.

'What is the meaning of this?' His voice betrayed his terror, but at least he had the courage to attempt a brave face.

Markov did not turn as he answered, but kept his eyes on the line of shocked girls. Amongst them was his quarry.

'One of these girls is an enemy of the state. Official telephone calls have been overheard and their contents divulged to subversive elements. She must identify herself immediately.'

The manager babbled. 'There must be some mistake. I cannot believe ...'

Markov gestured, and one of the Cossacks punched the manager full in the face, breaking his glasses. He was then pushed out of the room.

'I repeat, the traitor must give herself up at once. Otherwise...' He turned and nodded to the Cossacks. Smirking, they undid their baggy breeches and pulled out their erections. The young women visibly quailed, pressing back against the switchboards.

'Otherwise, each one of you will be violated. The criminal can save her friends only by confessing.'

There was a tense silence. The cool spring sunshine lit the room, and the heavy smell of the unwashed soldiers began to be noticeable. Some of the girls looked as if they were about to faint.

Then one stepped forward. She was in her early twenties, with thin, mousy hair. Her face was a white mask, and her lips struggled to speak.

'It was.. It is me. I did it for the sake... Do it to me, not them.' She gestured weakly at the other operators. Markov's cold stare silenced her. He spoke.

'Corporal!'

The leader of the Cossacks stepped forward and signalled to two of the soldiers. They advanced on the solitary girl, the two grabbing her by each shoulder and kicking her feet from under her. She fell backwards onto the floor, the men holding her down. Two more came forward from the rank, kneeling and grabbing an ankle apiece. Roughly they hauled her legs apart and pushed up her skirt. The white cotton of her drawers protected her decency only for an instant, for the corporal drew his dagger, knelt, and carefully cut the centre seam open. The lips of her vulva were exposed to the hot gaze of the waiting Cossacks, whose phalluses visibly hardened in anticipation.

It was the corporal who took her first, pushing in urgently and panting like a dog as he fucked his way to an orgasm. In strict order of seniority, the other soldiers took her one by one. Markov lit a cigar and smoked idly.     As the last man climbed off the violated girl, she was dragged to her feet and hustled back downstairs to the street. The Cossacks tied each of her wrists to a separate horse's saddle and the column set off at a walk. Markov led, the girl stumbling along between the horses behind him. People in the streets where they passed turned their heads to watch, but none said or did anything. One or two women stood transfixed, following the captive with their eyes until the horsemen were out of sight. Soon Markov and the Cossacks were passing beneath the double eagle of the Peter Gate.

The commandant had insisted that Markov's prisoners be processed like all the others that entered the fortress, and so the telephone operator was handed over to be logged, photographed, and given a medical inspection. Then she was handed over to Markov's Specials, and taken to the dungeon.

He was waiting for her by the rack as she was brought into the entrance. Now for Markov's additional admission procedures. The girl, silent and tear-stained, was undressed. Then, stark naked, she was fastened to the rack and laid on her back. A few turns of the cranks had her legs wide open and her sex displayed. Markov nodded, and one of the Specials came forward with an open razor.

The prisoner squealed in terror, but Markov shouted at

her to be silent. He continued in a quieter tone. 'You won't be cut. Not unless Felix is clumsy, anyway. I suggest you lie absolutely still.'

Markov had chosen the guard Felix for this duty because he had noticed how well shaved he was, and also the eau de cologne he used. Not unusual for an officer- Markov used it himself - but rare for an ordinary gendarme. Markov had judged well, for with a little soft soap Felix expertly shaved the pubic hair from the victim. The swell of her Mount of Venus was now smooth and bare, and beneath were the prominent lips of her sex, swollen and sore from the repeated use. A wipe with a moist flannel, and she was ready for the next stage.

The rather effeminate Felix yielded his place between the prisoner's outspread legs to an altogether more formidable figure. This guard was massive and thickset, with calloused hands. He was a former sailor, and the needle and ink-bottle he carried marked him out as a tattooist. He was illiterate, however, and Markov casually laid a paper with the prison number on the girl's stomach. This the guard slowly copied, dipping the needle in the ink and jabbing rapidly into the soft, shaven skin of her Mount of Venus. From now on she would be known only by this number.

This done, she was released from the rack, issued with knickers and singlet, and taken to a cell. There, wrist straps were put on her and Markov supervised the fastening of them to the chains at the head of the leather-upholstered bed. He locked the cell and went for a well-deserved lunch.

Afterwards he and Ignatiev took a stroll on the ramparts, gazing across the water to the Rostral Columns and the Winter Palace. Ignatiev lit a cigar and blew a jet of smoke.

'When do you think she'll be ready for interrogation?'

'Not until tomorrow morning, I think. Let the situation sink in, let her understand she's helpless. The whole power of the state is against her. By morning despair will have begun to set in.'

'Of course she won't know it's morning.'

'No indeed. Time will lose its meaning for her.'

They wandered along towards the Trubestskoy Bastion, where Ulyanov was being held. Officially, they had nothing to do with him, and they merely speculated on the best means of dealing with him.

'It ought to be out of the Neva Gate and then the trip to the Schusselburg condemned cell. We should hang him like we hanged his brother.'

'The death penalty is only for those whose plot against the Tsar's life. Anyway, Dr Konigberg considers hanging barbaric. A bullet in the back of the head is more direct.'

'Hanging was good enough in the past.' snorted Ignatiev.

Markov nodded, reflecting that there were execution techniques in the past that made hanging seem lenient. 'But even if we do, won't there be others to follow him?'

'Of course. We'll hang them too. A rope is the best way to silence the treason they spout.'

'Well, Ignatiev, we have our work cut out.'

That afternoon Markov changed and driving a light carriage he went back to the shoemaker's shop. Slipping on a mask before he entered, he was greeted by the same man. His manner was nervous, but he had the corsets and boots ready.

'You will find they are all of the highest quality. I had the girls up all night finishing them.' He produced a sample corset. 'Note how the lower part of the back is reinforced to protect the kidneys. The boots,' he picked up a pair 'are of the softest leather and use patent hooks to lace up the outer seam.' Markov waved his explanations aside.

'I am quite familiar with these items. How much are you owed?'

The price the shopman quoted would have been enough

to employ for a year several doctors or teachers for the poor of the city. Markov paid in gold coins without comment.

On his return to the fortress, he had the guards unload his purchases, and found a note from Ekaterina waiting for him. It asked him to come to a certain cafÈ at 6 o'clock. She would meet him there. He was to leave the evening free.

When he entered the cafÈ, Ekaterina rose from her seat. She was wearing a light grey suit, the sleeves of the jacket fashionably puffed at the shoulders. She looked as if something was preying on her mind, but her voice was confident and businesslike. They sat.

'I am grateful you came, Lieutenant. I know how important and demanding your work is, but I need your help for a delicate enterprise.'

'I would be glad to be of assistance in any way I can, dearest lady.'

'I have been approached by a friend, a lady friend, who wishes a young girl of her acquaintance to become a member of the Guild. The girl is willing, eager in fact, but has no experience of any kind. She really has led the sheltered life we women are all supposed to have had, and it would be disastrous if she were thrown into the hurly-burly of a Guild meeting without some preliminary ... training.'

'Do you mean she's a virgin?' Markov was intrigued, naturally.

'Oh yes, and intends to remain one. She is a student at the ballet school, and pregnancy would mean the end of her career. She is curious, though, and more than willing to experiment. Of course, I thought of you.'

'That is a compliment indeed, madam. One that I know must have cost you some pain.'

She smiled weakly. 'I know you well enough to understand that I cannot keep you to myself. If I please you, then you will want me.'

Despite his cynicism, Markov was touched by this devotion. He took Ekaterina's hand and kissed her fingertips.

For a minute she stared at the table, then lifted her head. 'We shall call her Correphallia. Her apartment is near the Mariinsky Theatre, not far from here. I have arranged to take you there at half past six.' She consulted a diamond-studded fob watch. 'I will introduce you, and suggest that we talk for a little while over drinks. When the time is right, you should give her some practical tuition. I will offer her the advice of one long practised in these matters.'

'Have you brought dilators?'

'Of course. Afterwards, I have booked a table at the ImpÈriale for dinner. I told them no specific time.' Markov inclined his head in a mock bow, impressed by the efficiency of her arrangements. Ekaterina continued. 'A word of advice. Don't hold back. Often the more chaste and innocent a girl is, the worse the treatment she desires.'

He paid the bill, and they walked the short distance to Correphallia's apartment. It was in an exclusive block, forming three sides of a grassy square. The fourth side was separated from the street by a high iron railing. They entered through the ornate gate and, finding the correct entry, climbed the stairs to the second-floor.

A young girl opened the door, looking rather apprehensive. She gave Ekaterina an anxious smile, but avoided Markov's eyes. She invited them in. The main room of the apartment was large, large enough for a grand piano to be tucked away in one corner. Half the parquet floor was left uncarpeted and the wall on that side had full-length mirrors and a barre. The walls were crowded with framed photographs of ballerinas, many of them autographed. In one corner was a silver-mounted icon of the Virgin.

Ekaterina introduced Markov. 'Dearest Correphallia, may I present Lord Hermes. He has come to instruct you.' Markov clicked his heels and bowed, and the girl dropped as graceful a curtsey as he had ever received.

Markov and Ekaterina were invited to sit on a sofa covered by an Eastern bedspread. Correphallia herself took the armchair opposite them, sitting nervously on the edge of the seat. Markov glanced round at the photographs.

'Have you always wanted to be a dancer?'

Correphallia looked at him shyly. 'For as long as I can remember. My governess wanted me to become a nun, but when I found that ballerinas were allowed to show their legs in public, I wanted nothing else.' She relaxed a little as she spoke. 'You cannot imagine how exciting it is to be here in St.Petersburg, it is just as if I had been resurrected from a tomb. But all the other girls talk of lovers and the things they do. I want to be part of it all.'

Markov nodded thoughtfully. 'Have you had sexual experience of any kind?'

'Not really. I have felt, well, urges: urges to show off, to be admired. I felt excitement, but I could not understand why. Since coming here I have learned the essential facts, that is all.'

For a while they talked about sex and power. The young ballerina was well informed in some ways, naive in others. She seemed eager to please, however, and politely asked for clarification on several points. Eventually Markov decided it was time for action.

'Very well. We will now all undress.'

Markov stood up and removed his jacket. Ekaterina hesitated, and then began to unbutton her clothes. Correphallia sat, tense and uncertain. Markov strode up to her.

'Stand up.' Given a direct order, she obeyed automatically. 'Now take your clothes off.'

Her fingers crept to her belt buckle and she started to strip. The room was silent but for the rustle of garments, each

156

absorbed in their own undressing as if the others were not there. Soon they stood naked. Markov gazed at her appraisingly. His cock began to rise.

Correphallia was slightly built, with a firm body, small breasts, and long legs. Her brown hair was pulled back into a bun, and her hazel eyes were downcast. She stood with her hands clasped in front of her sex.

'Hands by your sides.' Like a well brought up girl, she did as she was told. There was a light down of pubic hair at the fork of her legs. 'Turn round.'

Her bottom was tight and rounded. Markov noted the way she stood straight but supple, her feet slightly angled in the ballerina's way.

'Good. Now come here.' Correphallia approached him. 'This is my penis. Have you ever seen one before?' She shook her head. 'Touch it.'

She looked at Ekaterina for reassurance, who smiled encouragingly. The young girl extended her hand, and brushed the head of the uprisen sex with her fingertips. 'Now hold it.'

She clasped the shaft with both hands. The touch of the cool fingers made it stiffen still harder. Correphallia spoke, almost as if to herself.

'Once in the cherry orchard behind the house I caught a songbird. It was a living thing, between my hands.'

Markov laid a hand on her shoulder and applied a little pressure. 'Kneel down.' She sank to her knees, still clasping his penis. 'Suck it.'

Correphallia looked enquiringly at Ekaterina. The older woman knelt beside her and murmured. 'That's all right, dearest. Take as much in your mouth as you can.'

Correphallia complied, bowing her head. The knob of his engorged cock nudged her lips and she opened her mouth to take it in.

Ekaterina continued her advice in low tone. 'Be careful,

157

dearest, not to let it push too hard against the back of your throat. Now wet it thoroughly, using your tongue.' The young ballerina's saliva was liberally applied. 'Now suck it like a lollipop.'

Her lips closed round his shaft and she began a nibbling, sucking action. Ekaterina coached her technique. 'The most sensitive part is just below the head. Grip it gently with your lips and work it back and forth.'

Dutifully, Correphallia's head bobbed up and down. Markov felt his sperm begin to rise, but he had no wish to have his orgasm so soon. He pulled out of the dancer's mouth abruptly. 'That's enough for the first lesson. Now you will watch me sodomise Lady Anometia.'

The older woman fetched the lubricant she always carried in her bag. Markov made her go on all fours on the carpet, and got down behind her. Correphallia knelt beside them.

'This is how I will penetrate you in a few days' time, Correphallia. As yet, your bottom hole is too tight to be penetrated easily. I will have it stretched. On this occasion, I want you simply to assist and take note.' He handed her the small pot.

'Apply some of this to the head of my penis.' The biddable girl smeared the glistening knob. 'Now part Lady Anometia's buttocks.'

She gently separated the pale cheeks, offering the tight pucker of Ekaterina's anus to him. Markov thrust his hips forward and lodged the end of his cock in the tiny opening. Correphallia watched with bright eyes and half-open mouth as he slowly pushed into Ekaterina's bottom. The older woman spoke between clenched teeth.

'It always hurts a little, dearest, but if you push out with your bottom muscles, he can get into you more easily.'

Markov now began his regular thrusts. As he buggered Ekaterina, he reached out to the young ballerina kneeling

158

beside him and slid his hand up her naked thigh. Without pausing in his rhythm, he pushed his hand between her tightly-clasped legs. The compliant girl yielded to him, opening her legs. He found the lips of her sex, moist and open, and began to caress the soft nodule of her clitoris. It was as if his finger-tip was a magic wand, for the girl went rigid and a soft moan escaped her lips. With half his mind on sodomy and half on masturbating Correphallia, Markov needed all his sexual skill to do both successfully. By concentrating on pleasuring the dancer, he was able eventually to bring her to orgasm. As her shuddering gasps betrayed her climax, he returned his atten-tion to the woman in front of him. He gave himself to his own gratification. A few more rapid shoves, and his warm sperm was jetting into Ekaterina's bottom.

Markov pulled out, and all three lay on the carpet, breath-less. The evening sun still shone through the high windows. The 'white nights' of this northern city, with their long sum-mer daylight, were already beginning. There was peace for a while in the room, and Markov was aware of the scent of polish and a smell he did not immediately recognise. Then he realised it was the resin that ballet dancers put on the tips of their shoes.

He got to his feet, and began to dress. 'Well, Correphallia, I hope you found your first lesson instructive. I will return for the second when your rear passage has been widened enough to receive me.'

The young ballerina was gazing up at him as if he were a god. Her first orgasm had left her stunned and exhilarated. She seemed hardly to hear what he said. 'Widened?'

'Yes. Anometia will handle the details.'

The older woman went once more to her bag, and pro-duced a black rubber plug. There were leather straps attached. 'You must put this inside you, dearest. I will show you.'

The lubricant was applied again, and the rubber dilator

pushed gently up Correphallia's bottom. She winced at the intrusion, but accepted it meekly. Ekaterina buckled a strap around her waist, with another pulled tight in the cleft of her sex and anus. 'The straps will keep it in place. Wear it during the daytime, under your ordinary clothes. I will see you the day after tomorrow, to change it for a larger one.'

They completed their dressing and took a cab to the ImpÈriale. They had an excellent dinner, talking intelligently of dancing and sex. It seemed it was impossible to have one without the other: every young ballerina was beseiged by wealthy admirers, and most girls were happy to please them. It was pleasant for Markov to recall that one woman had her rectum full of a rubber plug, the other full of his semen. He had hoped Ingrid would be there to serve them, but she was evidently not on duty. He reflected that nothing in life was ever perfect.

It was the following afternoon that he judged it time to interrogate the telephone operator. He and Ignatiev went in uniform to the dungeon, where Nikolai and two other guards were on duty. The telephonist had been kept chained in darkness with only water for twenty four hours. The two officers went through to the torture chamber, and selected a whip each. They ordered the prisoner to be dressed in the leatherwear and brought to them. While waiting, they made a wager.

After a while she was led in, escorted by Nikolai and another guard. They had carried out their instructions carefully, and the black leather fitted her well. The thigh-length boots were tightly laced, contrasting with the pale flesh above them. The heels were fairly high, with the intention of raising her sex to approximately the height of a man's and thus making it easier to penetrate her standing up. The corset was firmly drawn in round her waist, exaggerating the width of her hips. Her breasts were forced up, as if being offered openly above the leather cups that supported them. She wore wrist straps,

160

and the collar engraved with her prison number was buckled round her neck. She was still blinking in the unaccustomed light, but gazed round in horror at the equipment in the chamber.

'Well, 1046, you understand your position. You will tell us all we wish to know or you will suffer the consequences.'

She met Markov's stare with the best courage she could muster and made an effort to look resolute. 'Do your worst. I will never betray my friends. I ...'

He silenced her with a violent slap. She bowed her head, one cheek reddening from the blow.

'We'll see, 1046.' He drove the handle of his whip into her crotch. 'Kneel down. Put your hands behind your back.' She sank to her knees and made no resistance as her hands were fastened together by the clips on her wristbands. Markov stood in front of her and Ignatiev behind. They struck.

The whips lashed down onto her back, her shoulders and her breasts in a merciless rhythm. The regular sound of leather cracking on soft flesh echoed in the chamber, as did the moans of pain that were wrung from the victim's lips. She writhed and might have toppled if Markov's boot had not pushed her back on her knees. The sight of her suffering made his penis harden.

The whipping continued pitilessly, scoring her pallid skin with brutal red welts. Tears welled up in her eyes. She screwed them shut, but the tears spilled out and ran down her face. This drove Markov on to harsher cruelty, laying on his blows with the full force of his arm. He paused, and Ignatiev stopped his beating also. Opening her eyes, she saw Markov undoing his breeches to expose his erection. She raised her tearful face to him in mute appeal. Markov's only response was to force his cock into her mouth.

Her sobbing was muffled by the shaft between her lips. He thrust his erection to the back of her throat, making her choke. Grabbing her hair and forcing her head down, he was able to penetrate deeper. She gasped for air as he worked his cock back and forth in the soft passage of her mouth. It wasn't long before his pent-up sperm rose and spurted deep into her throat. Markov pulled out to allow her to cough out some of the thick fluid that threatened to suffocate her.

When she had caught her breath, Ignatiev stood in front of her. He pushed his member into her mouth, slippery with Markov's semen. He repeated the act of oral sex, discharging his sperm to mingle with his friend's. The two men then returned to their positions to resume the flogging. However, the prisoner had had enough. She collapsed clumsily on the hard stone floor, her hands still pinioned. She spoke through her sobs. 'No more. Please, no more.'

Markov replied in a not unkindly tone. 'You have done all that could be expected for your friends. Now you must tell us their names, where they live and what part they play in the plot against the state.'

The demoralised girl was helped into a chair and her wrists unfastened. Markov questioned her calmly and systematically. She answered as best she could, in a low, hopeless tone. Ignatiev carefully noted her replies in a small notebook. She implicated students, secretaries, trainee teachers. Each name was recorded, with whatever detail they could extract. When satisfied she could tell them nothing more, he ordered the guards to return her to her cell. When they had left, Markov turned to Ignatiev and handed him some gold coins.

'You win this time. I thought she would hold out longer. Still, she's given us valuable information. Now it's up to us what we do with it.'

# CHAPTER EIGHT

## Notes from Underground

The typewriter clattered out the last few lines, and Ekaterina wound the page out of the machine to join the earlier ones. Markov sat on the corner of his desk, idly swinging a booted leg as he had done for the last hour. He had dictated the telephonist's confession, a report to Zubatov, and a series of orders and warrants to the police. These would result in the arrest of more enemies of the state, mostly young, mostly female.

Ekaterina opened the office door and called in the special messenger who had been waiting outside. She handed him the envelopes, embossed with official seals, with instructions for immediate delivery. As the door closed behind the messenger, Markov sauntered over to a drinks cabinet and poured them both vodka.

'That was very efficient. You would have made an excellent secretary.'

'I trust I shall, Lieutenant.' Ekaterina sat in a low armchair near the window and crossed her legs. This was an unusual thing for her to do. A well-bred lady did not sit with her legs crossed: the deportment classes at the Smolny Institute would have emphasised that. She was showing an ankle, and rather more of her leg than was proper. Then Markov realised why she was exposing herself in this way.

'The boots! You're wearing the boots.'

Ekaterina smiled. 'I wondered when you'd notice. I honestly expected you'd have your hand up my skirt within a minute of my arrival. However, you concentrated entirely on your paperwork as if I were an ordinary male secretary.'

'Well, business before pleasure, madame. Time now to relax. Does your wearing the boots mean there is a meeting of the Guild tonight?'

'Indeed, and I hope you will be able to come as well.'

'I would be delighted. I have nothing to do now except await developments.'

The long daylight hours were no friend to the secretive seeker after sexual decadence. Rather than go there together, the pair arranged to meet inside the Guild. When Markov entered he found that Ekaterina had not yet arrived. Penosugia, wearing a black silk dress, was in quiet discussion with Lord Corvus and another man, but stood up as Markov approached.

'Lord Hermes! I am so pleased you have come again - I hoped you might.'

'It is my pleasure, I assure you. Anometia is to join me shortly.'

Penosugia had a slight air of guilty furtiveness. From her cleavage she quickly handed him a small envelope, of the kind visiting cards are put in. It was sealed, and simply had 'Thursday, 11pm' scribbled on the outside. Markov saw that it was a little worn and creased. She must have brought it to the last meeting for him, he decided, and brought it again tonight in hopes of seeing him. He knew better than to open it, but slipped it into an inside pocket. Neither spoke.

He was sipping wine when Ekaterina arrived, masked but in her street clothes. Many of the Guild members were already there, but there were some he thought had not been at the last meeting he attended. It was hard to tell beneath the masks. The ladies withdrew to the outer room to prepare and returned in their soft leather corsets and thigh-length boots.

The evening proceeded much as on the previous occasion. Drinking and conversation were interrupted by episodes in which one of the ladies was beaten, humiliated and taken by one or more of the men. Markov noted that only one victim was abused at a time. For the duration of her ordeal, she and she alone was the centre of attention.

Markov made a mental note of any particularly interesting techniques. For example, he was intrigued by the man who made four women - one of them Ekaterina - go on all fours alongside each other, making a kind of table or couch on which he took his chosen woman.

The heavy figure of Lord Corvus approached him. 'Hermes?' The grunted question was in a friendly tone. Markov nodded.

'Please feel free to have any of the women that you want. Although Anometia introduced you, she understands the traditions of the Guild.'

'I will certainly do so. By the way, is our medical consultant, Lord Caduceus, coming tonight?'

'I think not. He is usually here at the beginning, if he comes at all. He's some sort of government doctor, I think, and his work takes him out of St.Petersburg.' Corvus stubbed out his cigar. 'Will you join me in Coitolimia?'

They went over to where Coitolimia was bending over Lord Satyr, filling his glass. Corvus pushed a finger up her sex from behind. She finished her task and straightened up, the finger still inside her. Corvus murmured in her ear. 'The bridge'.

Without a word, she put down the bottle and gravely walked into the middle of the room. There was something in her poise that made him wonder if she were a ballet dancer herself. The company fell silent to watch as the two men followed her, undoing themselves to expose their erections. Coitolimia lay on the polished floor then, raising her hips, bent her knees to place both boot heels flat on the floor. Then she brought her hands back above her shoulders so that her palms were also on the floor. Pushing up with her arms, she raised herself so that her body was bent backwards in a graceful arch. It looked easy, but Markov could sense the tension in the young girl's body. The leather of her boots creaked a little under the strain.

'Mouth or sex? Whichever you please, Hermes.'

Markov chose the mouth. He knelt. Coitolimia's head hung right back, and so it was into a mouth that was upside-down that he inserted his penis. A shove signalled that Corvus had entered her between her legs. The men then began to thrust in and out, making Coitolimia teeter a little in her tense pose. Markov found that her head being bent so far back meant he could only push his cock to the back of her mouth. Nevertheless she gripped his shaft firmly below the head, her breath hissing in her nostrils as he fucked her lips. Her posture must have been cramped and painful, and the thought of this gave Markov intense pleasure as the sperm gradually rose in him and finally jetted into her mouth.

He withdrew, and the thick fluid ran from Coitolimia's mouth to drip onto the floor. Corvus came to his own climax. As he pulled out of her, she collapsed onto the floor. For a moment she lay still as the men got to their feet, buttoning their flies. Then she stood up, stretching and rubbing her limbs. A quick smile to both men, and they returned to their seats. Ekaterina welcomed Markov back, seemingly without jealousy, and they clinked their glasses in a silent toast.

In the course of the evening, Ekaterina was used by two other men. The first had her on the bench and simply gave her a brisk fuck; the second put her on the whipping frame and Markov watched with professional detachment as the riding crop was wielded, lacing her buttocks and shoulders with livid weals. He smiled knowingly at the ease with which the man thrust into her sex once twenty good lashes had been applied.

Markov waited until he was back in the fortress before opening the discreet little envelope. It contained an engraved visiting card with no name, only an address. On the back was written 'Lord Hermes. The planets are auspicious. Please

come: it is an opportune time for worship. Your priestess.'
What could this mean? Well, time would tell.

During the night the police raided the addresses given
them, and arrested most of the suspects implicated in the
telephonist's confession. When Markov awoke in the morning, it was to hear Ignatiev talking to a messenger in the sitting room. He soon entered Markov's bedroom and sat un-
ceremoniously on his bed,

'We've got six, at any rate.'

'Only six?' Markov had hoped for more.

'The men are in the Trubetskoy, and two of the women
were rejected at the medical inspection. Gonorrhoea. They've
been sent to an ordinary prison. Still, six isn't bad.'

'Where are they now?'

'Still in the Commandant's House, but they will be brought
over when we're ready. I suggest you get out of that bed and
do some bloody work.'

Markov laughed. 'That's no way to talk to your superior
officer.' He readily forgave Ignatiev, though. He was the only
friend he had.

The morning was spent processing the new prisoners. Each
had her cunt shaved and tattooed with her number. She was
issued with clothing: the singlet and knickers for daily wear,
the leather corset and boots for more significant occasions.
Then she was locked in her cell, in the lonely darkness that
would do much to break her spirit.

As the door slammed behind the last, Nikolai, the guard
commander, approached Markov. 'Begging your pardon, excellency, I was wondering about 1046.'

1046? Ah yes, the telephone operator. He hadn't given
her a thought all day. 'What about her?'

'Well, sir, we was wondering, if there's no other plans for
her, if we might not, you know, if that would be in order.'

'You mean you want to screw her.'

'Well, sir, the Cossacks did.' Nikolai tactfully did not add that Markov and Ignatiev had also used her. Markov shrugged. Why not?

'Very well. But no venereal infection, or I'll castrate the culprit personally. I've no intention of catching some dockside disease. Chain her to the bed and let the men go in to her. No more than two at a time.'

Nikolai's salute was crisp and flawless.

Markov had arranged to meet Ekaterina at a small restaurant for lunch, and was surprised to see Correphallia arrive with her. The young ballerina was dressed primly in a plain but expensively tailored suit. Markov noticed that she sat down gingerly. She leant over to him and spoke in an undertone. 'I've got it in me now, under my clothes.'

Markov gave her an encouraging smile. 'What's it feel like?'

'A bit horrid when I actually push it in, but I soon get used to it. In fact,' she blushed and dropped her gaze 'I like the feel of the strap on the place where you touched me. I pull it quite tight, and it feels exciting as I walk.'

Ekaterina added 'we're going back to Correphallia's apartment afterwards to change it for a bigger size. You would be very welcome if you wish to come.'

Markov readily agreed. The shyness of the young dancer relaxed as the meal progressed, and he was able to probe a little of her background.

'When my parents finally accepted that I was going to train as a ballerina, then it had to be St.Petersburg. The classical tradition was more respectable, you see, though I prefer the more lively Moscow style.'

'And you hope to become a great dancer with the Imperial Ballet?'

'Oh yes! If only I could be like Kschessinka. She has the rank of prima ballerina assoluta, you know, she can perform thirty-two perfect fouttÈs in succession. Dukes and princes vie for her favours, the jewels they give her are celebrated, many from FabergÈ. Indeed, her royal connections mean that crawlers use her friendship to advance their own careers. There's an artist called Diaghilev, for example. He's very unpopular, though, and several influential people are trying to get rid of him. No, I don't think that Russian dance will hear of Diaghilev again.'

'So you have your sights set on royalty?'

'Eventually, I hope. Of course, I realise that I will have to be able to satisfy other men before I can aspire to the court. That is why I must learn that art from you. When I yield my virginity, though, it will be to a member of the Imperial family.'

Markov was impressed, despite himself. 'Well, my dear, you seem to have your future well planned.'

Back at her flat Correphallia undressed unselfconsciously. She stood naked in front of her visitors with only the narrow leather straps around her waist and between her legs to indicate that the dilator was in her back passage.

'I have to take it out when I practice my dancing. There's so much movement down there, of course, and it is too uncomfortable to have it in.'

Markov considered her youthful body. 'I'd like to see you dance.'

'Now? But my pianist isn't here.'

Ekaterina solved the problem. 'I'd love to play for you, dearest, if the piece isn't too difficult.'

Correphallia eagerly agreed, and left Ekaterina looking over the sheet music while she went to her bedroom to remove the anal plug and change into her dancing clothes.

She reappeared wearing cotton tights and a little knitted jacket that crossed over to tie at her waist. Her ballet shoes were firmly bound above her ankles with pink ribbon. She dipped the block toes of her shoes in a shallow tray of resin and stood ready. Ekaterina sat at the piano and after a false start began the introduction.

Correphallia rose to her pointes and began a simple but graceful sequence of steps to the melody. Markov lit a cigar and sat back luxuriously, drinking in the beautiful young body in motion. He was no balletomane, clustering around the stage door after a performance in the hope of meeting one of the corps de ballet. Nonetheless, he was not immune to the sheer sexuality of the dance, especially when the ballerina was dressed in such revealing clothes. The smooth swell of her crotch, the pert tightness of her buttocks were constantly seen in different ways as she moved. Markov felt the urge to penetrate the hidden orifices that lay beneath the smooth white cotton of her tights. The knee-length gauze skirts worn by the classical ballerina normally concealed these pleasures. Markov had attended in Paris a ballet where the dancers wore a daring costume in which the skirt was scarcely more than an organdie frill around the waist. These 'tutus' exposed a charming glimpse of closely-fitting satin below. He hoped the fashion would spread to St.Petersburg.

The piece ended with Correphallia balancing on one pointe, raising the other leg straight behind and her arms outstretched in a graceful arabesque. She remained motionless in this pose. Markov went up to her and fondled her crotch.

She smiled shyly and returned to a standing position, though Markov continued his groping between her legs. She wore nothing under the tights, and he could feel the swollen dampness of her sex. It seemed that the dancing itself had excited her sexually. He undid his trousers and pulled out the erection that had been straining for release as she danced. A drop of fluid gleamed from the head. He nudged against the gusset of her tights, leaving a wet stain on the white stretch cotton.

'It is somewhat frustrating that I may not enter you from the front, dear Correphallia. Allow me at least an imitation of the act.'

He pushed his phallus between her legs, clasped in the warm triangle between her crotch and the tops of her thighs. Slipping his hands down from her small, firm breasts he gripped her hips. Ekaterina rose from the piano and came over to watch more closely.

'Squeeze your legs together more, dearest. It will help him to have his pleasure.'

As he began his pelvic thrusts, Correphallia helpfully pressed her strong thighs together to grip the length of his shaft more firmly. As his cock slid back and forth, the purplish-grey head protruded and disappeared below the cleft of her bottom. The small ballerina laid her head on Markov's chest as his pace speeded up. Her body was warm and slightly perspiring, and her perfume was the more noticeable.

As his orgasm burst out, Markov withdrew his phallus so the first hot squirt struck the centre seam of Correphallia's tights.

'Ooh! You're wetting me!' The ballerina gazed down, her hands beside her face in astonishment. Then she gave an embarrassed laugh. 'I don't know what you must think of me. Of course I knew that stuff came out, it's just that I haven't seen it before.'

The young dancer left to remove her semen-stained tights. Markov had Ekaterina show him the anal plugs she had brought, and they decided on the next size. When Correphallia returned naked, they had her go down on all fours on the carpet. Ekaterina greased the hard rubber and gently inserted it. The young girl screwed her eyes shut, but said nothing as the dilator stretched the tight muscle of her anus wider.

Ekaterina looked up at Markov. 'Another day or two?'

'Yes, I think she will be ready then.'

Correphallia got to her feet and buckled the straps that held the plug in place. Slipping on a silk dressing gown, she showed the pair to the door. As Markov left, he fondled the ballerina's firm bottom beneath the silk.

'I will let you know when I'm coming. Be ready for me.'

The next morning was spent in some leisurely paperwork with Ignatiev. Markov was waiting until the prisoners' morale had been eroded by hunger and darkness before starting their interrogation. They treated themselves to an elaborate lunch, and over a particularly good bottle of wine they planned their campaign. A detailed question sheet was prepared.

'About twenty minutes for each prisoner?' suggested Markov.

'Yes. The doctor recommended a maximum of twenty minutes' beating before the pain begins to be numbed. Of course, the subject will think it's an eternity.'

Markov smiled and poured another glass. 'We'll give ourselves a rest between each, naturally. If we find we are getting tired, the guards can be trusted to carry out some basic flogging. And so we go on until each one cracks. We may need to continue tomorrow, so we must allow ourselves a good night's sleep.'

When they were ready, the black-uniformed men made their way to the dungeon. Their boots echoed in the underground corridor that led to the torture chamber. Markov wondered if the footsteps aroused fear in the victims who lay in the dark cells that lined the passage. He hoped so. In the chamber the two officers prepared their equipment. They were ready to face the first prisoner as she was brought in by two of the guards. '1050, excellency.'

She was in her early twenties, with dark hair and a pale, owlish look around the eyes that suggested she normally wore spectacles. Her face was pretty, but already wrinkles showed that her life had not been free from care. The leather corset constricted further a slender waist, and the tight lacing thrust up her modest breasts. The high boots were unfamiliar, and she teetered a little. In the electric light she squinted, but stood as upright as she could.

'I must protest against the treatment...'

Markov's fist slammed into her stomach, and she doubled over. The guards behind her grabbed her shoulders and pulled her straight.

'No, you slut, you must not protest at all. You must tell us exactly what your role is in this subversive group, and who your accomplices are. That is what you must do.'

One guard shoved her roughly forward. She stumbled into Ignatiev, who spun her round, twisting her arm up her back. The four men formed a square, roughly pushing her between them, jeering and insulting her. They pulled her hair and grabbed at her breasts and buttocks as she tried to keep her balance. She stopped, panting, in front of Markov, who calmly slid his hand between her legs. He found the little nub of her clitoris beneath its hood of protective flesh and squeezed it hard. She screamed.

A violent push from behind sent her pitching forward. She put out her hands to break her fall onto the flagstones. Markov stood over her, legs astride.

'Well, 1050? Are you ready to confess?'

'Please...' she extended a hand along the floor towards him. He pressed his boot down on her fingers.

'I repeat, filth, are you ready to confess?' The crumpled figure panted for a little, then spoke in a clear voice.

'I must protest against..'

Good for her, he thought. There's some fight in her.

'Up. Single chain.' Markov signalled to the guards without giving her a chance to finish.

She was hauled onto her feet and her hands raised above her head. The wrist straps were clipped together. Then one of the guards grabbed her round the waist and raised her off the floor, while the other attached the wrist straps to the chain. The guards stood back against the wall. Released, the victim could now just touch the flagstones if she stood on tiptoe.

Her upstretched arms accentuated the thrust of her breasts over the corset. Markov decided to dispense with it and had one of the guards unlace and remove it. He made sure her apprehensive eyes saw him take in the full vulnerability of her nudity, then he stepped forward and grasped her breasts, tweaking and pulling at the nipples, then letting them snap back. She wept with shame when they engorged, standing out hard and red against the tawny areolae.

'Please don't,' she whispered.

'There is nothing I can't do, and nothing I won't. Understand that.'

1050 nodded dumbly.

To his amusement he noted that the full realisation of her helplessness in front of all these men was keeping her nipples hard. Russian women only understood harsh treatment, he reflected.

He ordered the guards to start whipping her and told the prisoner to count the lashes. The extra touch of cruelty left the girl floundering and there were several false starts before she began counting after each loud crack of leather across her back.

He allowed the count to reach fifty before ordering a halt.

At a nod from Markov, the guards unfastened the dangling victim and lowered her to the floor. Markov and Ignatiev expertly unbuckled the wrist straps and massaged the purple flesh of her hands to restore the circulation. At this point she burst into tears.

'You beat me,' she sobbed 'then you make sure I am not too badly hurt. What is this all about?'

'We have no intention of injuring you, 1050. Even the

flogging was not too bad was it?'

He noted that her nipples were still betraying her. She saw where he was looking and glanced down in shame.

'I am quite serious when I say that all we want is that you should tell us what you know.'

She sat up and wiped the tears from her eyes with the back of her hand. Gazing silently at Markov for a minute, she finally spoke in a flat, almost lifeless tone.

'Very well.'

Sitting in the chair, she was given wine and a roll. She wolfed the bread with her eyes on the floor, as if aware that her hunger as well as her reaction to her flogging was on show to the group of men. Then she began to tell of her involvement with the movement, her rage at the injustice of society, her pity for the poor. Then came names, places, details. She described one shadowy figure who was known only by a code name, Spark. The interrogators had no need to prompt her, and by the end they had what amounted to the biography of a revolutionary. She was taken back to the cells.

Markov and Ignatiev went back to their apartment for a glass of tea. They compared notes. 'What did you think of her?'

'Intelligent. Articulate. A good memory for facts. Altogether a most useful informant.'

'Yes. Let's hope they're all of that quality.'

The next was not, however. They heard her screams before she was even brought into the chamber and the shrieking, blubbering figure flung herself on the floor.

'Please, please, anything. I'll do anything. I'll tell you anything.'

Markov felt a surge of disgust for the cowering, snivelling figure. He turned on his heel and hissed to Ignatiev. 'Please take 1048's statement for me. I have better things to do.'

Ignatiev found Markov in the office, taking notes from 1050's confession. '1048 was nearly useless. She gave me dozens of names, practically everyone she's met, I'd guess.'

'Damn. You might as well throw her confession in the bin.' Markov was in a bad mood when he returned to the chamber. When the next prisoner was brought in, his glare made her quail. Nevertheless, there was defiance in her eyes as well as terror.

She was young, perhaps twenty, and had the air of a student. Her brown hair was still neatly pulled into a bun, and she wore the corset and boots unselfconsciously. Forced up by the leather cups of the corset, her full breasts seemed about to burst out. Markov dropped his gaze to her crotch, where the number 1051 on the pale mount of her sex proclaimed her identity. He demanded a confession, but she made no reply. Fear had begun to fade from her expression, to be replaced by resolution.

Markov stepped forward and dipped his hand into the cup of her corset. He rummaged among the warm flesh until he found the nipple. This he pinched hard between finger and thumb. She gasped and screwed up her face in pain.

'The rack.'

The four men hustled her over to the long wooden frame, and forced her to climb onto the planking and lie down. With one at each limb, they stretched out her arms and legs, clipping her wrists and ankles to the cords that lay waiting. At a sign from Markov, the guards began to turn the rollers with long wooden bars. With the clicking of a ratchet, the cords drew taut and pulled the girl into a spread-eagled position. Markov stood at the foot of the rack.

'Well, 1051? What have you got to say for yourself, you dirt?'

She said nothing and Markov gestured to the guards. After a few minutes he asked her again.

She raised her head to look at him despairingly. He raised his hand to signal to the guards manning the levers, but she whispered 'No. No more. I can't stand it.'

'You'll talk?' She nodded, then let her head fall back on the wooden bed.

The girl was lifted from the rack with a curious gentleness by the guards. She was placed in the chair, given wine, and the interrogation began. Her story was similar in outline to 1050's, and included references to a leader known only by the name Spark.

The two officers walked back to their apartment. Ignatiev poured them both a drink - vodka for Markov and lemonade for himself. 'What about this Spark? He must be a professional, not like these amateurs.'

Markov settled into an armchair with a sigh. 'We'll see what we can get from the others. Tomorrow, I think.' He sipped his vodka. 'I have an appointment later tonight, and I want to be fresh for it.'

Penosugia's address turned out to be one of a terrace of grand houses. The windows were heavily curtained and no light showed. A flight of steps led up to an imposing door, and a pull on the bell roused echoes deep inside the house. He quickly put a mask on. The door was opened almost at once by a maid in a black dress and white pinafore. She, too, was masked, and when she spoke it was with a cultured accent.

'Lord Hermes? My mistress awaits you in her private parlour.'

He followed the maid. Was she one of the Guild? It seemed likely, but he couldn't be certain. The hallway was paved with black and white squares of marble, and the stairs they mounted were thickly carpeted in a burgundy colour. Markov was aware of a heavy, sweetish smell, something like church incense.

Penosugia, masked but unmistakable with her red hair,

rose to meet him as he was shown into a small room. It was so cluttered that it seemed even smaller. There was space for two armchairs upholstered in damask, a coffee table between them, and an electric lamp with a pink shade. There were shelves round the walls, with sideboards and chests of drawers below them. On every flat surface stood upright objects of some kind. Penosugia invited him to sit, and only when he had settled did she sit herself. The maid stood silently by the door.

He was offered coffee and it was only as he raised the cup to his lips that he realised that the objects that filled the shelves were phalluses.

With an effort, he prevented himself choking and spluttering, and Penosugia smiled at his astonishment. 'You see my private collection here, Lord Hermes. I have devoted nearly twenty years to it. It is an obsession, I know, but one that gives me pleasure.'

He craned round to take in the ranks of disembodied penises, carved and cast out of every imaginable material. Many were of ivory, with Chinese or Japanese characters engraved on them. Others were of ebony, jade, metal, rubber. Some had a pair of balls attached, others not. Some were faithful replicas, down to the veins and wrinkles, others were stylised, stubby pillars. Amongst them he suddenly recognised the large stainless steel sex he had given Ekaterina five days before.

'My phalluses. I have had every one inside me at least once.' She picked one up from a sideboard. 'Of course, one does have one's favourites.'

Markov cleared his throat. 'How did you begin such a very specialised collection?'

'In my late teens I became enchanted by the male member. I loved to suck my boyfriends' cocks, but I dare not let them penetrate my sex, much as I longed to. There were no diaphragms in those days, you understand. Then one day I was browsing around the back of an antique shop, and there was this beautiful ivory dildo. Chinese, from the last century. The shopkeeper was fearfully embarrassed when he found me examining it, but I soon reassured him. In fact, I sucked him off in his little office in return for it.' She put it down tenderly.

'That night it took my maidenhead. Since then I have acquired all these. I have never paid for any. Most have been gifts - Lord Corvus is particularly generous - but some were exchanged for personal favours.'

Markov took a sip of his neglected coffee. 'But it was not to show me this collection that you summoned me.'

'No indeed. It is because of your own sex, dear Hermes. What is an artificial organ compared with a warm, hard, living one? You must know that yours is exceptional: in fact Anometia told me of it before I confirmed it with my own lips.'

She rose and took a large folder from a drawer. It contained a chart or diagram, with a phallus depicted inside a five-pointed star. It was surrounded by curious symbols and annotations.

'The planets are so configured now, as the solstice approaches, that it is one of the best times in the year to worship the male's ascendancy over the female, the power of the sun as embodied in the phallus.'

Markov was mystified by this. 'What is it that I am supposed to do?'

'My acolyte will instruct you. Go with her. I go to prepare the temple, for the ceremony must commence at midnight.'

The maid opened the door, and led Markov down a corridor. He was ushered into a small dressing room. On the wall was a row of pegs, with a black gown hanging from one. 'You will undress here and put on the robe. You will carry the thyrsus,' she indicated a rod topped by a pine cone and tied

179

with a ribbon-bow, 'and use it to strike the priestess thrice when she offers her back to you'.

There was another doorway opposite the door he had entered, but this was covered by a heavy curtain. The girl murmured quietly. 'Enter the temple when the bell rings. The priestess will pay you homage. Take your place upon the throne.' She paused and the eyes behind the mask gazed into his with a kind of holy zeal. 'Remember that you are to take on yourself the embodiment of the masculine principle.'

Markov was left alone in the room. He undressed quickly but methodically. Naked, he surveyed himself in the mirror. His was a hard, young body and below the dark bush of his pubic hair the heavy length of his phallus was already beginning to stiffen at the thought of what lay ahead. He slipped on the black robe, the cool silk whispering across his bare skin. It hung open in front.

Then a bell rang beyond the curtained doorway. Markov hesitated for a moment and, picking up the thyrsus, drew the curtain aside.

The temple was a high, dark hall lit only by a few candles. At the far end a large wall-hanging dominated the room. It depicted a huge erect penis, beautifully and realistically embroidered, with the sun's rays streaming from behind it. In front of the hanging stood a throne flanked by two tall candlesticks, themselves in the form of phalluses. There was a velvet cushion on the floor in front of the throne, and to one side a low table like an altar. On it, between two candles, was a small silver pot or bowl and a silver plate with what appeared to be a posy of flowers on it. Somewhere incense was burning, and the heavy, languid scent filled the warmth of the darkened hall.

Penosugia stepped forward to meet him. As the priestess, she wore a simple white tunic that only reached to her waist and left her sex exposed. Around her neck was a phallic pen-

180

dant, and metal bracelets glittered from her wrists and upper arms. Her brow was encircled by a crown with a gold penis rearing from the front, above a silver crescent moon.

Gracefully, Penosugia sank to her knees, then lay on the floor in front of Markov. She kissed his bare feet, lingering to lick the toes. Then she rose and stood aside as he strode to the throne. Markov saw that the maid, in a similar tunic but without a crown, was standing in the shadows beside the throne. He turned and sat down, the robe parting as he opened his legs to expose his sex. Penosugia sank to her knees on the cushion prepared for her.

The priestess brought her hands together as if in prayer, holding Markov's hardening member between her palms. She bent her head and kissed the head of it. She spoke.

'I humble myself before the Sacred Phallus - strong, erect, and glorious. I worship this sacred symbol, the image of maleness, I acknowledge it as a representation of power. It is the proud god-image of manhood.'

She kissed it again. 'The penis is normally kept secret, hidden beneath garments. I am honoured by its exposure to me, the mysterious focus of maleness.'

Then she took his shaft fully into her mouth, gently sucking it as it stiffened and grew to a massive erection. The priestess gave a little moan, muffled by the thick flesh filling her mouth. Then silence, broken only by the wet sounds of Penosugia's saliva as his cock slipped in and out between her lips. Finally she disengaged from her fellatio and spoke again.

'Erection demonstrates the power of life, of masculine energy. The male organ dies and returns to life repeatedly. It rises in excitement, and in orgasm its energy pours out. After an interlude of rest, it arises again.' She sucked his cock reverentially.

'The penis is external, proud and open. The female sex is internal, private and passive, awaiting penetration by the male.

181

The feminine is soft, gentle, weak and dependent. The phallic male repudiates femininity. I acknowledge his superiority.'

The acolyte brought forward the bowl from the altar and the priestess dipped her fingers into it. It contained lubricant oil, which she applied to Markov's uprisen phallus and smoothly worked her fingers up and down it.

'I anoint the incarnation of the masculine, I make this offering to the superior male from the inferior female.' Penosugia was then passed the silver plate, and Markov saw that it held a tiny chaplet of flowers, carefully woven into a circle only a couple of inches in diameter. The priestess solemnly slipped it over the head of his penis and slid it down the shaft.

'I crown and encircle the phallus, symbolising the male penetration of the female. The inner god, royally erect like the rising sun, demands expression by entering the female and discharging his life-force into her body. I offer my body to be penetrated by the sacred phallus. I am a woman, a vessel for the outpouring of the male's sacred fluid.'

She then returned to her delicate massaging of his penis with her fingertips. 'The Male is the Sun, the power upon which all life depends. The Female is the crescent Moon, shining only by his reflected light. But just as the Sun casts shadows, so the masculine force has its dark aspects. Women are raped, beaten and abused by men. This also is acknowledged and accepted. The woman affirms her femininity by her suffering.'

The priestess lowered her forehead to the floor between Markov's feet, offering him her back. He struck her three times with the thyrsus. Penosugia moaned at each blow, but returned to her sucking. She spoke no more, but worked her firm lips up and down his shaft in a way that made Markov abandon self-control and give himself over to his pleasure.

The priestess herself had her hand between her kneeling thighs. The acolyte knelt down beside her as the climax approached.

Markov's orgasm exploded into her mouth in a gush of warm semen. It seemed to be the final stimulus for her own pleasure, for the shuddering gasp that convulsed Penosugia allowed a little of the fluid to escape her lips. She had milked the last drop from his cock and with her mouth full of sperm, she turned to her maid. They kissed, and Markov could see the maid swallowing as some of his semen was transferred to her mouth.

The two women then rose to their feet. The ceremony was clearly over. He got up from the throne, and they prostrated themselves as he walked between them back to the changing room. After he had dressed, the maid reappeared in her demure black and white uniform. She showed him out, but just before closing the door murmured 'My mistress asks you to say nothing of this to the Lady Anometia. She hopes you will come again to the Guild, and will contact you there.'

As he walked slowly through the night-shrouded streets to the fortress, he mused on the strange passions that can rule a life.

He slept late that morning, and the noon gun had rattled the windows before he had donned his uniform and entered the office. Ignatiev was at the desk, completing some paperwork concerning yesterday's interrogations. He turned as Markov entered and gestured to the samovar.

'Tea? Or something more sustaining?

'No, tea will do. Any news?'

'I've been to Fontanka 16 to see if they have anything on this Spark character. You've seen the card index. Thousands of suspects, but without a particular name there's nothing to go on.'

'Well, let's have a little lunch, then back to the chamber.'

The next prisoner's crotch bore the number 1052. She was tall and willowy, and the edges of the smallest corset nearly met where they were laced. Her pale blue eyes had a withdrawn look, as if she was not really there. She glanced with indifference at the rack and the chains, but when she saw the row of steel penises on the shelf, fear seemed to grip her. Markov consulted her medical report.

'I see you are a virgin, 1052. If you wish to remain one, you had better tell us of your criminal acts against the state and of your associates.'

She looked at him, her lips moving silently as if in some inner turmoil. Then she cleared her throat. 'I must decide which is more important, my silence or my purity. You must also decide. I believe I can resist any pain, but pain passes. If you take my maidenhead, that is something that can never be restored. It is like a death sentence. Defile me, and you have lost your power to terrify me.'

Markov was baffled for a moment. He had never before met a woman who had such a revulsion for sex. Then he reflected that considering the women with which he usually consorted, this wasn't surprising. However, he was equal to the challenge.

'Two chains. Spreader bar.'

The prisoner's wrists were raised and attached to two of the ceiling chains. A steel bar about a yard long, with clips at the ends, was fastened first to one ankle, then the other. As her feet were pulled apart, she was forced into an X-shaped position. Ignatiev selected a vicious cat-of-nine-tails, with lead pellets at the end of the leather thongs. He took up a position behind her. Markov remained in front, studying her. He nodded to Ignatiev.

The full force of his arm swung the whip against her back, with a thud that sounded like a slamming door. Markov saw no flicker in the pale eyes, even when bright red marks rose on the skin below her armpit where the lash had curled round from her back. He sighed and nodded ruefully.

'You speak the truth. It will have to be the other.' He went over to the shelf and picked out one of the smallest phalluses. Weighing it in his hand, he returned.

'Now you must decide. As I penetrate you with this, do you lose your virginity? Is this instrument merely a lifeless object? Or does it not matter whether you are violated by an artificial penis or a real one?' He nudged the head of the dildo between the parted lips of her sex and pushed.

The scream startled even Markov, but he continued to force it in. The helpless woman strained against her bonds, and he held the phallus deep inside her until she ceased to struggle. Her head sank on her chest, her breath coming in sobs.

When he pulled the dildo out, he was surprised to see that there was no trace of blood. Perhaps her maidenhead had been insubstantial. Or perhaps it required a larger member to tear it open. He returned to the shelf and chose a middle-sized phallus. He returned to the woman hanging in the chains.

He was about to insert the instrument when she raised her head. The pale eyes looked wild now, and the lips were moving again in that inward conversation. The words became audible, then spoken out loud. 'No, no. Dirty, dirty. Dirty little girl. Smack you. Whip you... '

The victim shook her head and then met Markov's gaze levelly. The madness faded from her eyes. 'You have won, torturer. I will tell you everything, on condition that you do one thing for me.'

'And what is that?'

'That you beat me until I lose consciousness.'

This they did. Markov decreed that the weighted 'cat' would curtail the flogging and instead selected a scourge. This woman deserved a prolonged beating and she would receive it. The corset was removed and while Markov flogged

185

her from the back, Ignatiev worked from the front. Chained as she was her body could not move much under the twin assaults but she writhed in her bonds to the limits of her ability and let out an orgasmic yell before fainting away, evidently well satisfied with her punishment.

When she had recovered, they took her statement. Markov and Ignatiev questioned her closely about Spark. She had only met him once, but that was with the telephonist in the apartment of a bearded student who had a girlfriend called Sonia. The two officers exchanged glances.

When she had been taken back to her cell, Nikolai came in. '1046, excellency. She begs to see you. I said I'd mention it.'

'Very well. Bring her in.'

The telephone operator was noticeably thinner and looked haggard. She knelt at Markov's feet and looked up at him.

'Please. I know I've done wrong. But I can't stand it any more. Is there any way, any way at all that I can leave here?'

Markov thought for a moment.

'There is one way.'

'What is that?'

'As my slave.'

# CHAPTER NINE

## Dead Souls

'Your slave?' The grovelling prisoner seemed not to understand.

'Yes. You will clean my apartment, carry out other domestic tasks, and sometimes cook meals and serve them. Of course, you will also do anything else I might order you to do.'

She pondered, but not for long. Perhaps it was the reference to food, or perhaps a longing to leave the cell which had become a brothel, but 1046 gave her agreement. It was an arrangement that would suit Markov and Ignatiev. The orderly who was supposed to clean their rooms was surly and negligent. With a supply of female captives nearby, it was logical to replace him.

Markov left the dungeon to discuss some routine matters with the commandant, and casually mentioned his plan to use one of the prisoners as a slave. Oddly enough, the commandant objected. This contravened the regulations concerning the treatment of prisoners. It could only be done, he insisted, if the woman herself signed a document agreeing to it. Markov shrugged. He was confident he could get anyone to sign anything.

When Markov entered the office, he found Ignatiev fucking Ekaterina. He had her bent forward over the desk, with her skirts up and her drawers down round her knees. Ignatiev gripped her hips as he thrust rapidly in and out of her from behind. He glanced over his shoulder as Markov came in.

'Hang on. I'll be finished with her in a minute.'

'Take your time. There's no hurry.' The black leather of the seat of Ignatiev's breeches stretched and relaxed rhythmically as he pumped in and out of the passive woman. Markov leafed through the daily intelligence summary while the muttered obscenities indicated that Ignatiev was approaching his orgasm. It came, and the officer pulled out of the lady's body with a sigh of satisfaction. Ekaterina, a little flushed and dishevelled, straightened her clothes and picked up her dictation pad as coolly as any office secretary.

Markov dictated some correspondence, including a note to Correphallia to be delivered by Ekaterina. He finished with a document for 1046 to sign that agreed to her use as a domestic slave. Ekaterina's eyes narrowed.

'Who is this intended for?'

He told her, and she made no comment. She was silent as she typed up the dictation. However, when she handed the slave's contract to Markov, she spoke calmly.

'I know that I am an aristocrat, lieutenant, but I assure you that I am quite capable of doing housework. I could help you here. It is not necessary to engage anyone else.'

Markov raised her hand to his lips and kissed her fingertips. 'My dear lady, your talents and your time are much better spent on more important matters.'

1046 agreed to sign the contract on the condition that the guards would no longer be allowed access to her body. This presented no difficulty, for the cowardly 1048 was available as a sex object. 1046 would be taken from her cell each morning to the apartment. During the day she would wear her singlet and knickers to clean. In the evening she would put on the corset and boots for more demanding duties. When the men had finished with her, she would be escorted back to her cell. Markov ordered that the cloak that hid her revealing costume be taken away after each trip, so that there was no clothing she could wear in an escape attempt. The arrangement was to start the following day.

The next morning, however, not one but two prisoners

were brought into the office. One was 1046, but the other's crotch marked her as 1049, one who had not yet been interrogated. She was slightly plumper than 1046, and wore her long, black hair in a braid or plait down her back. They both stood respectfully to attention as the guards removed their long cloaks. Beneath they wore the black knickers and white singlet, and carried their boots and corset in a neat bundle. Markov swung round in the swivel chair and glared at Nikolai.

'What's this? I don't remember ordering two.'

To his surprise, it was 1046 who answered. 'Please, sir, this is my friend. I got word to her that if she volunteered for this duty, things would be easier. I hoped you wouldn't mind.'

Markov stood up abruptly and faced Nikolai. 'The prisoners are not to communicate with each other. That was my instruction.'

Again it was the captive who replied. 'The guards refused at first. I had to let them... I paid dearly for their co-operation.'

'I thought it would do no harm, excellency.' Nikolai quailed before Markov's wrath. The lieutenant snorted, but then shrugged.

'Very well. But if anything like this happens again, I'll send the whole lot of you back to barracks and find others who know how to obey orders. Now get back to your duty.'

When the crestfallen guards had filed out, Markov turned to the two girls. Both were attractive, 1049 perhaps more so, with a heart-shaped face, large, dark eyes and a small nose. The closely-fitting stretch cotton outlined their figures to perfection, figures which the hunger of the last few days can only have improved, he thought. He addressed 1049.

'You have not yet made a statement. Are you willing to do so now?'

When she replied, it was with a trace of some foreign accent. 'I am willing. I have heard enough from my cell to know that sooner or later I must tell everything.'

Markov sat at the desk and wrote rapidly as she told her story in short sentences, with pauses for thought between them. Again the enigmatic figure of 'Spark' was mentioned. He laid the notes aside and took the slave contract from a drawer.

'You must both sign this.'

He laid it on the desk and pushed the inkstand with its pens toward them. They both came forward and bent over, reading the clauses that surrendered their bodies and their freedom, but not their lives, to the officer commanding the special interrogation centre. 1049 signed first, dipping the pen with shaking hand. 1046 took the pen firmly, and her signature was more decisive.

Markov rose and fixed them both with level gaze. 'You are now serfs. You may think that there are no longer any serfs in Russia. You are wrong. There are at least two.'

The girls instinctively stepped back as he approached them round the desk. He stood in front of them. 'You are to go down on your knees and knock your heads upon the ground. You are to say 'Thy obedient slave beats her head at thy feet, Great Lord."

The prisoners did as they were told, their voices quiet but clear as they repeated the ancient formula. They got to their feet.

'From now on, I and my colleague are to be addressed as 'lord', and you will obey every command that either of us gives.'

He then set them to work, and when Ignatiev returned, he was delighted by the arrangement. The apartment was cleaner than ever before, and the officers' laundry was carefully done. The two officers agreed that they should not have an individual slave each, but use both promiscuously.

They were professionals, however, and did not mention

confidential subjects in front of the women. They kept them locked in the apartment, and went into the office to confer. Ignatiev sat at the desk.

Markov lit a cigarette. 'We've got to track down Spark, that's clear.'

'Certainly. We should get headquarters onto it immediately.' Ignatiev pulled a sheet of paper towards himself and dipped a pen.

'No. Wait. I have contacts I can pursue myself. I may be able to get straight to him.'

'How will you do that?'

'I've been neglecting my studies disgracefully. It's time I became a student again.'

Rather than start at once, however, Markov calculated that he had time to keep his appointment with Correphallia. He would begin his pursuit of 'Spark' tomorrow. He changed into a smart civilian suit, but wore no underclothes. He took a carriage to the street next to the one where her apartment block stood and walked the rest of the way.

Correphallia opened the door, her face pale and nervous. She was wearing the silk dressing gown, and she gripped it tightly together at the front as she led him into the salon. Ekaterina was already there, in a lace-trimmed day dress. The samovar and glasses showed that they had fled to tea, as ladies do when under stress. They poured him a glass.

'You're frightened?' Markov's voice could be kind when he wanted it to be. Correphallia sat down and smiled weakly. 'I suppose a bit. I know it's going to hurt, but I've made up my mind.'

Ekaterina reached over and patted her knee. 'Don't worry, dearest. No woman enjoys it the first time. Just relax and let it happen to you.'

They sipped tea and made polite, if slightly stilted, conversation until Markov stood up. 'Well, it would be best if we are all naked.'

Markov and Ekaterina, well seasoned in debauchery, undressed swiftly and neatly. He made sure, for example, that he removed his socks before his trousers: no man looks well with his legs terminating in socks. There was no ugly underwear revealed when he pulled off his shirt. He stood naked, and found Correphallia's gaze a little bolder as she eyed his body.

Ekaterina, her bare flesh pale in the afternoon sunlight, helped the ballerina to remove her gown. She was naked beneath it, the red marks made by the straps still visible round her waist. The young body was perfect in its proportions, lithe and even muscular compared with the older woman's. Was there jealousy, or just resignation, as Ekaterina gave a barely audible sigh?

The women had already made preparations. A washstand stood against the wall, with a sponge, hot water and a soft towel. Several cushions were placed on the carpet, and on these Correphallia went down on her hands and knees. On the low table nearby was a pot of lubricant. Markov knelt behind her. Correphallia spoke quietly.

'I think I could stand it better if you spanked me first. Anometia recommended it, and I should like to see what it feels like.'

Without replying, Markov swung his hand hard down onto the firm flesh of the dancer's bottom. The smack sounded loud in the tense silence of the room. Then another and another. He continued his spanking, the buttocks glowing pink under the punishment. Despite her sinewy build her buttock flesh rippled pleasingly under the ringing smacks he delivered. She made no move to escape the punishment and only allowed little mews to emerge from her lips as the heat built up in her bottom. Ekaterina looked on with nothing but envy on her face. At last, his hand stinging, Markov paused. In the

192

hollow at the top of her thighs Markov could see the plump cunt lips, engorged and open. She had evidently discovered that spanking was to her taste and he regretted that that opening was off limits. Still her anus was virgin too and should provide a pleasantly tight fit.

Ekaterina sensed the time had come, and knelt beside Correphallia's bowed head. 'Courage, dearest.'

Markov dipped a finger into the grease and applied it first to the head of his cock, then to the tight pucker of the ballerina's anus. He pushed the finger in a little, and felt the ring of muscles grip it.

'Relax.'

The tip of his phallus pushed into the tightly clenched opening. Slowly, but with merciless pressure, he forced his way into her virgin bottom. She closed her eyes and bit her lip. Her ring was being stretched cruelly by the intruding member, and he felt her instinctively contract tightly against the unnatural penetration. Correphallia moaned. Ekaterina stroked her hair.

'Push out. Open yourself to him.'

The resistance relaxed a little, and after what seemed an age he got the full length of his member up her rectum. He paused for a moment, then gently began to withdraw. Halfway out he pushed back in, not so far this time. Then with increasing speed he began to push in and out of her tortured bottom. Short, rapid thrusts slid more easily now, and the grip of her ring just below the head of his penis drove him to greater and greater excitement. Finally with a groan the hot flood of his orgasm gushed into the secret passage of the young dancer's body.

Sweating freely, Markov remained still, impaling the young girl's bottom. Her anal muscles twitched convulsively, bringing extra pleasure to the softening member. As his breathing slowed, Markov became aware that Correphallia was sobbing.

He pulled out of her rear, the semen trickling wetly between her scarlet buttocks and soaking the soft hair around the lips of her cunt. Correphallia collapsed on the cushions, curling up as she wept. Ekaterina lay beside her, hugging her and murmuring reassurance.

Markov got up and looked around for some strong drink, but could find none. He finally took his brandy flask from his jacket and took a long swig. He sat down heavily, still naked, and watched as Ekaterina carefully washed and dried the violated bottom of the ballerina. She was helped into her gown and then the women sat down also. Nobody spoke for a while, as Ekaterina wiped the tears from Correphallia's cheeks.

'Well, what was it like?'

Correphallia managed a brave smile. 'Not quite as bad as I feared. Anometia warned me that you were bigger than most men. I'm sure it will be easier next time.'

'Next time?'

Ekaterina butted in. 'Yes, Correphallia is anxious to attend a meeting of the Guild. I will take her next time, though she will have to limit her activities to begin with.'

Markov frowned. 'Is this wise? The men of the Guild are not accustomed to restraint with women. Indeed, is that not the Guild's very reason for existing at all. How can you be sure they will not rape her?'

'I thought if I made a point of asking them to spare her maidenhead...'

Markov snorted. 'I hardly think that is going to have the desired effect. Quite the reverse. No, there must be a surer way.' He pondered.

'Correphallia, you must lock up your sex.'

'Lock? But how?'

'Two small holes in the lips of your vulva - it will only be

194

like piercing your ears, which I see you have already done. Then a tiny padlock. You will then be free to mingle with men, having only your mouth and your bottom available to them. When the right man, or should I say the right prince, comes along, you can make him a present of the key.'

At first shocked, Correphallia saw the sense in this. Markov agreed to supply the lock and carry out the necessary operation. They dressed, and Markov left. At the door, he took Correphallia's hand and kissed it.

Markov hailed a cab at the iron gates to the apartment block forecourt. He ordered the driver to take him to Bolshaya Morskaya 24, the new premises of C. FabergÈ, the court jeweller. He asked for the master himself, but it appeared he was in Paris for the Exposition Universelle. Instead Markov spoke to one of the master jewellers. He described the tiny padlock he wished to have made, though not its purpose. The craftsman was familiar with silver padlocks to secure valuable jewels, but Markov thought silver might tarnish. Steel was best, he suggested. This was not a metal the firm was accustomed to using, but Markov's ready agreement to pay any reasonable price concluded the matter. Before leaving the establishment, he asked some general questions of the man who pierced the ladies' ears. From this he gained some useful technical information.

Arriving back at his quarters in the fortress, he found that Ignatiev had kept the slaves busy. Apart from the main salon, it was not a large apartment and the housework required was well within the capabilities of two women. He had bought some food on the way, and handed it to the girls for them to cook for himself and Ignatiev.

'I know exactly the quantities there. If I discover that either of you have been eating any, you will go back to the cells for good. It is evening now, and you must change into your corsets and boots. And let your hair loose also.'

The girls retired into one of the bedrooms to change, though Markov wondered why they bothered. When they emerged they were more exposed than ever, the tight corsets thrusting up their breasts, and the high-heeled boots exaggerating the sway of their hips as they walked. The lips of their sexes were naked between the lower edge of the corsets and the tops of the boots ending at mid thigh. The contrast between the black leather and the pale skin was charming, and they had brushed out their hair to hang, rich and soft, halfway down their backs. The pair stood side by side in front of Markov, who reclined in an armchair. Ignatiev entered from the office and took another chair. It was Markov, naturally, who spoke first.

'From now on, whenever you enter or leave the room, you must curtsey to us.'

'Yes, lord.'

'And if you happen to be sitting or kneeling when we come in, you are to stand up. The only exception to this will be if one or the other of us has ordered you to remain in a particular position.'

'Yes, lord.'

'Any disobedience, or hesitation in carrying out an order, will be punished by whipping. Is that clear?'

'Yes, lord.'

1046, who it appeared was the better cook, was sent into the small kitchen to prepare the meal. The dark-haired 1049 remained standing. Markov ordered her to serve them drinks. As she bent to lay the sherry glass on the small table beside Markov, he took the opportunity to fumble between her legs. She made no comment, and took Ignatiev his mineral water. Once more, she was indecently groped. Her submissiveness only inflamed Markov's cruelty and his maleness rose hard in response.

He unbuttoned himself and pulled out his erection. He

clicked his fingers and 1049 came over. At his sign, she sank to her knees in front of him. Parting her lips, she lowered her mouth over his cock. She began to suck. He smiled down complacently at the glossy hair, which he stroked idly as her head bobbed up and down. He sipped his sherry until the rising pleasure that radiated from his sex grew so intense he could no longer ignore it. He carefully put his glass down before allowing the soft ministrations of the slave's mouth to bring him to ecstasy.

When he had discharged, she dutifully swallowed his semen and went to fill Ignatiev's glass. Markov demanded another sherry himself, but instead of dismissing her, he made her go down on all fours, sideways in front of his chair. Markov then placed his booted legs across her back, using her as a footstool as he sipped his second glass. Ignatiev, stimulated by the sight of a woman used as a piece of furniture, came over and exposed himself. Kneeling behind the motionless slave, he inserted his member into her sex and began his pelvic thrusts. Neither man exchanged a word. But the ease of his penetration spoke volumes to Markov about the essential nature of Russian womanhood.

When he had acheived his orgasm, Ignatiev rose and returned to his chair and picked up a newspaper. The girl remained as she was, the sperm dribbling out of her. She was like that when 1046 entered, and stopped in mid-curtsey when she saw her friend. She made no remark, however, other than that dinner would be ready in half an hour, and should she set the table?

Markov nodded and pushed his footstool over with his boot. He rose and went into his bedroom to change out of his leather uniform and put on a mess jacket. When he picked up his hairbrush from the dressing-table, however, he was enraged to see a few long brown and black hairs hanging from it. He stormed back into the salon.

'Have you been using my hairbrush without permission?'

The slaves, having finished laying the dining table, were against the wall, one on either side of the kitchen door. The colour drained from their faces at Markov's anger. 1046 confessed.

'It was I, lord. I thought you wouldn't mind. I brushed out her hair and then did mine.'

'I see. Well, for that you will have twenty-five blows with the brush itself.'

He made her kneel on a chair, facing its back and offering him her bottom. The ebony-backed brush had a handle, and Markov used it like a tennis racket, smacking it hard against the naked buttocks. Ignatiev sauntered over to watch, and made 1049 stand beside him to hold his glass when he wasn't drinking. She stood patiently, her downcast eyes watching her friend's punishment.

Markov had to admit that 1046 was good slave material. The buttocks were pleasingly broad and well rounded, swelling out attractively from the narrow waist and easily capable of soaking up the prescribed punishment. He swung the blows in hard and enjoyed the ripples they set up in the soft flesh. The girl made no move or sound as the tally mounted towards twenty, the loud smacks echoing round the room and the buttocks steadily turning a flaming red. But during the last few blows she made half sobbing, half mewing noises and fidgeted between strokes, but Markov didn't let that distract him. After the twenty fifth stroke, he stopped and 1046 got stiffly off the chair. Markov now insisted that she thank him for the beating. This she did in a subdued voice.

'You are a slave. Do not forget it. Your pain is a measure of your servitude.'

The girls then served the meal. The fruit bowl contained bananas, and after a little experimentation, the men proved that it was possible for a woman to serve at table with a banana pushed up her sex.

After the girls had cleared and washed up, the guards arrived to take them back to the cells. Markov lit a cigar, and Ignatiev left for a card game with some of his new cronies. Markov picked up the paper and glanced through it. The Chinese resented the European strangers amongst them, it seemed. No surprise there, and nothing a well-organised European army couldn't deal with. The English queen had her hands full in South Africa. Perhaps it was an opportune time for Russia to challenge her empire once more in Afghanistan.

The bell jangled at the door downstairs. A messenger perhaps? Markov went down and opened it. To his surprise it was one of the fortress officers, one whom he knew slightly as a drinking companion. He looked tense and apprehensive.

'Lieutenant, I must speak with you in private. May I come in?'

Markov ushered him upstairs to the sitting room. He indicated an armchair and poured a brandy for the agitated man. 'Well? What is it?'

The officer gulped half his brandy. 'Lieutenant, it is my regrettable duty to inform you that you have been insulted.'

'Insulted?'

'It was Tavrichevsky, the artillery subaltern. He got drunk in the mess just now, and there was talk of your interrogation methods. He said any man who beat a woman was a coward.'

Markov poured himself a brandy and sipped it thoughtfully. 'My methods are supposed to be confidential.'

'Lieutenant, you cannot expect anything within the fortress to remain confidential.'

Markov sighed and nodded. 'Very well. Is he still there?'

'He was ten minutes ago.'

Markov hurried through the twilight to the mess. Silence fell as he entered and strode up to Tavrichevsky. The young

199

artilleryman blenched when he saw the cold ferocity in Markov's eyes.

'I understand that you have called me a coward.' His voice was measured.

The subaltern met his gaze with bleary eyes. His speech was slightly slurred. 'Yes, yes I did. And I'll say it to your face. A soldier who beats defenceless women is no soldier, but a coward.'

He drew himself up to his full height, a little taller than Markov. 'I joined the army to fight men, armed men.'

Markov replied coldly. 'Then you shall.'

The spot chosen for the duel was in the wooded area beyond the western ramparts, near the Kronversky bridge at daybreak. Markov chose sabres as the weapons and nominated Ignatiev as his second. He returned to the apartment and when Ignatiev came in, he casually informed him of the arrangement.

'A duel? Are you bloody insane?' Ignatiev paced up and down the carpet. 'We have work to do, vital security work, and you challenge some drunken fool. Why, for God's sake? What if he kills you?'

'He won't, my friend. Anyway, you know I have no choice. One of the first things our new Tsar decreed was that an army officer who was insulted, or even others felt had been insulted, must fight or face expulsion.'

'I know all that. But you are not serving in the army now. You are detached to the Interior Ministry. That is enough to remove the obligation.'

'I do not look for excuses. Anyway, I tell you I shall beat him.'

There was thick mist from the river at dawn, and the small group of figures that met near the bridge could barely see the looming mass of the fortress. The two combatants removed their tunics and tested their sabres. There was no attempt at a

200

reconciliation, for none could be accepted. The seconds stepped back, leaving the swordsmen facing each other. They saluted each other with their swords, raising the hilts then sweeping the blades down to the right.

'En garde!'

They engaged their blades, and Markov immediately began to apply pressure, pushing his opponent's sword aside. The artilleryman wasn't standing for that of course, and pressed back just as hard. Then suddenly Markov flicked back his wrist, disengaging his blade. Tavrichevsky's sword, with nothing to resist his pressure, swung across to his left, leaving him open to Markov's cut. It slashed down, but the subaltern's reactions were tense and rapid: a parry up and to the right swept Markov's blade aside.

'Well, he's not a complete fool then,' thought Markov as he stepped back out of range of Tavrichevsky's riposte. They stood weighing each other up for a moment, then the subaltern lunged.

A lunge is not a common stroke with the sabre, its curved blade being more suited to cuts. The artilleryman would have been used to a straight-bladed weapon, rather than a horseman's sword. Nonetheless, it is a killing thrust, and would have killed Markov if he hadn't simply dodged to the right. With his weight on his back foot, though, Markov was unable to riposte with anything other than a crude overhand swing. It clipped Tavrichevsky's left ear.

The red drops splattered the artilleryman's shirt. A voice - it could have been Ignatiev's - shouted. 'First blood. That's enough. Honour is satisfied.'

The subaltern lost his temper at this, and closed on Markov, hacking furiously. 'Thank God, now I've got him,' thought Markov, easily parrying the heavy, clumsy cuts. He knew how he was going to finish the matter.

The brief and highly-specialised medical training which

formed part of Doctor Konigsberg's instruction had given him some sketchy knowledge of anatomy. Markov knew that the radius, the lower bone of his forearm, had nothing but skin over its outer edge. The arteries, muscles and nerves were all safely on the inside. He also knew something of the ligaments of the leg.

Markov stepped back, letting his blade fall to the right. It was an opening Tavrichevsky couldn't ignore and he lunged once more. Markov caught the blade on his left forearm. The shirtsleeve offered no protection from the steel edge, which dug into the flesh and skidded along the bone. He had blanked off his mind to the pain, fixed on his own riposte. The subaltern's right knee was now close to Markov, fully flexed as the lunge developed. Markov stepped in, hooked his sabre behind his opponent's knee and with a pull the back edge of his blade severed the tendon.

Tavrichevsky fell with a scream, crippled and helpless. The pain in Markov's arm flooded up instantly, and he stared as the blood soaked the white linen of his sleeve. Fury replaced the pain, and he raised his weapon above the contorted figure on the ground at his feet. Just then Ignatiev's hand gripped his sword arm.

'That's enough. That's enough, old chap. It's over.'

The doctors bustled forward, exclaiming over Tavrichevsky's injury. One offered to dress Markov's pouring wound, but he angrily dismissed them.

'Come on, Ignatiev. Back to the apartment.'

There Ignatiev bathed and disinfected the long, jagged cut. A strip of skin had been almost shaved off.

'It needs stitches, Markov.'

'Then stitch it, blast you.'

Ignatiev produced a military sewing kit, and clumsily drew the severed edges together with cotton thread. Then more antiseptic, a gauze pad and bandages. Finally he poured them both a massive brandy and they sat, both of them pale and shocked.

'I hope you're satisfied, you young fool.'

Markov was too exhausted to resent his friend's remark. 'Yes, I'm satisfied. I don't think any of them will dare insult me again.'

Ignatiev gulped his brandy. It was the first time Markov had seen him touch alcohol. 'At least they won't accuse you of cowardice. Still, having hamstrung one of their gunners, you are unlikely to be more popular with them, or I, for that matter.'

'Perhaps we need to make ourselves more welcome within the fortress.' Markov took a long pull of his brandy. 'I know, I'll have one or other of the prisoners made available on the rape rack during the hours of daylight. The entrance will be unlocked, but guarded, of course. Any member of the fortress garrison will be allowed to enter and use her.'

Ignatiev nodded judicially. 'That would certainly help. I'll write out the order.'

He was about to add something, but was cut short by the furious jangling of the doorbell. It was at least an hour before the slaves were due. Could it be a summons from the fortress commandant? Ignatiev went downstairs.

Moments later, there were hurried steps on the stair and Ekaterina burst into the room. Wild-eyed, she hurled herself at Markov's feet, embracing his knees. Her breathless voice betrayed her anguish.

'I came as soon as I heard of the meeting. I hoped to arrive in time to stop it, to get between you and your enemy. I heard you were hurt. I heard you were dying.' She collapsed in tears.

Markov leant forward and gently raised her head to his. He ignored the throbbing in his left arm as he cupped her face in his hands. 'I have a little cut, that's all. There's no danger.'

The expression of joy and relief that flashed into her eyes told him what he had long suspected. She loved him. Ah well, women do tend to love swine. It's part of their tragedy.

Ekaterina's countenance now took on an air of brisk determination. She got to her feet.

'Show me the wound.'

'But Ignatiev has stitched it and dressed it.'

'Come on. Let me see.'

This was a new Ekaterina, forceful and purposeful. Markov shrugged mentally and began to unwind the bandage. She blanched at the fresh blood, but bravely examined the wound. She considered the clumsy stitching quite inadequate.

'You will come to my house at once. My physician will attend you. I will nurse you until your wound is healed.'

'But I have so much to do here.'

'That can wait. You must come now. My carriage is outside.'

Markov reflected that it might be advisable to let the cut settle down before he embarked on the hunt for 'Spark'. He agreed to go.

It was clear that she no longer felt the need for great secrecy in their relationship. Her carriage, bearing her coat of arms and manned by her coachmen, drove him openly across the city to her house. Servants were ordered to prepare his room, and the family doctor, hastening to answer the summons of Lady Lementova, soon arrived. He too thought Ignatiev's needlework unsatisfactory, and made a professional job of it. The dressing, too, was better-fitting, although Markov rejected the advice to wear his left arm in a sling. He had lost a lot of blood, however, and the cool sheets of the grand bed were welcome as he slid naked between them.

When he awoke, he could tell by the sunlight from the tall

windows that it must be nearly noon. He lay gazing up at the embroidered canopy of the bed until Ekaterina's voice beside him started him out of his reverie.

'You are awake at last. I have some gruel keeping warm for you.'

He turned to the figure sitting next to the bed. For a moment he failed to recognise Ekaterina, for she was in a nurse's uniform, a plain white dress and apron with a headdress like a nun's. Only her face and hands were not covered by the fresh, starched cotton of this severe and puritanical costume, relieved only by a bright red cross.

'Where did you get the uniform?'

'One of my charities is a women's nursing corps. We receive some training, and will be expected to nurse casualties in the event of a war. I have never had occasion to wear it before.'

She rose and fetched a bowl that was standing on a small spirit stove on the table. 'We were taught how to make a nourishing gruel that would sustain the wounded.'

She dipped a spoon in the bowl and brought it towards Markov's lips. With a shock he realised that she wished to feed him like a baby. With a violent shove, he pushed her hand away, sending the grey sludge shooting over the bedspread. Flinging back the covers, he got out of the bed and confronted the cowering nurse. He grabbed her wrists.

'Now look here, you pious whore. Perhaps you're doing what you think best, but I won't stand for it. I'm as strong as I ever was, and I won't be treated ...'

The wide-eyed fear of the woman in white stirred the dark echoes in Markov's crotch. His penis began to stiffen as he dragged her from the chair and down on her knees. Still gripping her wrists beside her head, he nudged his cock against her lips. She opened them and took him in. Automatically, she sucked him to a rigid erection as the lust swelled within him.

He hauled her across the carpet, pushing her down. She turned on her side to rise, but he shoved her onto her back and climbed on top of her. He clawed at the hem of the skirt, the starched material rustling as he dragged it up. She had spared no expense, and both her stockings and shoes were white. His hand encountered the drawers. Of course, they were not of the open kind. No nurse, as demure as a nun and as white as a bride, would wear anything but closed drawers. She protested feebly, more about her clothing than her modesty, but his desire gave him the strength to rip the crotch of her drawers wide open. She surrendered, and opened her legs as he entered her.

He fucked her vigorously, until the tension of the last hours was released in his orgasm. The hot sperm jetted deep into her, leaving him drained. His naked body relaxed on the white-clad form. She stroked his hair.

'Yes, you certainly are as strong as ever, my lord. Nevertheless, you must return to bed.'

He got up, gazing down on the crumpled whiteness which contrasted prettily with the torn drawers that exposed the lips of her sex. They glistened with his semen.

'If I am to stay, it will be as your guest, not your patient. You will wear your ordinary clothes. There will be no more of this Angel of Mercy stuff.'

'Very well. I will not attempt to be an angel.' She carefully removed the elaborate wimple that shrouded her head, and then undressed completely. Both naked now, the nurse and patient slipped into bed and into each other's arms.

It was late afternoon when he woke once again, but found himself alone in bed. The pain in his forearm was less now, and there was none of the swelling that might indicate an infection. Someone had changed the bed cover. He savoured the smoothness of the fine sheets and the faint scent of

Ekaterina's perfume. The room was on the second floor, and the clop and rattle of the street traffic was far below. Once he heard the stutter and bang of a motor car. Bloody western innovations.

He let his imagination wander over the events of the last few days and the future to come. He remembered the slaves in the apartment and began to plan acts of humiliation and ill-treatment. Once more his penis, which had so recently violated the nurse, hardened with anticipation.

Just then the door latch clicked and Ekaterina entered, carrying a tray covered with a white napkin. She set it down on a side table and came over to sit by the bed. She was wearing a dark dress, and her hair was brushed out.

'Are you feeling better?'

'I am feeling exactly as I should.' He flung back the cover and exposed his naked erection to her astonished gaze.

'You really do seem unaffected by your injury.' She leant over and caressed the rigid member thoughtfully.

'Did not your nurse's training teach you how to bring comfort to your male patients?'

She laughed. 'Certainly not. It could lead to a dangerous rise in the pressure of the blood. But you are in no danger, I suppose.'

Her slender fingers curled round his shaft and gripped it firmly. Slowly she began to wank him, pumping her hand up and down. He moaned and writhed a little beneath her touch, then grew tense as she quickened her pace, her hand jerking him faster and faster. He gave a long low groan, and abruptly a hot jet of sperm spurted upwards. Its warm stickiness overflowed her fingers as she gently milked the last drops from his cock.

Rising, Ekaterina wiped her hand with a hand towel, then carefully dried his softening phallus.

'I've brought you some food.'

'Real food, I hope. But what I really need is a drink.'

'Nothing alcoholic. Doctor's orders. He's coming in another hour to check your progress.'

Markov had to be content with coffee, but the physician was pleased at the way his wound had stopped bleeding, and showed no sign of infection as he changed the dressing. He should be able to resume light duties the following morning. Very well, then. The hunt for Spark would start the next day. That night he and Ekaterina slept naked together. He, well-rested and well-fed, slept lightly, and roused her twice in the night to perform acts that were just as well concealed by darkness.

As day broke, he dressed in the least conspicuous of the General's civilian suits and returned to his student lodgings. The sparsely furnished rooms were as he had left them, and the landlady seemed to have ignored his absence. He had paid a month in advance, after all. A shave and a change into the crumpled and badly tailored student clothes transformed him. He swung his undergraduate's cloak around his shoulders - no university student would be seen wearing the grey greatcoat of the high school boys. He was ready for the chase.

He hoped Anastasia's dissolute life meant she was still in bed as he tapped on the door of her flat. He was rewarded by a muffled curse and eventually a tousled Anastasia unbolted the door. She sprang awake immediately.

'Ilya Ivanovich, thank God you're safe!'

'Safe? What do you mean?'

'Haven't you heard? The Okhrana have arrested many of our group. I heard nothing from you. I feared you were amongst them.'

Markov was ready for this. 'I have been in the Baltic with Dr Popov. We sailed to test the possibility of wireless communication between ships. I returned last night.'

'Come in, quickly. Who knows who is being watched or

followed?'

Over tea, Markov gently probed Anastasia to find out how much she knew. She confirmed that perhaps half the student revolutionaries had been apprehended, though oddly enough more women than men.

'By great good fortune Spark escaped them.'

'Of course, Spark. He's the important one. Where is he now?'

Anastasia looked strangely at him. 'Staying with Sonia, of course. After the raids he stayed put, and hasn't been out of her flat.'

Spark. The sharp-featured youth with the glossy beard. Spark, whom the young soprano had sucked off two yards from him.

'I'd like to go and see them.'

'Is it a good idea? I think we should all stay quiet for a bit.'

'Can it do harm? If the secret police suspected either you or Sonia, they would surely have raided your apartments before now.'

It took a little persuasion, and eventually a long screw, to get Anastasia dressed and walking nervously through the backstreets to Sonia's flat. It was at the top of an elegant block that obviously housed fairly well-to-do tenants. As they climbed the stairs, Markov remarked that Sonia could afford better than himself.

'Oh, Sonia was at the Alexandrovsky Institute, you know. A real bourgeoise like myself. We would have liked to go to the University like you, but we are women and must be content with the Bestuzhev Higher Courses.'

Anastasia tapped on the door. A frightened voice behind asked who it was, and it was an edgy Sonia who opened up and beckoned them in. The apartment was well furnished but untidy, and the grand piano in the main room was littered with sheet music. Spark stood behind it, as if using the bulk of the instrument as a protection.

'You remember Ilya Ivanovich, Spark?'

He gave a curt nod and moved from behind the piano. The four sat down awkwardly where they could. Markov shifted a box of phonograph cylinders to sit on an upright chair. Sonia bustled out to brew coffee.

Spark stared hard at Markov for an uncomfortably long time. He spoke.

'You weren't arrested, then? That was good luck. A lot of us were.'

Markov repeated his cover story of the scientific voyage.

'When did you say you left?'

'Ten days ago. Before all this blew up, it seems.'

Spark's gaze became a steely glare. 'Then how is it that you were seen dining at the ImpÈriale on Monday with two women?'

Keep calm. Bluff it out. 'That must be a mistake.'

'Ingrid was not mistaken. She knows you. She had been used by you.'

Spark's hand moved towards his inside pocket. A pistol. Time to get out. Markov lunged for the hallway and the outer door.

'Sonia, stop him!'

The white-faced girl, coffee pot in hand, appeared at the kitchen door. Grabbing her shoulders, he spun her around to collide with Spark. The boiling coffee deluged the outstretched hand and its revolver. The door was bolted and chained. The three seconds it took Markov to open it were the longest of his life, but he was aware all the time of the screech of the scalded man.

Then he was hurling himself down the stairs, his hands alternately gripping the handrails as his feet hardly touched the steps. It seemed an age before the first shot, but when it came it was almost an anti-climax. A popping noise, and he had no idea where the bullet went.

Then he was out in the street, a long, featureless one with no cover for a hundred yards in each direction. Thank God. A carriage on the other side. Two glossy chestnuts harnessed to a fly. The coachman was adjusting the halter of one of them.

Markov was on the driving seat and whipping up the horses before the coachman could yell a protest. He got the whip across his face as Markov whirred past. Then the second shot. This time he heard it smash into the woodwork at the back of the carriage.

What now? He had never even considered carrying a weapon himself, and he had gone alone, unsupported, right into the enemy's lair. Where were the Cossacks when he needed them most? Where was the power of an autocratic state, whose instrument he was? A sudden loud rattling sound made him glance over his shoulder. Oh no.

A motor car was emerging from the archway beside Sonia's apartment block. And there could be no doubt that it was Spark at the steering wheel.


CHAPTER TEN

A Hero of our Time

What Markov did now would determine whether or not he was to die in the next few minutes. His self-reproach lasted a moment, and even as he lashed the horses to a hard trot he was calculating rapidly. Much would depend on the speed of the motor car pursuing him. Was it faster than a light carriage with a pair of good horses? In the past he had deliberately ignored motor cars. Now it was vital he knew something about them.

The wheezing rattle was getting nearer, and a glance over his shoulder confirmed that Spark was gaining on him. The avenues on Vasilevsky Island were long and straight, with streets crossing them in a grid pattern. There were no short cuts or bends where he could abandon the carriage without being spotted. Should he drive towards the Strelka, where the guards at the Custom House or the Stock Exchange might intervene? Could he even make it across the Little Neva to the fortress itself, to which Spark would hardly dare follow?

At the next corner stood a large, dark-painted van with two horses. Some men were standing beside it. It might help to mask him as he turned. Markov hauled round on the reins, whipping the outer horse to speed up the turn. Then something happened which was entirely beyond his control.

The offside horse lashed backwards with a rear leg, kicking over the traces on that side. It stumbled and fell, bringing the nearside horse down at the same time. Markov was pitched forward off the driving seat and landed with a thud on the sweating horses below. Avoiding the flailing hooves, he rolled off and stood up.

'Comrade! Over here! Quick!'

In a split second Markov realised that the group of men were sailors, in striped undershirts and caps, and that one was holding open the back door of the van. He was across the street and into the dark interior moments before the motor car spluttered up to the group. It stopped.

'He ran off that way!' Through the half-open door, Markov could see the sailor helpfully pointing down the street as he shouted an answer to the invisible driver's question. He could also hear him add under his breath 'You fucking bastard' as Spark drove away.

The noise of the motor faded. The sailors clustered around the rear of the van, and one of them offered Markov a swig of brandy. He gulped it down, realising for the first time that he was shaking.

'Thanks.' He was about to blurt out the story, and order the sailors to pursue Spark. Then he remembered how he had been called to, and held his tongue. It was this that saved his life.

'We saw you coming. Anyone who is being chased by a secret policeman with a pistol is our friend,' muttered one of the seamen. Markov shook their hands.

'Comrades, I owe you my life. That was a treacherous Okhrana agent who had infiltrated our student group. I must go now and warn the others.'

One of the sailors, older than the rest, spoke up. 'That would be dangerous. The whole island will be crawling with police soon. I suppose your carriage was stolen?' Markov nodded. 'You'd best come with us to the docks, and we can get you across the river. They'll be watching the bridges. We have contacts with some workers' groups. They will hide you for a while.'

Hell. Well, better go along with them. The sailors piled in and sat on packing cases as the van rumbled and swayed. The sailors were based at Cronstadt, and belonged to a naval revolutionary network. It seemed that the Baltic fleet was simmering with discontent, and it was only a matter of time before there was a mutiny.

When the back doors of the van opened again, they climbed out into a paved yard next to a quayside. They must have travelled to the western side of the island. A small steamer was moored alongside, flying the ensign of the imperial navy, and most of the sailors went aboard her. The older seaman, however, led Markov across the yard to a low brick building. He unlocked a door and showed Markov into a storeroom full of brass lanterns and smelling of paraffin. If he waited, someone would come for him. The sailor left, closing the door.

With a shock, Markov heard the key turn in the lock. Perhaps they hadn't been fooled after all. Anyway, it meant he couldn't slip out and get back on Spark's trail. He paced the small room, nervous and impatient. It was nearly half an hour before the door opened again, and the same seaman beckoned him outside. There he introduced an elderly waterman with a long white beard. His face was brown and wrinkled with exposure, but the arms beneath his smock were powerfully muscled.

Quickly crossing to the dockside, they climbed down an iron ladder to a small boat moored alongside. The waterman cast off and took the oars. The boat was soon sliding past the shipping of the harbour, some of them naval vessels but most merchantmen that flew the flags of half the nations in the world. Tall, slender sailing ships appeared elegant but outdated amongst the squat, smoke-stained steamers. Coal was being unloaded into barges and great bales of cotton swung up by cranes. They pulled across into the mouth of the Fontanka river. The old man nodded towards two figures waiting at the top of a flight of stone steps.

'These two comrades will escort you from now on. Don't worry, they've got pistols if it comes to a shoot-out.'

This was bad news, but Markov tried to look grateful. He offered the waterman a kopeck, the usual fare for crossing the river. It was refused.

'I am too old to fight, but if I can help a lad like you to relieve the suffering people, I am content. Good luck.'

There was nothing for it but to climb the steps and meet the men, tough-looking types in workmen's clothes. They said little, but led him to a tram stop. When it arrived, they climbed up the stairs. It cost only three kopecks on top, as opposed to five inside. Money was precious. The horses were whipped up and the tram rumbled off. Markov's silent protectors were tense and alert as they travelled past the triumphal arch in

Narva Square and into the factory district to the south. They got off in a street of squalid industrial buildings; the side-walks littered with sunflower seed husks spat out by working men. One of his companions tapped on a peeling door in an otherwise blank brick wall. It opened a few inches, and there was a short, muttered conversation. The workmen stepped aside and indicated Markov was to enter. He went in alone and the door shut behind him.

'You will be safe here, comrade.'

It was a woman, perhaps in her early thirties but with hair already tinged with grey. She wore a blue cotton apron over her simple dress, and smiled encouragingly at him. From the hallway a stone staircase with an iron railing led upwards, and Markov followed her up it. Unlocking a door at the top, the woman showed him into a long room with beds ranged on either side and tables down the centre. A dormitory of some kind.

'I'm Tanya. It's better if you don't tell me your name.' She invited him to sit at one of the tables. 'You must be hungry.'

Only after she had spoken the words did he realise he was ravenous. She brought some of the buckwheat porridge that was the staple peasant dish, and it was quickly devoured. Then she led him to a window. To his surprise it did not give a view outside, but down onto the floor of a large textile mill. Rows of clattering machines were spinning cotton, tended by young girls dressed like Tanya.

'Those are my girls, my chicks. I look after them here, but their life isn't easy. They come from the country villages to work in Peter, but trade has fallen on hard times recently. Coal is dear and wages are low. Of course, women are paid less than men for the same work. That's why the employers use so many young girls.' She sighed. 'I try to keep them from prostitution, but they are young and lusty and need some excitement in their lives. Anyway, they couldn't escape from sex if they wanted to. Any man in the company, from supervisor to director, treats them as if they were a harem. The girls know their jobs depend on it. Look, look there. Boris the foreman. He's doing it again.'

A thick-necked man with a shiny bald head had grabbed a girl by the wrist and was leading her to the wall. He pushed her against it and reached down to unbutton his trousers. He pulled out his cock, and guided the girl's reluctant hand to it. She began to wank him without enthusiasm. Meanwhile, he was rummaging up her skirts. After feeling her for a while, he pulled up her clothes, exposing the pale thighs above her stockings. He made her part her legs and hold the bunched-up apron, skirt and petticoats while he bent his knees to penetrate her. The slick way he got himself up her spoke of long experience. He began his pelvic thrusts.

The other girls, facing their machines with their backs to the coupling figures, were carefully ignoring them. It was not long before he had his orgasm, for he pulled abruptly out of the girl and dried his glistening member on her apron. He then shoved her back towards her machine.

Tanya turned round angrily to Markov. 'You see how it is? They never leave the girls alone. If it's not rape, it's dirty suggestions and groping.'

He tried to compose his features into the correct expression of indignation, but Tanya continued. 'You are one, though, who would change all this exploitation. You will stay with us tonight. They'll never think of looking here.'

Having eaten, Markov now felt exhausted, and Tanya showed him to a bed behind a curtain. He undressed, slipped naked between the coarse cotton sheets and slept.

It was some hours later when he was woken by a bubbling of female voices. The shift must have ended and the girls had come to sleep. A face peeped through the curtains, young and pale, but quickly disappeared when he smiled at

216

her.

Tanya's voice spoke firmly. 'Leave him alone.'

'But he's awake, Tanya. He looks nice. Can't we talk to him?'

'I'll see.'

Tanya came in, and Markov sat up. 'I don't mind meeting the girls, Tanya, but I'll have to get dressed.' His words faded as he saw Tanya was only wearing a threadbare towel round her waist.

'Oh, don't worry about getting dressed. They're all practically naked themselves now. This isn't one of your student residences, you know.'

Markov pushed aside the curtain and silence fell, as a dozen or more girls turned from where they were undressing by their beds. They were young, but there was a boldness in the way they looked him up and down that was certainly not innocent. One of them stood in front of Markov, naked but for her stockings and boots, hands provocatively on her hips. Somewhat skinny to Markov's eyes, her breasts were small and a tuft of pubic hair adorned the fork of her crotch. The familiar urge flooded through him, and his cock began to rise and stiffen. There was an appreciative murmur from the girls as they clustered round.

'You are welcome, stranger.' She glanced round the giggling group. 'In fact I'll show you how welcome you are.' She sank to her knees at Markov's feet and, cupping his balls in her hands, guided his hardening shaft into her mouth.

Markov glanced at Tanya, who shrugged. 'If they must have sex, at least it should be when they choose to.'

'You're not the only one who can suck a cock, Olga.' Another girl pushed forward from the group and knelt in front of Markov. Olga, with his rigid member still in her mouth, glared sideways at the newcomer, but allowed her to nibble the side of his shaft while she concentrated on the head of it.

217

Two other girls, anxious not to be left out, stood on either side of Markov and guided his hands to their crotches. Three or four more pressed forward, angrily complaining that they couldn't get near him. Jealous looks were exchanged.

'Don't squabble, girls.' Tanya sounded more than ever like a schoolmistress. 'If everyone takes a turn, I'm sure you can all have a little fun.'

The first young fellatrices gave their places to two more and then another two. Each girl tried her best to improve on the technique of her rivals. It took all Markov's self-control not to succumb to the soft caresses of their mouths. He wanted to get as much stimulation as he could before the orgasm that was already building up finally erupted.

After about the fifth pair had risen to their feet, Tanya beckoned forward a girl with the olive skin and almond-shaped eyes of the southern provinces. 'Leila, I'm sure our guest would be interested in your party piece.'

Smiling shyly, she pulled a long bench from under one of the tables, covered it with a towel and politely invited Markov to lie full length on it. This he did, his rigid erection sticking almost vertically upward. One of the other girls began a war-bling tune on some sort of flute or recorder. Leila stood at the end of the bench and started to dance in a sinuous, snake-like way.

All the movement seemed to start from her hips, waves of almost fluid sensuality flowing through her body, along her arms and out through her fingertips. She moved forward, and as she did so her legs parted to straddle the bench. Without losing the rhythm of the dance, she flexed her knees and low-ered herself over Markov's feet. The delicate wetness of her vulva hovered over his big toes, gently brushing their tips.

Then further up him, until her swaying body was poised above his erection. The action seemed to focus now on her stomach, her navel gyrating as the muscles rhythmically convulsed. Then down on him, the parted lips of her sex teasing his knob for a second or two before sliding down over it.

Then Markov understood the true meaning of this belly-dancing. It was not the outward show of a young and supple female body. It was the erotic ecstasy that the muscular contractions evoked in the male penis that impaled that body. The undulating spasms milked him in a way no mouth or hand had ever done. It was no use fighting against it. His climax rose uncontrollably and exploded in a hot jet of semen that shot up into the dusky girl's womb. She slowed her pace, gently milking him, sucking the last drop from his phallus as she gripped it with her animated vagina.

The music came to an end and Leila dismounted. The semen ran out of her, splashing Markov's hot but softening member. The watching girls were obviously impressed, though one or two looked enviously at her. Tanya spoke.

'That's enough, girls. I'm sure our guest wishes to sleep, and it's time you were all in bed.' There was a murmur of disappointment as they turned away to complete their undressing. Tanya led him back to the curtained bed.

'This is my bed, in fact. I hope you won't mind if I share it with you.'

It would be the least he could offer, thought Markov, though I doubt she'll get much out of me after what I've just experienced. He misjudged his own sexual energy, however, and in the middle of the night he was able to give her a more than satisfactory screw.

At that time of year there was little darkness, and it was broad daylight when Tanya let him out of the street door. He caught the tram back to the next cabstand, then, with a few rapid changes, to the fortress. The slaves had not yet arrived and Ignatiev was still in bed. Markov had to steel himself to admit that his attempt to catch Spark single-handed had been a clumsy failure. Ignatiev took it well, perhaps not entirely

219

unhappy that the younger man had made something of a fool of himself.

Hurried reports and instructions were dispatched, but Markov knew that the trail was a day old and his quarry would have fled long before. His bad mood was made worse when he learnt that Ulyanov had been released.

'Why, in God's name? I risked my life to get that agitator behind bars, and now those bloody politicians have simply let him go.'

'At least he's still in the country, where we can keep an eye on him. Some say he should be sent abroad, and good riddance, but that's a mistake. In the west he can plot and scheme without surveillance. He'd be much more dangerous.'

It was in a foul temper that Markov changed into his black leather uniform and strode off to the dungeon. He needed an outlet for his frustration, and 1053 would be his victim. Ignatiev had apparently already obtained a confession from her, but Markov had not yet personally applied his expertise.

In the entrance hall he found the rack occupied by a recumbent form with widely parted legs. A glance at her crotch identified her as 1048. It was mid-morning and already the puddle of semen that had dripped onto the flagstones testified that her helpless body had been well-used. She lay staring at the vaulted ceiling as if in another world.

Markov stalked to the torture chamber and ordered 1053 to be brought there. After some delay, while she was being dressed in her leather corset and boots, the sullen prisoner was led in. She was a tall girl, a trainee teacher apparently, with brown hair which now hung loosely. She paled when she saw the look on Markov's face.

'I've told them everything, I swear it.'

Markov told her to shut up and get over the flogging block. The guards fastened the wrist and ankle straps so she was bent forward over the leather-covered block, her arms stretched downwards. Meanwhile Markov selected a whip. He chose a bullwhip of plaited leather that was still stiff and new.

The first blow landed full across the girl's back with a crack like a rifle shot. Her mouth opened wide in a soundless scream as she arched her body. The second lash came almost immediately, and now she found her voice. She yelled in agony as Markov struck again and again, criss-crossing the pale skin of her back and shoulders with angry red lines. In a frenzy of rage, he gave all his strength into the flogging. He grunted with the effort as he swung his arm. At each blow his anger grew less, though, and slowly the rapidity and force of his blows lessened. At last he stood panting. The girl had stopped screaming, and was sobbing. The tears ran down her cheeks and dripped onto the flagstones of the torture chamber.

Markov hung the whip back in its place and ordered the guards to release the girl. She was to be taken back to her cell and her injuries treated, if necessary. He returned to the office in a more relaxed mood. At least he'd given the conspirators a hell of a fright, and their organisation would be disrupted for a while. They had lost their telephone interceptions, and they would not know who among their number could be trusted. Maybe Anastasia would be blamed. Ah well, life is never fair, not even among egalitarians.

He took Ekaterina to lunch, though he was careful to avoid the ImpÈriale. She did not mention his disappearance the previous day: she seemed more concerned about the immediate future of the women in the dungeon.

He explained. 'They'll be passed on to the usual prisons in a few days, though I think I'll keep the two slave maids for a little longer.'

'But you'll get rid of them soon?'

'Possibly.'

Ekaterina did not seem pleased with this evasive answer. After lunch, she accompanied him to the jeweller's shop and then to Correphallia's apartment. When Markov presented the small, pale wooden box to the ballerina, she grasped it with delight.

'FabergÈ! How wonderful!'

The box, stamped with the imperial eagle of the court jeweller, contained a tiny metal padlock, burnished like a mirror, and two small keys. Markov told Correphallia to undress and lie on the table. He produced some instruments and a small bottle of spirits from a side pocket, and with Ekaterina's help arranged her legs so her sex was gaping wide. The actual piercing of the vaginal lips was straightforward, and the pain seemed less than he might have expected. The padlock was slipped through the bleeding holes and the key turned.

He applied a simple dressing and passed on the advice he had received. The young dancer climbed shakily from the operating table. She gazed at the two little keys cupped in her hands.

'I will keep one on a gold chain around my neck. The other I will keep in the bank vault.'

Markov reflected on the mercenary nature of this virgin's sexuality. Still, sex was often a means to an end, rather than an end in itself. Parting from Ekaterina, he returned to the fortress.

The commandant had asked to see him, and greeted Markov in a friendly fashion.

'We've had a complaint from some of the lady typists in the Mint. They say they do not object to the new underground urinal which has been established under the rampart. The number of the garrison who visit it every day testifies to its usefulness. However, they dislike seeing the men coming up the steps buttoning their flies. Could we insist they adjust their dress before leaving?'

Both men smirked. Markov solemnly undertook to see it was done. He was about to leave, when the commandant handed him an official envelope.

'Oh, by the way, this came for you an hour ago.'

It was from Fontanka 16. Headquarters was by no means displeased with Markov's efforts. Spark had certainly fled the city and the ants' nest was very thoroughly stirred up. Suspicion and distrust crippled the subversives' activities. However, Markov's description had been widely circulated round the revolutionary groups with instructions to kill on sight. Already one physics graduate of similar appearance had been badly beaten before the mistake was recognised. The strongest advice was to leave St.Petersburg for a while until the tension had eased.

If Markov wished, he could retire to a dacha, a country cottage that the Okhrana had outside the city. It was secluded and the perimeter unobtrusively guarded. A caretaker lived in a cottage some distance away, who could bring in basic supplies from the village. Otherwise the dacha was empty. Perhaps Markov could grow a beard as a disguise. It was expedient to close down the Special Interrogation Centre for a while. Perhaps Captain Ignatiev would accompany him.

Markov mulled this over as he made his way back to the apartment. If he had to leave the city, he would prefer to go to Paris, where so many of the social Èlite were visiting the great international exhibition. However, if he was to resume his unfinished business with Spark, Markov needed to be near at hand. Well then, it looked like another month in the country.

Ignatiev was not surprised to hear of the proposal, and agreed to go with him to the dacha. They spent the rest of the day on the necessary arrangements. Ekaterina typed the papers that transferred the prisoners to female gaols to await trial, and agreed to come into the office regularly to handle routine paperwork and forward important messages. However, he reported that numbers 1046 and 1049 would be detained for further questioning. In fact, they were to be brought to the dacha as slaves.

The following day saw numerous luxuries delivered to the apartment, including cases of champagne and handmade Turkish cigarettes. In the afternoon a closed coach left the fortress, heavily loaded with boxes and trunks. The doors were locked and blinds were closed across the windows. Two men sat on the driver's bench, both wearing full beards that did not seem to be their own.

The journey to the dacha took all night and most of the next day. They frequently checked to make sure they weren't being followed. There were few stops, and those only in the woods. Markov took the opportunity at one such stop to pass the reins to Ignatiev. He then got into the coach to have sex with the girls inside.

It was a cramped space, dark and smelling of the leather upholstery. It jolted as the carriage rolled along the woodland road. The two slaves were sitting on opposite seats, facing each other, and wearing the singlets and knickers of their daytime uniform. They watched meekly as Markov unbuttoned himself and got his cock out. Holding on to the roof strut as the coach swayed, he stood in front of one of the maids. In the gloom he did not know which one, and he did not care. The compliant girl shifted forward in her seat and took his erection into her mouth. She sucked him respectfully for a while, then he pulled himself out of her mouth. He turned round and made the other do the same.

As he received her dutiful ministrations, he pondered how best to screw them in the confined space. The two bench seats were only about four feet wide and set so close that the maids' knees were almost touching. He ordered the girl sucking him to get his shaft really wet with her saliva, and told the other to stand up and take off her knickers. This was awkward, but the elasticated pants were easily taken down. Markov slid down his own breeches and sat down, his well-lubricated erection jutting stiffly upward. He told the slave who was now naked below the waist to sit down on it.

Obediently, she turned her back on him and lowered herself, hands on knees. Markov guided his penis between the lips of her sex as she sank down. She gave a little intake of breath as the full length slid inside her. She was seated on his lap, impaled on his rigid phallus. He then commanded her to raise and lower herself on him. Flexing her thighs, she rode up and down on his shaft. However, it was clear that while the sensation was pleasing, there was little possibility of bringing him to an orgasm that way.

He made her dismount, and told the other slave to move forward to the edge of her seat and part her legs. He knelt on the floor between her legs, and hooked aside the crotch of her knickers with a finger. He was able to get his cock into her, but the narrow space between the seats and the height of the seat above the floor made it hard for him to get into a good position to screw her. Once more he withdrew.

Standing up, he turned to the half-naked girl and ordered her to kneel on her seat, facing its back. This she did without hesitation, offering her rear to him. This time everything was satisfactory. He entered her body from behind, pushing deep into the warm depths. He began to thrust, bracing himself on the roof strut against the lurching of the coach. As he screwed her, he felt the hand of the slave behind him touch his buttocks. He wondered for an instant if she was trying to pick the keys out of his pocket. However, she reached between his legs and caressed his balls as he shoved in and out of her friend.

It was a good orgasm, and afterwards Markov made the two sit side-by-side as he slumped on the other seat. He dozed for a while, the girls patiently keeping silent. He woke, took a few swigs from his hip flask and felt much restored. He was about to call to Ignatiev to stop, when Ignatiev himself shouted.

'We've arrived!'

It was large wooden house, with the typical carved decoration of the region. There was a long balcony across the upper floor, and a stable yard to one side. Markov got down from the coach and, with the instinct of a cavalryman, his first thought was for the horses. With Ignatiev's help he unharnessed them, rubbed them down and turned them out to graze in the paddock behind the house. Only then did he remember the slaves, and ordered them out to begin taking the luggage inside. There was a long, open shed along one side of the yard. It sheltered an old troika sleigh and two small carts with high wheels and slender shafts.

'What are those, Ignatiev?'

'Oh, those are trotting carts. Just seats and a pair of wheels, really. They're a western type, used for pony racing.'

Markov nodded thoughtfully. He entered the house. The girls had opened the French windows at the back of the main room, giving a view of the birch woods beyond the paddock. A piano stood against the wall, and Markov bent to see the sheet music on it. It was the imperial anthem. Markov sat down at the keyboard and began to play. He hadn't touched a piano since hammering out drinking songs in the Lifeguards' mess, but it was in an easy key, without many sharps and flats.

'Great God the terrible...' The heavy, sonorous chords stirred him as they always did, cynical, cruel and self-indulgent though he was. Everyone must have something to believe in and at that moment, with the slanting summer sunlight and the scent of the meadow, it was his homeland.

Life quickly settled into a lazy routine. Letters and reports still had to be written and received, the old caretaker acting as postman and errand boy. He had fought in the Crimea and against the Turks, and the officers would sometimes entertain him with vodka to listen to his tales. Markov was pleased with the way his beard was growing, and tried with some success to introduce Ignatiev to hard drinking. They gambled at cards, which Ignatiev usually won, and chess, when Markov usually came out on top. Their main entertainments, however, were the girls.

The slaves were always on hand, in stretch cotton by day and leather in the long summer evenings. They would cook and serve, clean and launder, and do everything a man expects a woman to do about the house. Including, of course, being available for sex at any time it was demanded.

As well as these normal feminine duties, the maids would be required to perform more unusual services. On some evenings one or other of them was made to lie on the dining table with her legs raised and parted, chained to the ceiling so she could act as a living candlestick with a lighted candle sticking out of her sex. On these occasions, Markov was careful to ensure the hot wax caused no serious damage to the soft membranes of the vulva. However the girl would twitch charmingly whenever a scalding drop landed on her inner thighs or trickled down her anal cleft. The men imposed a long and detailed series of household rules, and mercilessly beat the girls for the smallest infringement. Supper had to be ready by eight in the evening, for instance. Once the officers had been out shooting in the woods, and the light was good enough for them to stay out until nine. The maids were flogged for serving a dry, overcooked meal.

Flogging was almost part of the daily routine. A pair of wrist irons had been attached to the post that supported the staircase as it came down into the main room. To this one or other of the girls was fastened so the men could wield their

227

whips. It was rare that this did not excite them to the point where they would want to enter the sufferer from behind. And as the days went by it became increasingly obvious to the men that the girls were responding well to their treatment. Passive obedience began to be replaced by willing and respectful subservience, and after each flogging, if a vagina was entered it was always found to be moist and eager. Through frequent use the girls' anuses had stretched and were also easily penetrated. Both men were pleased with the enthusiasm and expertise the girls demonstrated when called on to perform fellatio, which was frequently. Markov developed a taste for combining lunch on the table with shooting his sperm into a warm and soft mouth below it.

During the second week, Markov proposed a new wager to Ignatiev. Why not harness the girls to the trotting carts, and race them against each other while the two men lashed them on? It seemed a good idea, and they put the plan into effect at once. The maids changed into their long boots and corsets, so their bottoms and shoulders would be exposed. Meanwhile, Markov set to work with a sharp knife and some rivets to adapt two old pony bridles for human use. They led the girls out into the stable yard and harnessed them by passing a strap round the back of their necks, under their arms and down to the shafts of the carts. The men then climbed on board, reins in one hand and whip in the other.

The drivers flicked the girls' shoulders and, like rickshaws, the carts were pulled out of the yard to the starting point. A count of three, then crack went the whips across the naked flesh. The slaves leant hard into their harness straps and broke into a jogging trot. The high-heeled boots were not very practical footwear, however, and they stumbled often. Ignatiev cursed his slave as she staggered. The lashes cracked onto bare shoulders and buttocks as the two carts raced side-by-side across the meadow. Markov flicked his whip over his girl-pony's shoulder so that the lash stung her breasts. With a sudden spurt, she broke into a run and had drawn ahead of Ignatiev as they passed the tree that was the agreed winning post.

Ignatiev, flushed and angry, called across to Markov. 'Best of three?'

Markov agreed and they were hauled back to the starting point. The next race was faster, the maids becoming more familiar with their task. Both men applied their whips forcefully. It was striking to see how the pale skin contrasted with the red marks that soon almost covered the exposed areas. This time Ignatiev won by a short head, having threatened his slave with terrifying punishments if he lost. All depended on the final race.

From the start Ignatiev took the lead. Markov was determined to win, but how? He contemplated the firm, tight bottom and the pumping thighs of the slave girl pulling him. Then with the skill of an experienced horseman, he flicked the whiplash up between her legs so that the end curled up and stung her clitoris. It was a risky tactic, for the whip could easily become entangled and trip her up. Markov struck unerringly, however, and the maid squealed and bolted forward to get away from her tormentor. He had to do the same twice more before the finish, which saw him win by a comfortable margin.

That evening Ignatiev handed over Markov's winnings. It was Markov's pony girl who served dinner, for the loser was hung spreadeagled by chains from the ceiling. Under constant tension, she had to watch hungrily as the men ate at the table below her. Markov asked Ignatiev if he was really going to do to her all the things he had threatened.

'Of course. I have never issued a threat without intending to carry it out. That would be weakness.'

Markov agreed, but said he would like to have regular

pony races. To make it fair, the men would use the girls alternately. This would even out any difference in strength or fitness. It would then be a test of the driver's skill. That being so, the punishments Ignatiev had planned would not affect the slave's performance. Ignatiev glared up at the silent figure suspended above them, and reluctantly consented. However after their dinner it seemed to both of them that the opportunity to administer a good thrashing was too good to waste and accordingly it seemed only fair to give both girls thirty lashes, which would punish the loser and handicap the winner, resulting in an even contest the following day. The floggings were administered at the customary post and afterwards the girls performed enthusiastically with their mouths, sucking at the erections of their masters and then presenting their sexes for use while they knelt on all fours. Markov was only too glad to allow Ignatiev to win the race to ejaculation. He enjoyed thrusting deeply into 1049 who bucked and wriggled her broad hips against him pleasingly while his fingers dug and clawed at the weals on her back.

And so the weeks passed in relaxation and sport. However, despite the comfort of the house and the spacious grounds, Markov felt as if he were a prisoner himself. He would take walks in the woods, sometimes bringing one of the slaves along on a lead. He would go fishing, taking a girl to act as a seat. He had to acknowledge, though, that he was bored. Ignatiev was friendly enough, but even his company began to be tiresome. He wanted to get back into action.

Then came a letter from Zubatov. It was considered safe for him to return to St.Petersburg. The university term had ended, and most of the student radicals had left the city. There were several new female prisoners, arrested following the confessions obtained by Markov, waiting to be transferred to the Special Interrogation Centre. Would he report to Fontanka 16 the day after tomorrow?

It was with an eager heart that Markov set the maids to pack for the return journey. The last of the champagne was drunk that night, with a competition to see how far an empty bottle could be pushed up a vagina. The following day they departed for the city in a lighter mood than the one in which they had left it. They arrived at the fortress the next morning, to find Ekaterina in the office. She rushed to Markov, as if she would embrace him, then sank to her knees to kiss his dusty boots.

'There's something different about you. Oh yes, the beard.'

Markov was proud of the neat goatee and moustache, and was exasperated that she had hardly noticed it. Some disguise. After a bath and a change of clothes, the men returned to the office. Orders were given for 1046 and 1049 to be sent to normal prisons for trial, and plans made for the reception of the new captives. He then went to see Zubatov.

'You have achieved a lot in a short time, young man. However, it was foolish to have gone to Spark's hideout alone. For the last arrest you made, you had a troop of Cossacks.'

'I was overconfident. It will not happen again.'

'No, it won't. I am ordering you to limit your activities to the Special Interrogation Centre. Just forward the reports to us and we'll handle the rest.'

Markov, never happy to take orders, coldly acquiesced. Zubatov relaxed and there was even a trace of a smile. 'As I say, we're pleased with you. I have recommended to the army that your rank be raised to Captain. They have agreed.'

Well, that will make me Ignatiev's equal, thought Markov. Zubatov poured them both vodka and toasted his promotion.

'By the way, captain, why were you so anxious that Ulyanov receive a passport to leave the country? I was undecided, but your opinion tipped the balance.'

Markov stared at him in astonishment. 'What do you mean?'

'I mean the letter you sent urging that he be released and sent abroad as soon as possible.'

'What? My letter?'

'Yes, here it is.' Zubatov took a paper from a drawer in his desk and handed it to him. A chill flowed through Markov's blood. There was no doubt it was from his office. The letter-head, the official stamp. But the signature was false, copied by someone who knew it well.

'This is a forgery! It would be disastrous to allow Lenin to go to the west. Great God! We must stop him.'

'Stop him? But he's already on his way. He's at Warsaw, I believe, and will be out of Russia soon.'

Markov thought wildly for a moment of riding hard for the border, but realised it would take days. The telephone! Call the border guards to stop Lenin as he tried to cross!

'Can we telephone the border to prevent him leaving?'

Zubatov picked up something of Markov's urgency. 'Well, yes, if you think it wise.'

'Wise? I've seen this man. Unchecked, he could stir the whole of the working class to revolt.'

'Very well.' Zubatov cranked the handle of the instrument on his desk. 'Get me the railway border post on the line to Vienna.'

There was a long wait, and Zubatov had to repeat his instructions several times to different operators. There was confusion and unbearable delay before Zubatov, one hand over his free ear, strained to hear the reply from the border so many hundreds of miles away.

'We're too late. He's already crossed, on his way to Switzerland.'

Markov stood up, burning with rage and frustration. 'I'll make the culprit pay for this, I promise you.'

He stalked out of the room and, fuming, made directly for the fortress. Mounting the stairs two at a time, he flung open

232

the office door, sending it crashing back against the wall. Ekaterina looked up, ashen faced, from her typewriter.

'You filthy bitch! You treacherous whore! This has all been a sham, hasn't it? You are one of them. You've made a fool of me the whole time.'

Ekaterina stood up and then sank down, embracing his knees.

'No, no. Please believe me. I truly wished to serve you. I wanted to give myself totally to you. But I just couldn't bear you treating those wretched women worse than you treated me. I thought if I did something to make you angry, you would be as hard on me.'

Markov's anger was suddenly checked by this astonishing declaration. He replied in a cool tone. 'Then you have succeeded. You are under arrest.'

Obediently, she followed him to the dungeon, where he instructed the guards to process her. On the cold flagstones of the chamber she took off her smart secretary's clothes and was led unresisting to the rack. Her pubic hair was shaved, but there was the question of what number to tattoo in its place. Ekaterina had not been officially admitted as a fortress prisoner, and it occurred to Markov that this was no bad thing. He ordered the imperial eagle to be permanently marked on her Mount of Venus. Then he had her taken to a cell overnight while he considered the punishment she would face.

In the days that followed, she was mercilessly beaten and abused.

On her first morning she had the chance to try out the flogging block with all the alterations she herself had suggested. But Markov now knew that if he himself administered the beating she would derive too much pleasure from it. He detailed off two anonymous guards to strip and flog her, but in mid-morning he dropped by to see how matters were progressing. As he entered the chamber he was greeted by the satisfying sound of leather smacking down onto female flesh. Ekaterina was well marked on buttocks, thighs and back and the guards had worked up quite a sweat. He let them take a well-earned rest, then poured a glass of wine lifted her head by grabbing a fistful of hair and allowed her to take a small drink. She swallowed with difficulty but was able, when he asked her again, to repeat her story that she had only acted as she had in order to provoke him into the course of action he was currently following. Still holding her head he addressed the guards.

"Continue for another half hour then let her rest before the afternoon session, during which you will hang her by the ankles and attend to those areas you haven't dealt with yet."

He heard her whispered thanks then let her head fall back before stalking out and closing the door on the sounds of the flogging getting under way again.

He looked in twice during the afternoon and spent some time watching her body twist and jerk as it hung helplessly and the guards duly attended to breasts, stomach and the fronts of her thighs. On his second visit he squatted down and interrogated her as he ordered one guard to flick his whip down onto her open crotch. Between squeals and sighs of what was plainly ecstasy she managed to look him in the eye and repeat her story.

On the second day she endured the rack in the morning and the clamping of her nipples and labia whilst hung by her wrists in the afternoon. But never for a second did she deviate from her story and looked at Markov with nothing but the plainest devotion as he watched her suffering. She spent the whole of the third day staked out for the garrison's use and it seemed that the continual use of her body by the men, which resulted in thick crusts of sperm coating her thighs and breasts only provided her with complete fulfilment and she managed a wan smile for Markov when at last he surveyed her battered form at the end of the day. She repeated her story one last time before fainting.

He had to be satisfied that she really was loyal to the Tsar and even more, it seemed, to Markov himself. What should he do with her? He still needed a secretary, and at least one maid to serve in his apartment. Ekaterina could do both tasks and be trusted not to attempt an escape. Since she was not an official prisoner, he was answerable to nobody for what happened to her. So Ekaterina's life became that of a slave.

He made her move into the apartment, only releasing her from time to time to attend her charity meetings and religious events. They attended meetings of the Ladies' Guild together, where her tattoo was much admired. To her acquaintances her life seemed unchanged, though she seemed to be more tranquil. In the fortress though, she submitted completely to her master's demands. He indulged his cruel pleasures without pity, and expected total compliance. She submitted to every form of violation, abuse and humiliation without complaint. As well as Ignatiev, she had to open her body to any man her master permitted to use her. Many came to the apartment on business or pleasure. They would force themselves as they willed into the openings of her body; her mouth, her sex, her anus. She was constantly sodomised and raped. Markov even had some chains installed in his bedroom so that he could flog her whenever the mood took him.

Her only duty was to obey. When not carrying out an order, she would stand silently beside him, eyes respectfully downcast. Often when he was writing at his desk she would kneel below it and suck his penis. Shielded by the desk, she was invisible to any visitors and continued her ministrations even during business meetings.

For one of those meetings Zubatov himself came. It showed his approval of Markov that he didn't simply summon him to headquarters. Markov did not wish his boss to use his slave as the others had though, and she was banished beneath the desk to fellate him during the discussion.

The general situation was reviewed. How long could the Romanovs, who had reigned for nearly three centuries, resist the forces of democratic change? How could modernisation and western industrialisation be introduced while still maintaining the old order? How much of a threat was the exiled Lenin?

Markov felt less concerned than he had been before. After all, the present troubles were nothing new. Throughout its history, Russia had been in a constant state of internal war. Casting a complacent glance down at the woman grovelling at his feet with his phallus in her mouth, he felt confident.

'It doesn't matter what this Lenin does. Russia will always remain a land of masters, a land of slaves.'

Here is the preface to next months title "THE STONEHURST LETTERS" by J.L. Jones.
Sorry there isn't more, I just couldn't fit it in this month!

The letters in this volume were written in 1832, but they were suppressed until just recently as they contain detailed information concerning one of those periods of history that many of us would rather forget, a time when falsehood and hysteria overrode reason.

An educator by the name of Derek Hunter authored these letters while he was on sabbatical from Rosewood Academy for Girls, an institution where corporal punishment was approved of and used in liberal doses, and the letters are addressed to one of his fellow teachers at the academy. Both men enjoyed birching the bare buttocks of errant students.

Hunter's sabbatical took him to the home of a friend and former Rosewood colleague, Neville Olford. Olford lived in a remote section of the country and had become the Chief Magistrate of his village. In this area, young girls were being persecuted, legally being put to the whip and even sex-tortured because much of the populace believed that these girls had become infected with some sort of evil spirit, an evil that had caused the crops to fail for several years and thus causing a blight on the entire vicinity.

Olford had taken delight in thrashing the Rosewood students when he was headmaster at the academy, and, in his position as magistrate, he was in a position to mete out much more severe punishments to the girls brought into his courtroom, sentencing them to naked public floggings and having them put into the village stocks nude. The man took pleasure in this even though it was his duty to do it. He would go so far as to take some of these girls under his roof as wards of the court, acting as their sole guardian and disciplinarian.

The cover photograph for this book and many others are available as limited edition prints.
Write to:-

Viewfinders Photography
PO Box 200,
Reepham
Norfolk
NR10 4SY

for details, or see,

www.viewfinders.org.uk